TREAT THEM AS BUFFALO

A NOVEL

Blair Palmer Yoxall

ALGONQUIN BOOKS OF CHAPEL HILL
LITTLE, BROWN & COMPANY

The characters and events in this book are fictitious. Any similarity to real persons, living or dead, is coincidental and not intended by the author.

Algonquin Books of Chapel Hill / Little, Brown and Company
Hachette Book Group
1290 Avenue of the Americas, New York, NY 10104
algonquinbooks.com

First Edition: May 2026

Algonquin Books of Chapel Hill is an imprint of Little, Brown and Company, a division of Hachette Book Group, Inc. The Algonquin Books name and logo are trademarks of Hachette Book Group, Inc.

ISBN 978-1-64375-680-6
LCCN 2025948876

Printing 1, 2026

LSC-C

Printed in the United States of America

Advance Praise for *Treat Them as Buffalo*

"A harrowing adrenaline rush, a wild river of a story. My heart clenched in worry for the young narrator, a Métis tribal member named Nikosis, determined to rescue his dear relative at a time of kidnappings and violence. The book is billed as an anti-Western, sidestepping well-worn tropes and caricatures. The author succeeds on all fronts—Blair Palmer Yoxall is a force!"

—Mona Susan Power, author of *A Council of Dolls*

"Blair Palmer Yoxall enters the foray of Indigenous literatures equipped with the oratories of Louis Riel and Métis matriarchies. With excellent control over historical fiction and his inquisitive child narrator, Niko, Yoxall creates a world of Lac-aux-Trois-Pistoles that is rich with verisimilitude and the dueling emotional states of hope and rage. For fans of *Blood Meridian* and *Prairie Edge, Treat Them as Buffalo* is a refreshing addition to our canons with its historical weaving that makes so precedent the political issues of Indigenous peoples today."

—Joshua Whitehead, author of *Jonny Appleseed* and *Making Love with the Land*

"*Raw*, rowdy, and unflinching in its portrayal of a Métis community under siege amid the tumult of the North-West Rebellion of 1885. Yoxall's vivid storytelling immerses us in twelve-year-old Niko's world of friendship and feasts, buried secrets and hard truths, trust and betrayal. Brilliantly turning the Wild West myth on its head, the novel refuses to look away from the terrible cost of colonial violence on children and families. Unforgettable."

—Thomas Wharton, author of *Wolf, Moon, Dog*

"A fierce and beautiful work, a page-turning adventure that is impossible to put down. Yoxall brings to life a world filled with revolution, brutality, and madness. It is narrated by Niko, a young Métis child who is coming to understand the violence of his history and also the depth of his own bravery and sensitivity. He is a boy raised by a family of women. And the women are wild with resilience and pride, and are glorious monsters who terrorize those who try to steal the legacy of their children."

—Heather O'Neill, author of *The Capital of Dreams*

ᓂᒪᒪ
i did my best
i hope you are proud

ᑳ ᒫᔭᐦᑲᒥᑲᕽ | kâ-mâyahkamikahk

A Cree translation for the North-West War of 1885.*
Literally, "when bad things happened."

"I wanted to treat them as we would have buffalo."

Gabriel Dumont discussing the Canadian soldiers at the Battle of Tourond's Coulee/Fish Creek. For more, see Marilyn Dumont's poem in *The Pemmican Eaters*.†

---

* *North-West War* refers to the concurrent Métis conflict and Cree insurgence with Canadian forces in the District of Saskatchewan in spring 1885, usually called the North-West Resistance or North-West Rebellion. This text uses *North-West War* to respectfully acknowledge the consequential legacies of these conflicts on Indigenous Peoples across the Northern Plains.

† Marilyn Dumont, "I Wanted to Treat Them as We Would Have Buffalo," in *The Pemmican Eaters* (ECW Press, 2015).

DESJARLAIS FAMILY TREE

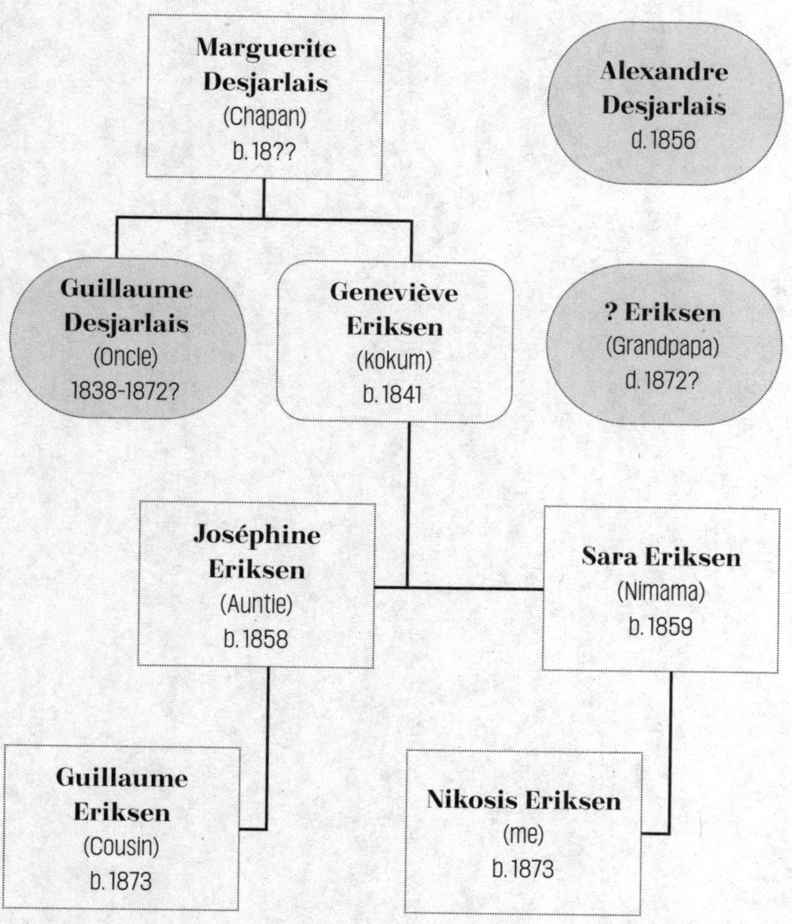

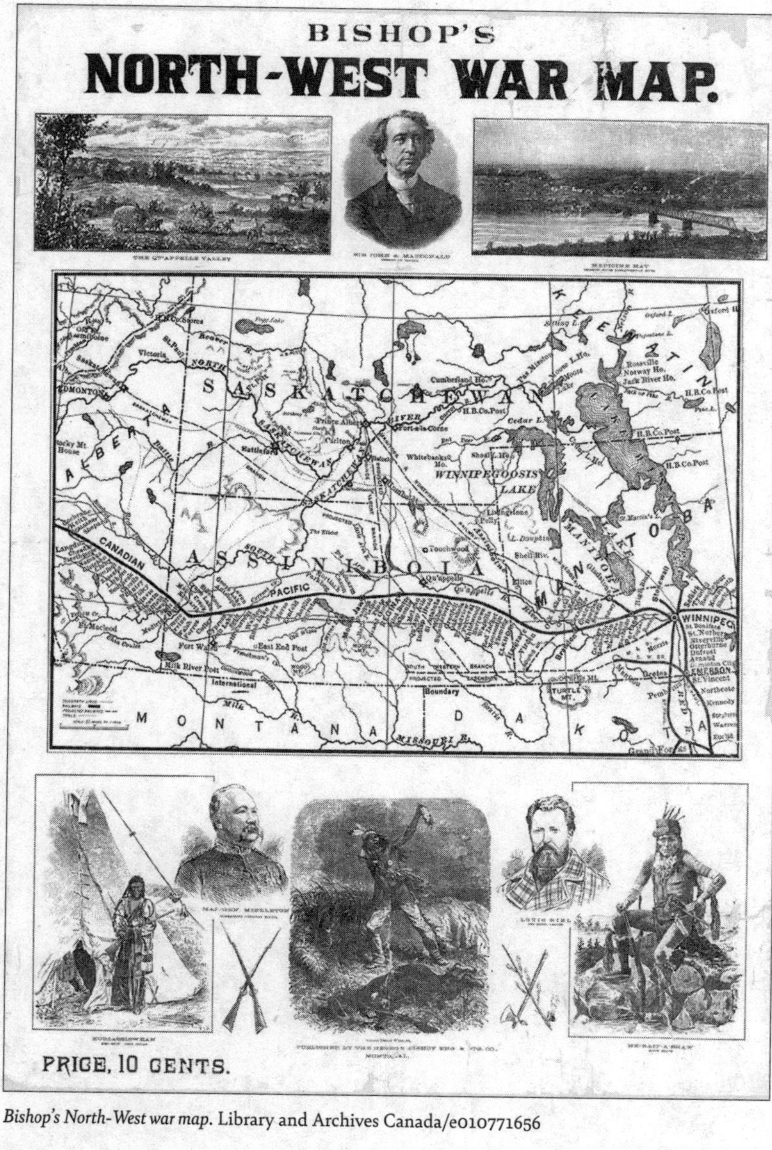

BISHOP'S

NORTH-WEST WAR MAP.

PRICE, 10 CENTS.

Bishop's North-West war map. Library and Archives Canada/e010771656

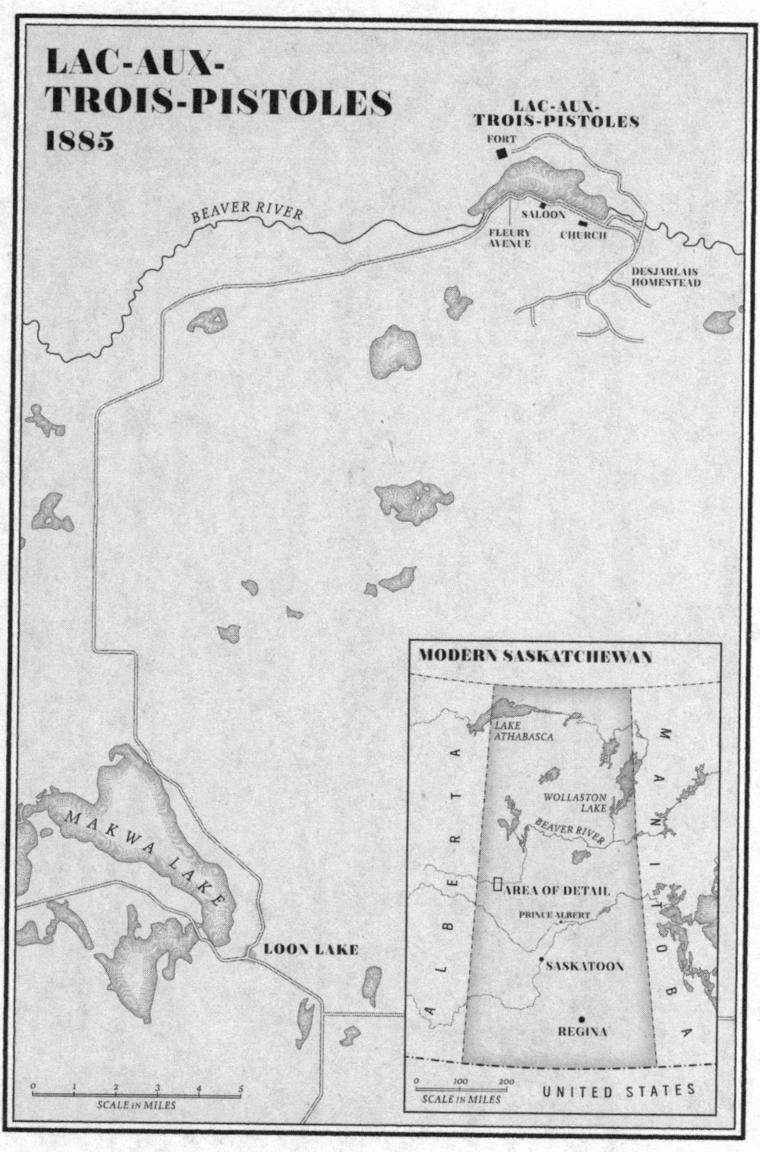

LAC-AUX-
TROIS-PISTOLES
1885
LAC-AUX-
TROIS-PISTOLES
FORT
BEAVER RIVER
SALOON
FLEURY
AVENUE
CHURCH
DESJARLAIS
HOMESTEAD
MAKWA LAKE
LOON LAKE
0 1 2 3 4 5
SCALE IN MILES
MODERN SASKATCHEWAN
LAKE
ATHABASCA
ALBERTA
MANITOBA
WOLLASTON
LAKE
BEAVER RIVER
AREA OF DETAIL
PRINCE ALBERT
SASKATOON
REGINA
0 100 200
SCALE IN MILES
UNITED STATES

TREAT THEM AS BUFFALO

NOTE TO READERS

This novel contains descriptions of physical and sexual violence and of abusive power structures. Please take care in your reading.

CHAPTER 1

WHEN BAD THINGS HAPPENED

WEDNESDAY, MARCH 18, 1885. LAC-AUX-TROIS-PISTOLES, DISTRICT OF SASKATCHEWAN.

Everything turned to shit when Cousin got took. It all happened like this: I rode Pony bareback, Cousin marched beside me. We was walking the trail from the burn scar in the forest back to the homestead after playing buffalo hunters. Me and him was making chit-chat about how good of buffalo hunters we would've made. Then I seen a coyote startle in the bush.

"Cousin! A coyote!"

I looked to Cousin beside me. He was gone. Me and Pony spun around and around looking for him. Couldn't see him nowhere. Couldn't even find his tracks in the snow.

"*Niko! Run!*" Cousin yelled from deep in the bush. A hand smothered his mouth.

I tangled my fingers into Pony's mane, clicked my tongue, and clapped my heels against her sides. I held on for dear life. We raced home.

I led Pony straight to the corral where Nimama watered and fed Auntie's horse and our mule with help from our three-legged mutt, Barney. Pony trotted with her hooves high to not squish the squirrels scrambling beneath her.

"Whoa! Where's Guille?" Nimama stabbed a pile of hay with a pitchfork. Her springtime breath cast swirly shadows on the mud.

"Cousin's gone!"

"Gone? Where?"

I slipped off Pony's back and splashed the not-as-froze-as-it-looked mud all over my moccasins.

"Me and Cousin was playing buffalo hunters in the burn scar and I was riding Pony and Cousin was walking beside me and I seen a coyote but Cousin wasn't there then I heard him scream but I couldn't find him, it's not my fault, I'm sorry, it was all on accident!"

"Whoa . . . Niko . . ." Nimama grabbed my arms. She looked me square with them bright eyes of hers. Blue as my own. She calls our blue eyes "Desjarlaises" even though me and her is Eriksens by last name. I don't get why she won't call them Eriksen Eyes. Only Chapan's last name is Desjarlais. And Chapan's peepers ain't even blue.

"Take a breath. Tell me what happened."

I took a big inhale and outhaled slow. A hunk of heartache blew up in my throat.

Nimama bent closer to my height. I'm pretty small for a twelve-year-old—not much over four feet tall.

"I was riding Pony and Cousin was walking beside me. We was coming home from the burn scar. We was talking the whole time. Then I seen a coyote in the bush. I went to tell Cousin. But he was gone. Then he yelled for us to run. So me and Pony raced home."

Nimama tugged me into her. I wiped my nose all over the shoulder of her tweed jacket she'd won at the Fleury Hotel and Saloon playing faro. "Is Guille okay?"

I tried to say something. Harder than I ever tried saying anything before. But nothing came out my mouth. I tried breathing through my gagging heartache. But my lungs jammed shut.

I buried my face into Nimama's burn scarred neck. I cried until nothing was left. Someone stole Cousin.

Nimama grabbed my hand and dragged me to the homestead. I stumbled over my feet.

"Joséphine!" Nimama called to Auntie. "Kokum!" she called to Chapan. "Get out here!"

"What's going on?" Chapan stepped onto the boardwalk of our two-story, white-like-angel-wings homestead. Félix the cat and Miss Kitty scurried out from between Chapan's legs and bounced into the bush. The homestead has "circus windows," we call them—windowpanes so droopy, everything looks melty and gooey through them.

"You need to take Nikosis." Nimama pushed me toward Chapan with her palm. Soft like a breeze. I waded into Chapan's bosom and wrapped my arms around her. "Guillaume disappeared not five minutes ago. I'm getting my sister. We're headed to the burn scar. Niko stays with you until we all come home."

"I still don't know what's going on." Chapan looked terrified.

"Look after Niko until we get back." Nimama burned past us into the house. She cussed to herself as she lifted the Winchester repeating rifle off the mantel—a family heirloom, she calls it, even though the rifle's same age as me and Cousin. She stuffed her pockets with bullets. "I'll be back with Guille and Josey."

Nimama ran off with the gun to the old cabin near the corral where Chapan lived before the homestead got built. Auntie uses it as her workshop nowadays. It's where she hides with her beads and books and sewing kits. She paints there too.

Chapan led me to the table. Before I could sit down, I heard Auntie scream from inside her workshop. I ran to the window and watched Auntie crash out the old cabin with the door swinging behind. Barney raced after her. Auntie tripped in the snow and mud and bounded into the corral. She leapfrogged over her horse's rump and gave him three solid kicks to the belly. She held his mane. He zipped up the trail. His hooves hurled waves of slush behind. Nimama mounted Pony and clambered after them with the rifle slung over her back.

Arf! arf! arf!

Barney raced after them.

"What's happening . . ." I said to the window.

Chapan hopped outside and closed the corral gate before Huckleberry the mule could take off. I pulled a chair at the table and sat down in front of a cup of elderberry tea Chapan had made for herself.

I leaned over the steamy tea. I thought about how them dried elderberries turn my tongue blue. How them seeds *crack!* between my teeth. How someone stole Cousin.

Hard as I tried distracting myself, Cousin was all I could think about. Tea was useless.

Who's to say we won't find Cousin? Auntie and Nimama will scour everywhere for him—even if the bush is endless from Lac-aux-Trois-Pistoles to Buffalo Narrows to Fort Battleford.

My thoughts felt heavier than lead. I looked around the homestead. Smelled wood everywhere. Wood boxes nailed to wood walls to make wood cabinets. Wood staircase to the wood upstairs with wood beds. Wood bookcases chock-full of maps, letters, newspapers.

Almost every nook and cranny in the homestead is stuffed full of books and maps and letters and everything papery in between. Everyone calls the homestead "la bibliothèque" because we got so much to read and share. La bibliothèque always smells woody and lived-in at the same time. Like Maman Earth, smudge, lumber, and old paper breathing together. On the walls, Chapan nailed old snowshoes for decoration, newspaper headlines, whitetail and muley antlers, medicines for drying, lots of old paintings of prairies and people and everything pretty.

"Pray a cigarette never falls from your lips," one of Nimama's guests once said. "Or this place'll be razed."

Ever since forever ago, Chapan's been the one trusted to use fire to change the forest. Burning them spots here to make better blueberry bushes. Burning them spots there so there ain't no fuel nearby for when the Big Fire happens. When lots of other half-breed people from this place called Red River moved to Lac-aux-Trois-Pistoles in the 1860s and '70s, they hired Chapan to clear land along the Beaver River or in the bush near the lake so they can live like they did back home on the open prairie.

Most farmers didn't have no money to pay Chapan. So a few years before me and Cousin was born, Monsieur Xavier Fleury got everyone in L-T-P together to build Chapan one of the nicest homesteads in all the North-West—a proper two-story house big enough for her whole family. They fund-raised to buy Chapan pretty things like glass windows and a stove. Even built a bazillion bookshelves for Chapan, giving her proper space to store her library.

People didn't leave Red River because they wanted to. They left because buffalo was disappearing and lots of folks from Out East was settling the prairies. New Canadian law said our land in Red River didn't belong to Indians or half-breeds no more because Canada bought all the North-West from the Hudson's Bay Company. Ottawa wanted to fill the prairies with European farmers. Indians and half-breeds had to go.

It started a big uprising before Christmas in 1869. This guy called Louis Riel took over Fort Garry and made a government for half-breeds in Red River to keep our land. They even executed a guy from Ontario. Everything was bad. No one knew what would happen next.

Then Ottawa got involved. Agreed to turn Red River into the Province of Manitoba when it all ended in 1870. But Manitoba became dangerous for Indians and half-breeds. Posses of vigilante soldiers from Ontario got violent. Men was murdered. Women and girls too. Chapan even framed an old newspaper article all the way from Minnesota calling it a "reign of terror."

So lots of Indian and Métis people moved from Red River to all over the North-West where their ancestors worked and lived—Fort Benton, Pembina, St. Paul, Qu'Appelle, Batoche, Lac-aux-Trois-Pistoles, Île-à-la-Crosse, Fort McMurray, Fort Edmonton—to build new homesteads, to meet new people who looked and talked like them, to reconnect with old family, to marry new family, to trap in the bush, to farm riverlots. Nowadays there's about a hundred or so people living within ten miles of Lac-aux-Trois-Pistoles in cabins and homesteads in the bush, then another hundred-fiftyish people living on riverlots along the Beaver River. We live in the bush just east of town. Chapan's lived in L-T-P damn near all her life.

Since the uprising ended, Lac-aux-Trois-Pistoles has become one of the biggest towns in the whole District of Saskatchewan. So big that the North-West Mounted Police started converting the abandoned fort on the north side of the lake into a police outpost last fall.

Chapan misses olden days when Lac-aux-Trois-Pistoles was nothing more than traplines, the lake, and the fort. But she also adores how much town has grown up with her. Nowadays there is lots of French-speaking families, Cree-speaking families, English-speaking families, many-language-speaking families, trapper families, horse-boarder families, trader families, farmer families, freighter families, devout families, traditional families, Catholic families, Protestant families—even a few "Not-estant" families.

"Kate McCannon calls me a Not-estant," Chapan once

said. I ain't never understood. Chapan comes to Mass and ceremony. Smudges and prays. Goes through all the motions. But, in secret, she don't believe in God. "But don't ever say that in front of Père Brisson. Okay?"

Cousin couldn't've disappeared at a worser time. No siree. Chapan says she didn't hear of no family in all Lac-aux-Trois-Pistoles who didn't lose at least a third their crops or gardens to drought and frost last year. There was even less game than Nimama'd ever seen. Chapan's been cooking up ham hock soup all week because that's all that's left of our poor pig, Percy.

We got a fancy root cellar in the homestead—a latch in the floor covered with a bearskin rug so nobody trips on it. Usually the cellar is stocked full of potatoes, sacks of flour and sugar, bottles of vinegar, seeds, dried berries and meats, pork pemmican, bear grease, duck fat, pickled eggs and carrots and onions and cucumbers. But there ain't much food this year. To make it worser, half our in-the-ground carrots was spoiled by rabbits this summer, half our in-the-cellar potatoes was spoiled by a family of rats Cousin discovered around Christmastime, and half the in-the-sack pork pemmican was spoiled by the same rats who made babies we didn't know about.

Chapan used to say no animals in the house. But after them rats broke her rule, she started keeping the cats inside. Problem is Félix and Miss Kitty always sneak outside whenever Chapan opens a window or door.

We finished building the church two springs ago. Nimama says the church got finished right when we needed it most. Life's got awful dark for us in the North-West. The church gives us a place to be together. Gives us a symbol of hope.

Chapan says them buffalo hunts was a time for all half-breeds to be together for a few months on the prairie. Even for us bush-breeds in Lac-aux-Trois-Pistoles, there ain't enough coyotes or martens to make good money selling furs to feed everyone without meat from buffalo hunts. Me and Cousin ain't never even ate buffalo meat before. We was little kids when the buffalo died in Saskatchewan forever. Chapan says when we lost the buffalo, we lost a family member.

Chapan's afraid we'll have another death in the family soon. She says the North-West is real sick. We need each other more than ever.

For one thing, nobody's sure how they feel about Louis Riel being back in Batoche. There's talk he'll lead another uprising. Bigger this time. Holier. Some folk say he's a saint. Others say he's insane. It's like half the families in Lac-aux-Trois-Pistoles think Riel's come to save us from tyranny like Jesus Hisself; the other half think he's bound to damn us all to Hell.

Like I said: Cousin disappeared at the worst time ever.

I opened my eyes. Chapan rubbed my tight neck muscles. I cupped my tea like a fledgling. Brung the porcelain to my lips. Devoured a mouthful of elderberries. Each and every seed *crick-crack!*ed between my teeth.

A few minutes passed like this—me sipping tea and Chapan massaging my shoulders like they carried the weight of the world. It was peaceful. Almost like Cousin never got took. Like he was napping upstairs.

I would've stayed like that forever. God as my witness.

When all the tea was drunk and them elderberries was in my belly, I left the table and hankered upstairs to the loft where most the beds is. Me and Cousin sleep in bunk beds: me on the top bunk and him on the bottom. My bunk begged me to crawl up the ladder and cuddle myself in the blankets. But I was too dang tired. So I tumbled into Cousin's bed instead.

Sometime in the night, when I lay trapped under Cousin's stinky blanket, I heard the door downstairs open and Nimama and Auntie hop inside. Nimama told Chapan they searched well past sundown. Even recruited some of the neighbours to help. She said all the footprints in the bush got so tangled together, the snow looked like a marching ground. There was no doubt Cousin got stole. But no sign of his kidnapper.

I got out of bed and snuck down a couple stairs, careful to hide in shadows. Nimama, Auntie, and Chapan sat around the candlelit kitchen table with numb faces. When I seen Auntie's dark eyes sunk in deeper than two wells to Hell, I knew she was going to be bonkers forever—or at least until we bring Cousin home.

CHAPTER 2

HALF-BREEDS ARE NOT PEOPLE!

THURSDAY, MARCH 19, 1885.

In the morning, I eavesdropped on Nimama and Auntie from the stairs while they talked to Chapan and sipped their coffees. A plate of bannock and a pot of lard and saskatoon berry pudding goop steamed in the middle of the table. Two sloppy cigarettes rested on an ashy saucer next to two burned braids of sweetgrass and sage. Chapan must have prayed with Nimama and Auntie—them to God, but Lord knows who Chapan prayed to.

Auntie shook her hair out its bun. Her hollow eyes examined the tips in the sunlight. She snipped the split ends with her nails.

Nimama pulled one of the cigarettes off the saucer. She lit a match. Smoke flowed out her nostrils. The paper looked extra white on her radishy skin.

Even though they's a tad sunburned looking all the time, both Auntie and Nimama got milky skin compared to Chapan's. In the summertime, the skin on Nimama's hands drinks up sunlight, making her brown and raspberry-like come August. Auntie'd look like that too, but she prefers hiding from the sun in her workshop. She likes to say she got dark white skin. But Chapan says her and Nimama is both creamy brown.

I don't know what Nimama thinks about the way she looks. Maybe it's because them flaming blue eyes make her look kind of Europeanish. But the sun don't scare Nimama like it scares Auntie. Out in public, Auntie's careful to keep her bun pulled tight so no one can see she got "wily half-breed hair," she calls it—a mess of blackish-brown curls that feels more like a fistful of moose fur than anything else. Nimama though, she braids her hair, then mats the fuzzy top down with Oncle's Stetson hat. Oncle—my kokum's older brother who disappeared just before me and Cousin was born—gave it to Nimama for an Easter present.

It's pretty neat: me and Cousin was born not two weeks apart after New Year 1873. But we ain't got no clue who our papas could be. Ain't even allowed to ask about them. Nimama and Auntie don't like talking about being so young and pregnant. They don't even talk much about their own papa. All me and Cousin know is their papa was some Norwegian fur trader with the surname Eriksen.

But I know Nimama and Auntie grew up in Dakota Territory with their papa and maman until their house burned down. They was just kids then. Chapan says that my kokum died in the fire. But Nimama says that's a lie. She says my kokum got so angry at the world she burned the house down and ran away when everyone else was sleeping inside.

After the fire, Oncle invited Nimama and Auntie and their papa to live with him on his farm in Red River. He needed a new business partner.

When they got to Red River, Oncle and my grandpapa farmed and traded furs together. That meant Nimama and Auntie went to be schooled at the Couvent-des-Sœurs-Grises.

School was hard. Between Nimama and Auntie, people always said Auntie was the homely one. I don't see it. But it don't matter what I see, I guess. When Auntie was getting educated at the convent, some of the nuns called her "Joséphindienne" in a not-so-nice way—to her face even.

Nimama and Auntie was home for summer after the uprising in Red River ended in 1870. Oncle and my grandpapa was one bad day away from losing their business. Auntie asked Chapan in a letter if her and Nimama and Oncle and my grandpapa could move home with her to Lac-aux-Trois-Pistoles. Chapan mailed back a handmade postcard. Her response was one word.

oui

When Monsieur Fleury heard that Chapan's son, son-in-law, and grandgirls was coming, he ordered everyone who owed a debt to Chapan to build her the finest homestead in the North-West. Even got all his nephews who worked at the livery to help.

Nimama and Auntie was happy to be with Chapan. Oncle and my grandpapa operated a new trading business out the old cabin that Chapan lived in before the homestead was built—the one Auntie uses as her workshop. Everyone says it was a quiet couple years. Stable too.

Then something real bad happened. Christmastime 1872. Just weeks before me and Cousin was born. Oncle chased our grandpapa off with a hatchet. They found their horses and bloody coats by the riverbank. Red splatters all over the ice. Cracks and exposed water. Both presumed dead since.

The pink morning shined through the windows. I scooted to my corner at the top of the stairs, careful not to make so much as a peep.

Everyone around the table sat quiet. Cougar quiet. The only hearable sound was the cigarette burning between Nimama's lips.

"The police have to help us." Chapan shifted in her chair uneasy. She rested her hand on Nimama's wrist. "Look, the Ducharme boys will be here after lunch. When they get here, take Niko and your sister to the outpost and report Guillaume missing. I'm sure the pol—"

"You really think they care about some missing half-breed boy?" Auntie tossed her hair and glared at Chapan. "They say we're all in it with Riel."

"How do you know that? You haven't even met them yet."

"Haven't you been reading the *Herald*?" Auntie snipped harshful. "We're one gunshot away from war!"

"The police's job is to look after the *people* of Lac-aux-Trois-Pist—"

"Half-breeds are *not* people!" Auntie knocked her chair flat on the floor as she blasted to her feet. She panted like a dog and clenched her fists. "They treat us like animals. If Ottawa thought half-breeds were people, they wouldn't fill our land with settlers!"

I sat on the stairs a long time. I didn't know what to think about what Auntie said. Them words bounced around my brain over and over and over and over: "Half-breeds are not people! Half-breeds are not people!"

Auntie ain't never escaped the shame of being Indian or Métis. Won't talk Cree in public. Won't wear her own beadwork out the house neither. She spent all her money on men's boots even though she makes me and Cousin warm moccasins with rabbit fur on the insides and beaded flowers on the outsides. I know it hurts Chapan's feelings when Auntie calls the old ways "*their* ways"—as if *they* is someone *we* ought to be ashamed of. As if *we* ain't *them*.

"Any sign of Cousin?" I walked down the stairs pretending I just woke up. I rubbed my eyes and yawned until real tears dripped down my cheeks.

"Niko! You're awake." Nimama met me at the bottom of the stairs with a bear hug. The kind she's famous for. She looked tired from up close. Smelled tired too. Like the only reason she was awake was the hot coffee and cigarettes boiling her blood. "No sign of Guillaume yet. We're going to find him though. Okay? Eat some bannock."

Nimama led me to the table where I hugged good morning to Chapan and Auntie. I rubbed their backs a long time. They needed some good hugging.

I sat beside Auntie. At the table I smeared a hunk of goop all over my bannock. But, for the first time ever, I wasn't hungry. Cousin disappearing took my appetite.

"What d'you figure, Guille?" Auntie rubbed my ears and twirled my hairs. She didn't notice she called me Cousin's name on accident. Which was good for her, I suppose. She'd go even bonkerser if she knew she called me Guille.

I didn't want to finish my bannock. But I did anyway. I hoped I wasn't about to give myself a tummy ache. That's the worst part about being hungry all the dang time: it's like your body punishes you for starving, then it punishes you again once you eat just for good measure. Chapan tries her darnedest to keep us well-fed—puts extra lard in all her cooking, lots of sugar from the store so our tummies don't growl so much. It makes her feel bad seeing her babies being hungry. She wishes there was more food to cook us.

I cleaned up the plates and scrubbed pans with Chapan. Auntie tied her boots with her mittens by the door. Nimama slipped into her tweed jacket and Stetson. She slung the repeater over her shoulder.

"We're going looking for Guille. We'll be back for lunch."

"Can I come?" I set a handful of plates on the table.

"You're safe here with Chapan."

"I get to come to the police outpost though. Right?"

Nimama buttoned her jacket slow. She looked at me suspiciousful. Auntie waited at the door. I knew I was about to get myself caught for eavesdropping. But I need Cousin back.

"We'll see what the Ducharmes say after lunch."

Nimama and Auntie stepped into the cold morning. I watched them ride off through the window. Chapan drank tea and read the latest *Saskatchewan Herald* at the table.

After a few minutes, I went upstairs to the loft to grab some stuff for me and Chapan. I brung down a deck of cards and the cribbage board Oncle made out of a moose antler for Auntie's thirteenth birthday. If I couldn't be out looking for Cousin, I needed something to take my mind off him being gone.

"Want to play?"

Chapan folded her newspaper and wiped her fingers on her apron. I set the cribbage board on the table and handed her the cards to shuffle. I reset the pegs on the board from when me and Cousin played yesterday—a lifetime ago. It felt wrong pulling the pegs from where Cousin played them last time. Felt just as wrong putting them back at the beginning to start a new game without him. Like we was moving on without him.

Me and Chapan played for hours. Then Nimama and Auntie came home for lunch—without Cousin.

CHAPTER 3

GUN SMOKE IN THE HALL OF MIRRORS

Even after all the coffee she drunk and them cigarettes she smoked at lunch, Nimama fell asleep in her chair with her head pillowed on her arms on the table. Auntie made it to the downstairs bed by the wall near the fireplace at least. She lay with her back to us reading *Leatherstocking Tales*. The pages rustled when she turned them like a windchime telling us she was awake. Me and Chapan splashed water as we washed the bowls and knives.

I felt wound tighter than a fiddle waiting for the Ducharme boys to show up. We hoped Cousin would be with them. Even if we didn't expect it.

Arf! arf! arf!

Outside, Barney barked his poor lungs out. Some young voices greeted him and told him how good a boy he was. A few seconds later we heard them at the door.

"Madame Desjarlais?" I turned my attention to Georges Ducharme standing at the doorway with his little brother, Charlo. Georges tipped his head to me and Chapan. He looked over to Nimama sleeping at the table and Auntie in the bed and tipped his head to them too. "Mademoiselle Eriksen. Mademoiselle Eriksen."

Even though Georges was sixteen and Charlo was eleven, they was about the same looking. Excepting in size. From afar they looked like twins in different phases of development. They shared the same reddish burned wood colour all over their skin. Even their black hair carried charred strands of red.

"Madame Desjarlais, we're sorry. We seen no sign of Guillaume."

"What time is it?" Auntie rose from the bed. She ambled to the table. Her toes stepped lazy-like over each other.

"Half past noon, Mademoiselle Eriksen." Georges glanced at a watch in his pocket.

"I made tea. Let's make chit-chat. You boys must be exhausted." Chapan waved for the Ducharmes to come into the house. She waddled to the stove.

Georges sat next to me. Charlo sat across the table next to Nimama. His face looked like he thought she was dead.

Auntie glared at Nimama sleeping beside Charlo. She balled her fist and *bonk!*ed the table next to Nimama's head. "Sara!"

Nimama shot up in her chair. Her braids was loose and fuzzy. She nodded sleepy hellos at Georges and Charlo. "Sorry, boys."

"No problem, mademoiselle." Georges nodded at Nimama. He loosened his collar's choke hold and swallowed. "Listen: I think it's reasonable to conclude that . . . well . . . There's no sign of Guille nowhere. We need help. We need bona fide search parties."

"Absolutely." Chapan brung over a couple cups. She poured each boy some tea with a fancy smell I ain't smelled in months—a tea made from dried muskego leaves, currants, saskatoons, blueberries. "We have to tell the authorities."

"Funny you should propose just that." Georges raised his cup to thank Chapan and blew a wave into the bluish-gold tea, shooing the steam away before he brung the china to his lips. "Me and Charlo thought we could go report Guillaume missing on your behalf. You'd have to ride past our place to get to the outpost anyway. Me and Charlo will head out after tea if that works."

"That's kind to offer. But Josey and Sara should really go with Niko. He was there. Besides: we need to speak to Père Brisson."

"Why don't we take Charlo home on our way to the police outpost?" Auntie asked. The room fell quiet. "Georges can summon Père Brisson."

Georges and Charlo looked tensionful at each other. Charlo nodded subtle.

"Sure . . ." Georges wiggled his jaw and gestured to Nimama and Auntie with his chin. ". . . if you take Charlo home."

Chapan nibbled her lip. Her eyes bounced between Georges and Charlo. "I'll wait for the girls and Niko to come home from the outpost. Then we'll all go to the rectory together."

"It's okay, madame." Charlo sunk into his shoulders as he reassured Chapan. "Georges can go."

"I don't know." Chapan ran her fingers over the lip of her teacup. "I don't want him alone out there."

"I'll be fine." Georges sat up in his chair like he was a little taller than he truly was. Stuck his chest out like his shoulders was a little broader. Raised his chin like he was a little braver. "If you're anxious about me riding by myself, lend me your gun. Honest: I'm the spottest-on shot on either side of the Beaver River."

Georges was right. He was the finest young marksman in the whole District of Saskatchewan. His papa, a seventy-or-so-year-old buffalo hunter by the name of Nishecabo Ducharme, taught Georges when they moved here five years ago how to drain a repeater in twenty seconds, all while nailing a flying pigeon damn near every shot.

Georges wasn't always the best marksman in L-T-P. For ages that distinction belonged to the boy's legendary father hisself. Nishecabo was one of the greatest buffalo hunters in all Indian Country.

Last spring, Nishecabo got struck with his malady. Made him not able to talk no more. Not able to walk neither. Even made part of his face slump to the side.

Everyone around L-T-P gets right anxious talking about Nishecabo. Me included. I confess. It ain't right the way we make behind-the-back chit-chat about him. Like he ain't alive no more. Like he can't understand us. But it's hard not to. People say it's tough picturing that man deserving what he's going through. Nishecabo had it all: a young family, wartime heroics, feathers, pigs and horses and sheep, land to farm along the river, strawberry bushes. All he had against him was time.

I ain't convinced Nishecabo prays for hisself like other people pray for him. For all I know, maybe he ain't one to think of his life as "right tragic," like some call it. Maybe for Nishecabo this is just the way his life is and there ain't nothing wrong with it unless God Hisself says so.

Then again, maybe not. God don't make much sense nowadays.

Nimama says it's hard on them Ducharme boys with such a sick pa. She can only imagine. She says I better remember that because they must be struggling.

It ain't fair. I deserve a papa to struggle over. Me and Cousin's papas should be in our lives. At least Nimama and Auntie had a papa, even if he wasn't no good. Someday I will be the best papa in the world. Total opposite of *my* father.

"That okay with you, Mademoiselle Eriksen?" Georges waited for Nimama to wake up a little. He pointed at the repeater on the mantel with his chin. "Lending me your gun for the day?"

"You didn't bring yours?"

"Maman donated our guns to the men in Batoche," Georges said, frustrated. "She says I got to stick around and look after papa."

Nimama lit a match and smoked a cigarette she lifted from the saucer. She pointed at her Winchester repeating rifle on the mantel. "Bring it back tomorrow morning."

"Sure thing."

Chapan walked to the fireplace and took the rifle off the mantel. A standard Winchester Model 1873. Nimama's favourite. Chapan carried it like a newborn to the table.

"Shooting pigeons ain't like shooting people," Chapan said to Georges. "Killing people hurts the soul. Kipapa knows what I mean."

For a sixteen-year-old, Georges ain't got much of a soon-to-be-a-man type body: the coppery whiskers on his chin is thin like Charlo's; Georges's Adam's apple is still a seedling.

Georges shuffled in his chair. He brung his tea to his lips and *slurrrp!*ed. "You can trust me: I won't be shooting first. Not unless there's immediate danger."

Chapan laid the gun on the table soft as a bundle. She grabbed a braid of sweetgrass, lit a match, and laid the smoky braid down.

Smoke flowed to the ceiling. Chapan washed her hands in the stream. She splashed plumes over her head, her ears, her eyes, her lips, her heart. She grabbed the gun off the table. She bathed Winnie over the smudge smoke. Washed the barrel, the stock, the lever, the trigger.

Chapan laid Winnie between her and Georges. "Take care of each other."

THE FAMOUSEST GUN IN ALL LAC-AUX-TROIS-PISTOLES IS KATE McCANNON'S gun—a side-by-side shotgun with the stock and barrels sawed off like a pistol. She calls it "Li P'chii." Li P'chii never leaves Kate McCannon's side. She's the only person in all Lac-aux-Trois-Pistoles who walks around with a loaded gun and a bandolier of shells—only person in L-T-P who, like Kate McCannon herself says, "carries fire."

Not everyone in L-T-P is keen on Kate McCannon bringing Li P'chii with her everywhere. Papa Brisson's devoutest followers scoff at Kate McCannon. They don't shine on seeing a sawed-off shotgun in public. On a woman in particular.

Truth be told, before Cousin got took, I didn't think there was no need for carrying fire. But Kate McCannon's always had her reasons, I suppose.

One time in February when me and Nimama was at Cunningham's store buying flour and coffee and such, I overheard a couple women say Kate McCannon wearing her gun around town is nothing short of a scar on Lac-aux-Trois-Pistoles's wholesome nature—a reminder of what she done to Papa Brisson.

"Fitting how she chopped the barrels off," said one woman as she inspected a tin of candy, pretending she could afford it. "As if seeing the father isn't reminder enough of Kate McCannon's penchant for chopping."

"Truer words were never spoken," the other replied, thumbing her nose. "Makes me worry for poor Tom."

"I wonder what he knows."

"About the cuckoldry?"

"Yeah."

"I doubt anybody who likes their hands will say much else," said the nose thumber, turning to Cunningham behind the counter.

Me and Nimama loaded Oncle's old Red River cart and squeal-wheeled back home. I hate riding in that thing. Can't hear nothing. Stupid cart wails like a mermaid fighting a rougarou.

Screeeeeeech! screeeeeeech!

I asked Nimama what the women at the store talked about, what cockledoodlery was and why it made Kate McCannon's husband, Tom, so poor. But I couldn't hear Nimama explain nothing over the awful *screech!*ing of the wheels. Didn't help none Huckleberry got a habit of farting wet-like on the regular. No regard for us in the back. Poor guy made the whole ride home a stinky, screechy, cold-as-hell trip to buy only enough goods to half-fill our bellies.

Kate McCannon's only ever drawn Li P'chii on someone once. They say one of them new Mounties pulled his pistol on Kate McCannon when they argued at the saloon around Christmastime. The bald, moustachioed policeman said something about her being a pagan and a whore. He wagged his gun like he shook his pissing pinger at her.

Kate McCannon snatched the barrel of the pistol with one hand. She whipped Li P'chii out her holster with the other. While gripping the barrel of the Mountie's gun, she swung Li P'chii high like a hatchet and hacked his wrist, severing the revolver from his mangy hand.

"Next time won't be so lucky." Kate McCannon re-holstered Li P'chii. She tucked the revolver into her bandolier. Then backed out the saloon doors and faded into the early-evening winter moonlight.

Kate McCannon's been on the lam ever since.

WE WAS ON THE TRAIL HEADED TO TAKE CHARLO HOME BEFORE GOING TO THE OUTpost. It was a cool, breath-be-seen afternoon. Springtime sun shined hot on my black hair.

Lac-aux-Trois-Pistoles is shaped like a revolver with the grip of the gun on the west arm of the lake and the barrel on the east. Inside the west arm is Fleury Avenue—home of the livery and hotel and saloon and town's heart. Monsieur Fleury opened his livery and saloon and such after Chapan cleared bush for him and his family when they arrived before me and Cousin was born. Now Fleury Avenue's home to a couple general stores, a smith, even an icehouse.

Inside the east arm of the lake is the community's soul—the church and rectory. Then southeast of town in the bush is where us and the Ducharmes and a few other families got our homesteads.

At the hammer of the revolver on the north tip of the lake, overlooking Fleury Avenue and the church to its south, is the new police outpost at the old fort. Tall wood walls surround the place like a castle. You can only get there by fording the river east of the lake. Otherwise the outpost blends in with Maman Earth.

Me and Nimama rode Pony—me in the front of the saddle and Nimama in the back. She wrapped her arms around the blanket over my shoulders.

Auntie swayed back and forth in the saddle of her stallion, Viking. Viking's real high-strung, but a pleasure to ride. A handsome steed too: solid white with black spots and a black mane and tail, and eyes darker than Auntie's.

Charlo sat silent behind Auntie's saddle with his arms wrapped around her waist. He stared empty at the trail below him.

We dropped Charlo off at home with his maman and papa. Then we continued back up the trail a long time. The trail ended at the wide ford in the river. The water was froze.

The ice was bunchy and trying to thaw. Hoofprints from all kinds of animals dotted the snow crossing the river.

We dismounted the horses and led them careful across the ice. Once we was safe on the other side, we mounted back up and continued the trail to the fort.

We seen the fort from afar. It looked like a wood castle perched high up on a hill, away from the muskeg, overlooking the lake across Fleury Avenue and the church. A tall fence surrounded the buildings. I couldn't say how many buildings there was because some of them was being tore down. It was clear that back in olden days, the fort was busier than anything them Mounties would ever need. A Union Jack waved way up high on a pole.

Nimama and Auntie dismounted at the gate. Side by side, they led their horses to the office at the far end of the fort. I wiggled my butt and reclaimed the saddle space where Nimama sat. Being in the front of the saddle's painful business—dang horn always squishes my pinger. It's the worst part about sharing a saddle with someone bigger. Won't be long until I'm too tall for me and Nimama to ride in the saddle together.

I imagined what life must have been like for Chapan back in olden days. Unwashed men rustling around with furs on their shoulders and sled dogs yapping at their ankles. Campfire and tobacco smoke polluting the fresh air. Women spit-roasting whole pigs and thin-cut buffalo strips while grease sizzled over a fire. Canvas and buffalo hide teepees surrounding the fort. Kids my age tagging each other, hiding behind buildings and tanning racks.

A couple buffalo-coated policemen shared a cigarillo by the stables. They watched each step we took across the fort.

After tying the horses to the hitching post at the office, Nimama helped me off the saddle and led me by hand up the stairs to the front door. My moccasined feet was careful not to trip. I felt nervous meeting the police. Even if we wasn't in no trouble.

Auntie opened the door for me and Nimama. We entered the office. Took no more than a half-dozen steps when Nimama stopped dead in her tracks.

"Holy Mary, it's you."

Nimama wide-eyed a young Mountie standing near the desk. The man looked about same age as Auntie. Had big brown eyes and curly black hair under his tilted pillbox cap. Clean-shaved cheeks, fat eyebrows, spongy lips. Tall and handsome too.

He squinted confused-like at Nimama. Auntie too. Then his eyes flashed when he recognized them.

"*Sara? Josey?*"

A senior policeman with triangular cheekbones and flaming blue eyes sat at the desk. His eyebrows crawled up his forehead. Frail lines led to his pointy, fiftyish-year-old chin. His skin was pale and tight like hand drums. "You already know each other?"

His slender hands oozed out the red sleeves of his serge onto his desk, messy with pens, maps, inkwells, letters, candles, cups, spittoons. All sorts of knickknacks. The red serge looked heavy on his bony body.

"You could say that." Nimama didn't look away from the young officer she recognized. Couldn't believe her eyes. Auntie looked at the young constable just as awestruck as Nimama.

The young constable surveyed me with surprised eyes. Familiar and worried eyes. "Who's this?"

"Niko's my son."

Blood drained from the young policeman's raspberry cheeks. He looked dead as the world continued around him. Like I was somehow bad news.

"How rude," said the senior officer behind the desk. "We haven't met. Ladies, I am Sergeant Paul Wagner. This is Corporal Bruno San Luis seated across from me."

A third officer sat in the fancy chair across from Sergeant Wagner's desk. He was a barrel of a man. Bald too. Buttons on his red serge looked like they would pop if he took too deep a breath. He had a boring face excepting brown cross eyes and a twirly pepper moustache. And his holster carried no pistol. It was Kate McCannon's now.

"And your friend here is our latest arrival, Constable . . . um . . ." Wagner snapped his fingers at Campbell.

"Campbell Palmer, sir."

"Yes. Right. He's a Métis." Wagner inspected my blanket, my hair, my skin, my mocs. "Like you three, I presume."

The sergeant retrieved a cigar from the ashtray resting on his desk. He twirled the tip over a candle flame as he inspected Oncle's Stetson on Nimama's head. "That's quite the hat you wear, miss. I understand that harlot Kate McCannon wears a similar hat. Although hers, I believe, is an old Civil War cavalry hat. You know, I'm not accustomed to ladies wearing hats like yours. European ladies wear different, more refined chapeaux than Métis.

"If I may satiate my curiosity: this custom of wearing men's hats, is it—how can I phrase this sensitively?—a tradition amongst your people?

"Campbell, do you know? Do women's hats have some

sort of Métis cultural significance?" Wagner waited for the silence to slither past. He supped his cigar.

Campbell shuffled his boots.

"How disappointing." Wagner batted ash off his cigar. "I'd like to have known. Your people, your culture, are delights to observe.

"As I'm sure you're well aware, our Mounted Police rankings lack officers of—what's the polite phrasing?—Indian pedigree. Being a Métis like you, Campbell is a welcome addition to Lac-aux-Trois-Pistoles's detachment. He brings necessary insight into your people's special needs."

Campbell dug his thumbs under his gun belt. A polished Enfield revolver popped out the holster on his hip. He tried looking tough. Like a gunslinger. But he couldn't. Something about him made me think Lac-aux-Trois-Pistoles was the last place he wanted to be.

"And what brings you ladies to my office?" said Wagner.

"We're here to report my son missing."

"A missing Métis boy. Of course." Wagner pulled a notepad from a desk drawer. He opened to a new page and dabbed his pen in the inkwell. The cigar burned in the ashtray beside him. "We'll find him right away. Now tell me about this young man. What's his name?"

Auntie sighed. "His name is Guillaume Eriksen."

"Eriksen?"

"Yes."

"*Eriksen?*"

"*Yes.*"

Wagner flung his pen onto the desk and leaned into his chair. Ink splashed on the notepad.

"Master Eriksen has, in fact, already been reported missing."

"By who?" Auntie's veins popped out her forehead.

"I cannot divulge sensitive information about an ongoing missing persons investigation. Be grateful a community member has a mind on your well-being."

"This is about my son!" Auntie smashed her fist against the desk. "Who reported Guille missing?"

"We have an open investigation into Master Eriksen's disappearance. Campbell begins his community patrols . . . Corporal San Luis, what's the date?"

"Thursday."

"Not the *day*, the *date*."

"March 19th, sir," said Constable Palmer. He looked like he had razors in his boots.

"Yes. Right," said Wagner. "Campbell begins patrols on Fleury Avenue next Monday. You can report information to him directly if you prefer."

Wagner retrieved the cigar off the ashtray. He puffed smoke toward our faces and leaned in his chair.

Campbell looked sad at me. Regretful even. Powerless. He had that look Cousin gets when he knows something I don't.

"We best go. You men have paperwork." Nimama spun me around to face the door.

"Corporal San Luis will see you out." Wagner chewed the end of his cigar. He fluttered us out the door with his stringy fingers.

Campbell stood still as a statue. Soon as our toes stepped onto the porch on the other side of the door frame, San Luis latched the door behind us.

CHAPTER 4

THE LAC-AUX-TROIS-PISTOLES RUMOUR MILLERS' UNION

Nimama's breath shot out her nose in a bullish cloud. We rocked with each of Pony's steps. "I can't believe Campbell's a fucking Mountie."

Pony and Viking stopped at the edge of the trail. We was tucked away in the forest. My breath froze all over the blanket. Kinky white swirls crusted the wool. If it ain't been for that sun, I'd have shivered until my teeth was dust.

Auntie pulled her hair out its bun. Crooked strands fell on her shoulders like lightning bolts. She dallied her reins around the saddle horn so she could pluck her split ends.

"We were kids back then." Auntie sounded annoyed. Cousin being gone and all, she only had so much patience left. "Kids grow up."

"Why are you defending him?"

"I'm not."

"Then what are you saying?"

"Nothing."

Nimama took off her Stetson, wiped her forehead, then put it back on. She looked good with her hat because Nimama felt good with her hat. Probably felt just as good wearing that tweed jacket because she'd won the thing even though it was uglier than sin.

At home, Nimama's indoor clothes ain't no different than Auntie's. Auntie makes all our clothes: knitted, beaded, sewed. Both Auntie and Nimama like their flowy dresses and high-waisted skirts. Both wear moccasins inside even though Auntie wouldn't be caught dead in public wearing beadwork or leather.

Nimama rubbed my knee and thigh. Like she was making mental notes of what my body felt like so she could never forget. "That couldn't have gone much worse."

"Sergeant Wagner has to be in on this. There's no other way they could already know Guille's missing."

"Don't talk crazy."

"It's not crazy. We'll see what the father says when we get home."

Nimama looked Auntie sour. The forest hushed around us. “I don’t trust him . . .”

“Be honest.” Auntie leaned into her saddle. She looked Nimama deep into her core like an anchor. “You don’t *really* believe what people say about Père Brisson. Do you?”

Nimama stalled. Inspected the trail. Took off her hat and fiddled the brim.

“Answer me.”

“I don’t fucking know!” Nimama grabbed the brim with both hands and stuffed her head into the hat. “Why else would Kate McCannon chop off the father’s hands?”

“Kate McCannon’s had it out for him since he got here.” Auntie tied her hair back into its bun. She undallied the reins from the horn. “Charlo doesn’t need his name dragged through this. What happened between Kate McCannon and Père Brisson’s their business. If Kate McCannon really cared about Charlo, she’d dismiss this bullshit. But that woman won’t deny any rumour that grows her legend.”

Nimama sat stiff in the saddle. I massaged Pony’s neck with my palm. Her muscles rolled like waves. “Would you still trust Père Brisson with Guille?”

Auntie didn’t say nothing. After a minute, she gripped Viking’s reins and kicked him forward. They started back up the trail. Me and Nimama followed.

“Let’s get going. Him and Kokum are probably waiting.”

LAC-AUX-TROIS-PISTOLES AIN’T NEVER MET SOMEONE LIKE KATE McCANNON BEFORE. Her and her husband Tom moved here not five years ago from the Great Sioux Reservation in Dakota Territory. A niece of Nishecabo hisself. If they got kids, they either grown up or they ain't brung them. But I ain't convinced they ever had kids. Kate McCannon's too friendly with us young ones to be a maman and Tom's too cold with everyone to be a papa.

Kate McCannon ain't no follower of Christ neither. Kind of like Chapan. Excepting Chapan's still part of the church community. Kate McCannon ain't no "Not-estant" like Chapan. Kate McCannon not only ain't no believer of God, she ain't no believer of *nothing*. Not even the old ways. Even before she got banished from church grounds, she ain't never prayed at Christmastime. Never brung a plate to Easter feast. Never washed in holy water. Always allowed to pass on smudges. Heck, the only Lent that Kate McCannon ever observed is Corporal San Luis "lent" his revolver to her—forever.

There's a chapel at the fort we used to go to before the church and rectory was built. Ever since forever ago, even in them years the fort was abandoned, a priest came to the chapel to preach to all the followers in Lac-aux-Trois-Pistoles. The priest who came before Papa Brisson wasn't well-liked. "Father Whatshisnuts," they called him. He preached until Papa Brisson got sent to us from France.

Kate McCannon sat in the chapel before service visiting with friends one morning. It wasn't unusual for Kate McCannon to visit with people before Father Whatshisnuts started his sermons. She sat at the end of the pew beside her number one friend, Hélène Ducharme. Somehow Father Whatshisnuts ain't never noticed Kate McCannon before. So when he did, he took it upon hisself to make introductions.

"Who are you, madame?" he said, not-that-nice-like, in particular because she wore that black cavalry hat indoors and had a wet cheek full of tobacco.

"Kate McCannon."

"Remove your hat, Madame McCannon."

"*Kate* McCannon."

"Take off that hat, Madame Kate McCann—"

"*Kate McCannon.*"

"That's what I said, Madame K—"

"Kate McCannon!" Kate McCannon stood and wagged her finger at the priest. "Say my name, for Christ's sake!"

"Do not use our Lord's name in vain like that, Madame Kate McC—"

"Say my name!"

"Madame Kate—"

"Say my God damn name! Call me Kate McCannon!"

"You can*not* say our Lord's name like that!"

"I am your Lord, you son of a bitch!" Kate McCannon shoved her nose not a feather's width from the priest's. "Call me Kate McCannon."

"Will you leave us then?"

"Call me my name and I leave forever."

"Then leave us forever, Kate McCannon."

No one called Kate McCannon nothing but her full name after that. A couple women Kate McCannon sat with in the pews, Hélène included, left the chapel with her. They never came back to pray with Father Whatshisnuts. Waited for Papa Brisson to arrive. But after what she done to Papa Brisson's hands, some of Kate McCannon's people don't come to Mass at all no more.

When Papa Brisson came to us two years ago, he'd heard

lots of behind-the-back chit-chat about Kate McCannon. Good things. Bad things. Even good things that was bad things. Ain't nothing straightforward with Kate McCannon.

Papa Brisson said Kate McCannon was his mission when he came to Lac-aux-Trois-Pistoles. He would say out loud to hisself she was a hell-bent woman with a moral code rigider than iron. She was ripe for salvation. But she was worser than a pagan: she was a nonbeliever.

Papa Brisson had a hell of a time tracking Kate McCannon down. Didn't get to her until last spring when he boarded her young cousin, Charles Ducharme. Charlo was Papa Brisson's first boarder. His maman sent him to be with Papa Brisson when Nishecabo got apoplexy and Georges broke his ribs and ankle falling off his horse. Hélène was too busy taking care of Nishecabo and Georges to look after Charlo too. So Charlo boarded with Papa Brisson for a couple weeks until Nishecabo's health was stable and Georges could take care of hisself.

All was fine. Kate McCannon even went to the rectory from time to time to check on him.

Then Charlo went back to living with his family. People started to whisper all sorts of things. When the Ducharmes stopped coming to church, the rumours got worser.

So Kate McCannon visited Papa Brisson for the last time. Alone. She brung herself a hatchet and two buffalo horns—one full of gunpowder, the other full of fire.

When the bishop asked Papa Brisson why he ain't got no hands to hold the rosary no more, Papa Brisson said he cut his hands so bad they got gangrene. So Kate McCannon chopped them off and seared them shut with hot metal and fire.

PAPA BRISSON'S WAGON WAS PARKED OUT FRONT WHEN WE PULLED UP TO THE homestead. We dismounted and led Viking and Pony through the barn doors to be with Papa Brisson's horse. We took off the saddles and tack. Brung the saddles to the saddle racks. Pony sweated where her saddle was. Steam rose off her body. She inhaled the oats in her pail. Gulped her water too. I brushed the dust off her legs. Picked snow, ice, mud, poo out her shoes. When I put my ear against Pony's neck, I listened to air pass through her windpipes. Blood *blub-blubb!*ed through her veins. I stood under her chin and wrapped my arms around her nose. I buried my nostrils into that shiny jawline of hers and sucked in the musty power that coated her body.

Nimama seen me hugging Pony's head. She shot me a quick smile. Then she grabbed my elbow and marched us out the barn toward the homestead. Barney dashed out the workshop. Barked loud to say he missed us. His lippy grin slobbered on the ground. I scratched behind his ears. His stinky dog dust stuck to my hands.

Me and Barney got lots in common. Lots of different breeds of ancestors to make a one-of-a-kind pupper. "Métis mutts," Chapan calls us. Excepting some people around town call me "quadroon" and "octoroon." But I ain't too sure what them words mean.

Félix and Miss Kitty waited for us up in the window to open the front door so they could escape. We opened the door. They slided through our legs outside.

Chapan sat at the table with four teacups, a teapot, and a couple rolled-up newspapers. Papa Brisson sat across from her. His boarders, Étienne and Jean-Baptiste Ghostkeeper, sat beside him.

"Nikosis, my son." Papa Brisson uncrossed his legs. He stood tall. His cassock used up twice as much cloth as any regular-size man's. He waved his sleeves for me to come close.

I waded into his belly. Nervousful. I wasn't always nervous around Papa Brisson. He's the closest thing me and Cousin got to a papa. But my heart gets a little sick with him ever since what happened.

Papa Brisson smiled at Auntie. Hugged her long too. "Your grandmother told me about Guillaume. We'll find him. Keep faith in God."

Papa Brisson bowed at Nimama. Smiled at her. "Mademoiselle Eriksen. I trust you are well. It was wonderful to see you at service Sunday."

Nimama ignored him. Instead she removed her hat and bowed to Étienne and Jean-Baptiste. Me and Nimama took our seats beside Chapan. Auntie sat at the end, straight across from Papa Brisson.

Étienne sat closest to Papa Brisson. He's about Charlo's age. Well-dressed in his black vest and shirt. Black, frizzy curls. And eyes browner than topsoil. "Bonjour, tout le monde."

"Taanshii," said his thirteen-year-old brother, Jean-Baptiste. His deep voice wanted to crack like ice. He wore a hot red sweater picked clean of lint and pilled balls. He was healthy and well-fed like his brother too.

"No use beating around the bush, mesdames." Papa Brisson slicked his thin hair back with a halo of bear grease. His wrinkles carried sixty-odd years of prayers in their folds. "Guillaume's disappearance may not be isolated. Two other boys have gone missing this week."

"The first was reported in the *Herald*." Chapan unrolled a newspaper, opened to a page near the back, and slided the paper across the table for Auntie to see. "But it got buried in the rumours section. All the other reporting's too caught up with Riel."

"What happened?" Auntie asked.

"Mademoiselle Bella Gervais's nephew didn't come home from checking his squirrel traps Monday night. Then on Tuesday, Madame Elinore Morin's grandson disappeared cutting firewood with his sister. Bella and Elinore spoke to the sergeant at the outpost yesterday morning."

"What'd he say?"

"He was already aware of the boys' disappearances. He thanked Bella and Elinore and sent them away."

Auntie shook her head. She grinded her teeth like an anxious horse. Everything was making less and less sense. "That's what happened to us too."

"Anything else?" Nimama put her hat back on her head and slided back her chair. "Otherwise me and Niko are happy to get your wagon ready while you gentlemen make chit-chat with Kokum and Josey."

"Stay put." Chapan tugged Nimama's chair back toward the table. She looked disappointed and annoyed with Nimama. "You're being rude."

"There *is* something else, Sara. A man came to the rectory on Sunday evening before the boys vanished." Papa Brisson shook his elbows so the sleeves of his cassock slided down his forearms. His patchy scars glowed in the candlelight. He flashed his wrists over the table like he showed off bejewelled rings and bracelets. "He wore these beautiful beaded gauntlets. From his wife, he said. I thought it would be worth a laugh if I tried them on. Then I noticed how scarred his hands were when he put the gauntlets over my wrists. Terrible burn scars."

Nimama put her hand on her blouse. Her fire-kissed fingers traced her own burn scars on her neck and chest.

Chapan had little burn scars on her hands too. Excepting hers came from keeping fire.

"Do you know who he was?" Auntie's frown dripped down her cheeks. Her, Nimama, and Chapan had the same scared look. The look they get when they share a secret.

"He wouldn't say. But he was very deliberate in telling me the Indian commissioner and the police superintendent hired him to control the coyote population in Lac-aux-Trois-Pistoles. He said they negotiated a lucrative contract in Prince Albert to sterilize the pups this spring."

Auntie's lip trembled. Tears escaped her heavy eyes. She looked to Nimama. Nimama hid her eyes behind her hands. Chapan rubbed Nimama's shoulder. They cried soft. What did they suspect?

Papa Brisson rose from his seat. He walked to Auntie and crouched in front of her. He soothed her knee with his forearms.

"He was around my age. Well-spoken with a European accent of sorts. Coppery white hair. And a chaotic soul. His hands aside, he was like any other old fur trader."

Auntie couldn't hold the weeping in no more. Her fear, her sadness bursted out of her. She dug her fingers into Papa Brisson's cassock and dug her face into his chest. She wailed into his sleeves. She couldn't stop. He rubbed his forearm against her back.

"Everything's going to be okay. We'll find your boy. We'll find Guillaume."

CHAPTER 5

EXOVEDATE

SUNDAY, MARCH 22, 1885.

All week I wanted to ask Auntie who the hell she thought Papa Brisson met for her to get so scared. Nimama and Chapan too. Like losing Cousin ain't scary enough. But I knew if I asked, I'd be dead. Auntie been going bonkerser every day since Cousin got took. Lashing out at all us like her words was whips. It's better not knowing than crossing her.

This morning Nimama said I could leave la bibliothèque to go to church with Chapan. But her and Auntie didn't come with us. Them and Hélène and Georges Ducharme was out searching for Cousin instead.

Me and Chapan drove Huckleberry with the Red River cart to church. We parked at the hitching posts and water troughs across the road in a pocket of spruce trees. The church got pearly paint brushed careful along each plank, around each fancy arched window frame for stained glass. The nave is shaped like a ginormongous rectangle with a fancy roof and bell tower plopped on top. The inside's decorated real nice with paintings and gold trimmings and wood panels.

Me and Chapan sat near the stove. Late-morning sunlight beamed through the colourful glass onto the backs of the pews. The church was half full of anxious faces waiting for Papa Brisson to start his sermon. Whole families with sick babies and hungry grandparents huddled together. Even Campbell Palmer, out of uniform, sat at the back.

Papa Brisson hovered over the pulpit. A ginormongous crucifix loomed over his shoulders. The altar behind Papa Brisson was decorated with flowers and candles and books. One corner was overseen by a pale statue of Jesus. The other Mary with her baby in her arms.

"Dear friends. May the Lord forgive us this morning for we cannot congregate as a whole. As many of you know, three of our sons have disappeared since we met last Sunday. Our flock is vulnerable.

"In this bitter climate of fear and hostility, a false shepherd threatens to lead us hungrily astray. Men in Batoche gather arms; other men in Ottawa rattle their sabres. The spectre of war with the Dominion looms on the spring horizon.

"Like you, I ask God for answers. How I would rejoice should He reveal Himself, in flesh and blood, and guide us to salvation! I understand the desperate temptation to follow this shepherd in times of such uncertainty. But by coming together in God's home, you've committed to Jesus as our shepherd. You've committed to each other.

"We have much to pray for. And now, on the precipice

of irretraceable change across the North-West, we must also pray for the safety of our sons. We need the love of Jesus's holy protectress. Together let us appeal to the mother of our Lord, O most gracious Virgin Mary, to intercede on our behalf."

ME AND THE GHOSTKEEPER BOYS AND LIZETTE MORIN, MADAME MORIN'S GRAND-daughter, stood around the soggy boardwalk outside the church. The air was still. The sun was warm. Winter wasn't over. But spring was winding up to crack its frozen shell.

The church and rectory was spaced fiftyish yards apart. A solid boardwalk and white picket fence connected the church and rectory with a vegetable garden in the middle. Most of the lot was cleared of forest excepting some brush by the garden and hitching posts. Chapan and her friends was making chit-chat across the road by the wagons and carts and such.

"My kokum told me about Guille." Lizette buried her hands into the armpits of her way-too-big wool coat. The top of her forehead sweated where her hairs was pulled tight into a bun. Her eyes frowned at the ground. She missed her brother. "The feeling's terrible. I know it good."

"Thanks." I wiggled my toes in my moccasins. The beaded flowers on the tops rolled like waves. "Any sign of Michel yet?"

Lizette shook her head. She rolled a snowball with her foot absent-mindedful. She's a year younger than me and Cousin. He's been in love with her for long as I can remember.

"How'd he disappear anyway?" asked Étienne.

"*Hey.*" Jean-Baptiste smacked his brother's ribs. "Think before you talk."

"Ain't no mind," said Lizette. "Me and him was sawing up a tree out back. He went to pee. I turned back around, he was gone. *Poof!*"

"You didn't see or hear nobody?" I asked.

"Not a peep." Lizette stopped toeing the snowball at her feet. She lifted her eyes just enough to look at me. "My kokum says you think Guille got stole?"

"Yeah. He yelled for me to run when it happened."

"I hope Michel got stole too." Lizette returned her eyes to the snow under her toe. "He couldn't survive out here alone."

Tweeeeet! "Lizette! Time to go!"

Madame Morin waved from over by the parked wagons and carts. Her and Chapan was making chit-chat with Bella Gervais and a few other folks.

"I gotta run." Lizette whipped her finger out her armpit and pointed serious at me and Étienne and Jean-Baptiste. "Don't any of you go disappearing now. Okay?"

Lizette spun on her heels and jogged across the road to her family's wagon. The dangling sleeve of her coat waved goodbye to us while her family drove off.

Étienne sighed. His breath made a big cloud. He made a *V* with his fingers and puffed a pretend cigarette. "You think her and Guille's going to get married someday?"

"I don't know." I stuffed my hands in my pockets and kicked around the ball of snow Lizette left. "We got to bring him home first."

I HOPE MARY LISTENS TO PAPA BRISSON'S PRAYER. I DON'T KNOW IF GOD LISTENS TO anyone else's prayers at all no more. Every morning, every meal, every night I pray for Him to keep Cousin safe and bring him home. Cousin's the person you want around when bad things happen. His soul is the kind you want near when yours is breaking. It ain't fair he's gone.

I know I should be grateful the Lord looks over me. And I am. But sometimes I wish I had a real papa looking over me too. Even if it means him dying one day and leaving a hole in my heart. I know Étienne and Jean-Baptiste ain't been the same since their papa died. Georges and Charlo been different since Nishecabo got sick too. But I'm jealous. Hell, I'm even jealous of Nimama and Auntie. At least they had a papa before him and Oncle killed each other. Even if their papa deserved it. I wonder what's worser: a dead papa, an evil papa, or no papa at all.

Auntie went out searching with Nimama when we got home from church. Me and Chapan played crib at the table. The whole time we played I thought about the men at the police outpost. Campbell in particular. Why did he look at me so weird?

"Can I ask a question?"

"What is it?"

"How do Nimama and Auntie know Campbell Palmer?"

"He grew up here. Him and his family moved to Fort Edmonton the summer before you were born. They used to work at the livery."

"What was he like?"

"Him and his brother used to borrow books from me when their maman was teaching them to read. They were good kids. They were all friends back then."

I almost asked Chapan if Campbell was me or Cousin's papa. Or if maybe his brother was. It made sense. Even time-wise. Why else would he act so guilty to meet me?

Chapan looked at me worried. I had a worser question.

"Who was that guy Papa Brisson talked about?"

"Could've been anybody." Chapan's eyes flittered around my cheeks. She couldn't look me square. Like my eyes was flames that would burn hers.

"Why don't I believe you?"

"That's enough, Niko. Your turn to cut the deck."

"*Chapan*."

"I told you." Chapan leaned into her chair. She folded her arms and squinted at me. "Could've been anybody."

"Most anybodies don't got hands that was burned real bad."

Chapan flashed her own hands. Old fingers crooked like autumn branches with little burn scars on the knuckles. "Anybodies like me do."

"Anybodies like you ain't no suspects in no kidnappings. Right?"

Chapan broke eye contact. She leaned on the table.

"Tell me, Chapan."

"That man sounded a lot like Odin."

"Who's that?"

"Odin Eriksen. Kimama and Auntie's papa."

I felt the weight of God sink into the room. He had a name. Odin. Odin Eriksen. Nimama and Auntie's papa. Grandpapa to Nikosis Eriksen. The serpent in my family tree.

I looked at my hands expecting to see blood. Like God wanted me to know it was something in me that made me guilty.

"I thought my grandpapa was dead?"

"There was so much blood, Niko. I don't know how anyone could survive what happened." Chapan shook her head. Her spine didn't have the strength to keep her chin up. "But if he did survive, then we got real problems."

CHAPTER 6

MEET THEM WITH POWDER AND BULLET

THURSDAY, MARCH 26, 1885.

Today started ordinary enough. I prayed for Cousin first thing. Then I lay in his sheets waiting for everyone else to wake up. It's been more than a week without him already. Me and him's supposed to be buffalo hunters together.

On the bright side, ain't no more boys disappeared since Cousin got took. On the bad side, ain't been no sign of nothing since he got took neither. Everyone's tired. People got lives to attend to. God was supposed to stop the world when Cousin got stole. But He kept it moving anyway.

The police ain't been by once since we tried reporting Cousin missing. Ain't done nothing to help find him neither. Or anyone for that matter. So Nimama and Auntie chatted with Constable Palmer about the situation on his patrol yesterday when they was searching for Guille.

"Did Campbell say how the sergeant knew about Guille's and them's disappearances?" Chapan inquired at breakfast. She made us all the biggest bowls of porridge and dried berries she could. But she only had enough to fill them halfway. Even with Cousin gone.

"He was being cagey again . . ." Nimama looked at Chapan forceful. Her after-breakfast cigarette roasted between her fingers. "He was real upset by it."

Auntie pushed her bowl of porridge away. She left more in the bowl than she spooned into her belly. "We should talk to the sergeant ourselves again."

"After what happened last week?" Nimama looked stunned at Auntie. It's easy to forget Auntie can't think straight. She's even more desperate for Cousin than the rest of us. "If I wanted to be treated like shit, I'd set up shop in the outhouse."

"That language, Sara. We're at the table," Chapan *tsk!*ed. "Did you ask him if he knew anything about that fur trader Père Brisson met?"

Nimama raised her chin. She looked frail in her authority. Her and Auntie still don't know Chapan told me about Odin. Chapan made me promise never to tell.

"No. Didn't remember to. You can ask him yourself when he comes by sometime to borrow some books. He gets bored a lot. Fleury Avenue's not exactly downtown London."

After we ate breakfast and me and Chapan cleaned the bowls together in the kitchen, Nimama and Auntie readied up at the door. Nimama slung the repeater over her shoulder. Auntie tied her boots and slipped on her mittens.

I want to *do* something. Anything. I can't live with myself doing nothing all the time when Cousin's out there facing Hell.

Before they headed out, I begged Nimama over and over and over and over to let me come help find Cousin. But, as always, she said no.

"Why can't I come?"

"You're safer here with Chapan."

"You need my help!"

"Another time. Okay?"

After Nimama and Auntie left, I sat at the table alone. Then Félix fell asleep on my lap. Wouldn't let me move none. I had to fiddle with the crispy braid of charred sweetgrass Chapan left in the saucer. I sketched the forest with that sweet-smelling black char on my fingers on the table. Then I wiped it all away with my sleeve like a fire.

Past week been brutal. Nothing takes my mind off Cousin. I should be out there looking for him! Instead I'm stuck in the dang homestead all the time. I ain't never been so bored in my life. At least I'm allowed outside to feed the animals and play with Barney in the corral under Chapan's supervision. But I'm so bored, sometimes I catch myself wishing it was me who got stole instead of Cousin. At least then I'd have a little action in my life.

I know. Don't judge me. I understand it's sinful to think them thoughts. Even on accident. But I can't help it. Being crammed in here all day is like being the good guy stuck in jail. Chapan's got tons of bookshelves loaded with letters and books and such. But I can't read good. Not even the Bible.

It's funny that Chapan has not one Bible but a whole church full of Bibles and she don't even believe in God. I asked Chapan why she smudged and went to ceremony or celebrated Christmas and Easter if her soul don't care.

"I don't know." Chapan made her face all scrunchy like she ain't thought about it in a long time. "Just things I was raised to do, I suppose."

"Then who you praying to for Cousin to come home?"

Chapan didn't expect me to say that. It was at that moment I noticed how all them years of smiling took their wrinkly tolls on her old cheeks. Cheeks so wrinkly, they look like ripples on the lake.

It ain't fair. All Cousin did was play buffalo hunters with me in the burn scar—a big arena Chapan made for us to ride in, deep in the bush. We was taking turns racing from the forest at the edge of the burned-out meadow to the lonesome charred wood post in the middle.

It was my last try. Game on the line. Whole point of buffalo hunters is you have to mount Pony bareback without crushing or dropping the snowball in your bare hand, kick her to a full gallop, then hurl the snowball at the charred post before you pass it. If you crush or drop the snowball at any time, you lose; if you pass the post without throwing your snowball or your throw misses the post, you lose; and if your throw is spot on and the snowball explodes all over the post, winner winner chicken dinner. First to win four times wins the game.

Cousin waited at the far end of the burn scar. The post stood between us. Pony waited anxious beside me. She was ready to run. I held my snowball careful. Cousin gave the signal.

"Go!"

I took a running start and leaped my belly onto Pony's back. I grabbed her mane with my free hand and swung over her body. I cocooned the snowball in my palm and gave Pony three solid kicks. We galloped for the charred post in the middle of the burn scar. I bounced wild.

We was coming up on the post. I pretended it was the hump of a fleeing buffalo me and Pony was chasing on the open prairie. All the trees around us was other buffalo and buffalo hunters in capotes and leather jackets.

Parrup! parrup! parrup! parrup!

I lifted the snowball over my head like I was shouldering a rifle. Me and Pony rode up beside the buffalo. I aimed my gun at his hump and threw my snowball with all my might.

SPLAT!

The snowball exploded. Snow shot everywhere. All over the sooty ice behind the post.

"Got it!"

"Damn!" Cousin threw his hands on his head. "Thought you was gonna miss."

Me and Pony trotted over to Cousin at the other end of the burn scar. I looked down my nose at him and chuckled. "How's the weather down there? *Loser.*"

"I ain't no loser." Cousin didn't want to walk home. But that's the punishment for losing buffalo hunters. Rules be rules. Losers walk home. Winners ride. "I won yesterday."

"That was then, nitôtem. This is now."

Cousin stroked Pony's nose and let her lick salt off his

palm. Him and Auntie look lots alike. Excepting Cousin's missing one of his front teeth. And instead of having dark brown eyes like Auntie, he got gold eyes like a cat.

Me and Pony walked out the burn scar together onto the main trail. Old snow crunched beneath her hooves. Cousin walked beside us. We was on our way home.

"Me and you would've made good buffalo hunters," he said.

"Yeah. Real good."

A minute later, he was gone.

CHAPTER 7

WHITE MEAT

SATURDAY, MARCH 28, 1885.

War broke out Thursday. Just outside Duck Lake near Batoche. Hundred-odd Mounties led by their superintendent was met on the Carlton Trail by more than twice as many of Gabriel Dumont's men. Like two prizefighters in the ring. Thirty minutes later, the police was in full retreat with a dozen deaths and as many wounded—a quarter their men.

Could've been worser too.

Not all Riel and Dumont's men was unscathed. A bullet grazed Dumont's skull. Poor guy even lost his brother. But even with a few casualties, there's no doubt: Riel and Dumont won.

Word flooded town. It's all anyone can talk about. Most everyone got an uncle or cousin fighting under Dumont's command. God spared most all them. And He punished the police and bad guys from Prince Albert too.

The prime minister has to sit down with Louis Riel now. No one wants more blood spilled on Indian and Métis land.

More than anything, I hope this is God's way of saying we'll find Cousin soon.

When Monsieur Fleury learned his nephews won at Duck Lake, he spread news all around Lac-aux-Trois-Pistoles he was hosting a bunny-hop at the saloon this fine Saturday evening to drink to Métis victory and good fortunes and such. We all need something to look forward to. We got to celebrate every victory God gives us.

Me and Chapan sat at the table eating porridge with Nimama. Auntie left before sunrise to search for Cousin. Rosy morning light spiced the cabinets.

"You sure your sister's up to go tonight?" asked Chapan.

"We'll leave early if we have to."

"Could be a lot for her. Hasn't even been two weeks since Guille disappeared."

"She needs to get her mind off things for a night." Nimama dropped her spoon in her scraped-empty bowl. "It'll be good for all of us."

Chapan swirled the watery coffee in her cup. I know she wanted to ask about Odin. But saying his name would give away to Nimama what I ain't supposed to know.

"Niko, can you promise me something?" Nimama threw her tobacco pouch and matchbook on the table. She rolled a cigarette over the empty bowl. "Don't go running off tonight. Okay?"

"Can I still go be with my friends?"

"Of course. Just make sure we know where you are. We don't know who's out there."

"I'll be fine."

"I know." Nimama sealed her cigarette with her tongue. "I trust you."

Nimama finished her coffee and cigarette. Then threw on her jacket and boots and headed out the door to catch up with Auntie.

I was excited for the bunny-hop. Eating. Dancing. Games. All our old friends. It's been so long since we had anything worth celebrating. We'll throw an even bigger and better party when we find Cousin and the war ends.

After breakfast I lay around in Cousin's bed upstairs trying to nap. I could hear Chapan downstairs scrubbing Nimama's and Auntie's sheets against the ribs of the washboard.

"You aren't a bad mother, Maggie," I overheard Chapan whisper to herself. She spoke gentle like she was her own sad friend. "How could you have known?"

Chapan won't never accept my kokum burned down her own house with her husband and two girls sleeping inside. It's easier for Chapan to say her daughter died in that fire than to accept she started it and ran away. Breaks Nimama's and Auntie's hearts when Chapan lies about my kokum.

But Chapan also ain't never forgot how Odin saved Nimama and Auntie from the fire. Much as Chapan hates Odin for whatever he did that made Oncle try to kill him, he'll always be Nimama and Auntie's papa. Their saviour of sorts too.

I don't think I'll ever know what my grandpapa did that made Oncle try to kill him. Nothing makes Nimama and

Auntie and Chapan more upset than when me or Cousin ask. Can't imagine how they feel thinking he might be alive. Might've stole Cousin too.

My own grandpapa. How could he do this? Ain't nothing make sense no more.

God damn . . .

At least Oncle was a good man. Chapan's late husband too. But they wasn't no old men when they died. Oncle and my kokum was still young when their papa passed away. Being a "successful" fur trader and buffalo hunter and such, Chapan likes to say her husband left lots of money to look after her, their horses, their home, their babies. Says the same about Oncle too. But nowadays I ain't sure there was much to leave behind.

Growing up, I believed Chapan. Had no reason not to. I lived in a nice house my whole life. We got a well. Glass windows, a library, a kettle, cupboards, a cellar. All sorts of fancy stuff. Life been stabler for me and Cousin in ways it ain't for lots of folks. Nimama and Auntie even.

But since before I can remember, Chapan's been particular about me taking too much sugar with my morning porridge. Or Nimama drinking coffee in the afternoon. Auntie buying too many beads. I always figure we'd get extra from the store next time. But I suppose we never do.

NIMAMA AND AUNTIE CAME HOME RIGHT AT SUPPERTIME. ME AND CHAPAN RAN outside to feed and water the horses and Huckleberry and get him hooked up to the cart so we could go to the bunny-hop. Nimama and Auntie sipped ham hock soup and nibbled bannock for supper. Then they got washed, dressed, hair-coiffed for going out.

Couple hours later, a half-dozen wagons and carts arrived at the livery en masse like a caravan. Us included. The livery is a ginormongous compound: two gargantuan barns for boarding everyone's horses. Each barn is the size of two churches smushed together.

A few hundred yards down the road is the Fleury Hotel and Saloon. The saloon is the biggest business in all L-T-P. So tall that ain't no one got ladders sturdy enough to fix its broken shingles. The main floor is the saloon where you eat and drink and play cards. The top floor is the hotel where you bathe and sleep and such. You can even get a haircut.

The Fleurys tickled with excitement for the bunnyhop. They smuggled in whisky and beer from south of the Medicine Line. Smoked moose meat from a lean bull shot last night. Roasted fresh ham. Pickled roots. All the cans of fruit in syrup from the Little Bulls' and Cunningham's stores that money could buy.

Excepting the cakey mud all over our knees from boarding Huckleberry and the cart, both Auntie and Nimama looked sharp in their best clothes. Nimama's dress shimmered the same shade of blue as her eyes. Auntie greased her hair for the first time in ages, rolling the stragglers into a perfect bun. Her black shawl looked good on her too. Matched her black blouse and skirt. Her shiny metal crucifix pendant hung from her neck. She looked fancy and mournful like Queen Victoria.

On this Saturday evening, I was a right handsome gentleman. Looking sharp in my favourite yellow sweater Auntie knitted, still stinky with soap. Stiff leather suspenders. Plaid pants. And, of course, my favourite mocs with them wild roses beaded on the tops. They even looked good caked in mud.

A half-dozen men lounged around the saloon porch. They cussed and laughed. Tobacco smoke flooded their lungs.

"Looks like the passenger train arrived!" said the tallest man. He was skinny like all he ate for supper was cigarettes. His bushy salt and pepper beard hid half his throat. "And on that train comes the famous Madame Marguerite Desjarlais and her beautiful family." The tall man flicked his cigarette into a muddy puddle and clapped his hands together as he skipped down the steps toward us.

In the background I heard a band playing inside. Their instruments sounded muffled from the thick wood walls. Guitar, fiddle, harmonica, banjo, cello, double bass, accordion, piano. The Fleurys got a troupe that plays on the stage each weekend. They call themselves the Unregistered Indian Band.

The slender man approached Chapan. He held her beaver-colour hand in his brownish paws. The man holding Chapan's hand didn't look much past forty-five. His breath reeked of whisky. But he still seemed like a family man.

"It's been years, Mesdemoiselles Eriksen." The man bowed to Nimama and Auntie. Then he bowed to me too. "An old fart like me forgets things. What's your name again, son?"

"Niko."

I shook the man's hand. He wore a dusty red sash tied in a jiffy around his thin waist. The knot bulged under his belly button. Braided tips tickled the ground between his moccasins.

"My name's Laurent Callahoo. I'm Angélique and François's papa."

"How's the party?" Nimama asked.

"There's tons of folks inside eager to see you. Everybody's here. Even Nishecabo. You should talk to him."

"Kate McCannon's here too?"

Laurent's brow crunched over his eyes. "Now I think of it, I haven't seen her. Talk to Hélène. She might know where Kate McCannon is. Not like her to miss a party. You know?"

Nimama tipped her hat to Laurent. "Have a good night."

"Whoa. Wait a second . . ." Laurent looked at us confusingful. His finger pointed beside me like I held hands with a ghost. "Where's the other one?"

"There's no other one," Auntie shot like a reflex. "What do you mean?"

"There's two of 'em." Laurent looked just as surprised at Auntie as me. My jaw hung. Why was Auntie lying about Cousin? "I know there is."

"No." Auntie shook her head fast. Me and Chapan held our breaths. Cousin wasn't no secret. Why wasn't Laurent allowed to know? "Just Niko."

Laurent rested his hands on his hips and shook his head like he'd accepted his fate as a man gone bonkers. "I must be losing it . . ."

"It's fine, Laurent." Nimama patted his shoulders and winked at him. "I plan on getting so drunk tonight I mistake my own sister for the queen."

"Expect it, mademoiselle. They got enough liquor in there to drown a whale."

We left Laurent with his friends and pushed through the saloon doors into a room so smoky I thought the walls was papered in chubby white and grey swirls. The place bounced with boozy bodies. Some danced. Some ate. Some talked. All was joyful and loud. Rows of long tables was jammed together throughout the entire main floor, decorated with saucy plates and foamy beer glasses. Chipped ashtrays and copper spittoons dotted the lengths of the tables. People leaned over the second floor railing. On the stage played the Unregistered Indian Band. Tables and chairs was cleared away for people to polka and jig and two-step with their whiskies held high overhead to not splish even a teensy splash.

Me and Cousin would have a right good time if he was here. We'd get all the kids together and have a big game of war. Take turns playing Dumont versus the Dominion on the stairwells. Maybe even get the older kids to sneak us some wine.

"La famille Desjarlais!" shouted a woman's voice high over the harmonica wailing and banjo twanging, the fiddle fiddling. Jigging footsteps hammered the floor like a dizaine of horses. "Vous arrivez! Laissez-moi vous embrasser!"

Madame Hélène Ducharme and her forty-odd-year-old smile beamed at us. Red hairs was tucked away in that mess of blackish brown tied up in a loose bun on the top of her head. Her teeth was piss orange.

"Joséphine, ma chère: on behalf of all of us . . ." Hélène inhaled Auntie into a hug. She placed her hands over Auntie's cheeks. Auntie looked uncomfortable with Hélène's fingertips on her skin. "We'll find your boy. Okay? I promise you."

She moved on to hug Chapan, then Nimama. Hélène's face twinkled when she looked at me. She whipped her arms around me. Picked me up and shook me back and forth in a hug so tight she damn near pinched the poo out of me.

Hélène planted my feet to the floor. She beamed her near rotted teeth. "Nikosis Eriksen, let me peck your cheeks!" She bent at the back and shot my cheeks with a couple kisses. Her breath tasted sweet and sour like rum and water. "I'm so happy to see you are well, young man. Ever so grateful. Stay strong, young man. We all believe in you. La famille Desjarlais, come come. We have a table."

Hélène reached behind her for Auntie's hand. They fanned smoke out their faces as they slithered between shoulders and around faro and dice tables. Nimama dragged me and Chapan behind. The air smelled dizzy and drunk.

Ain't no gracious way of putting it: no people can party harder than us half-breeds. Our homesteads right breathe with fiddling and guitar picking come partytime. Open windows puff the sticky smoke of roll-your-own cigarettes and roaring laughter. Ain't no family on Earth can host a village of half-drunk half-breeds and their up-all-night kinfolk better than the Fleurys.

"Mes fils," announced Hélène to her two boys seated at a table, hunched over plates. Georges and Charlo turned to face us with bannock and meat in their hands.

Shrivelled at the head of the table, Nishecabo nodded to acknowledge us. His ancient shoulders was lopsided against the tall back of his handmade wheelchair. His face looked heavier on one side than the other. Hélène got him dressed spiffy in a wool jacket made of thousands of threads, buttons sparklier than crystal, a red sash tied at the waist draped between his legs. His once dark skin was lightened from seventy-odd years of growing sun-bleached and weathered. A bright white beard straggled down his chest. He had arthritisy hands like buttes on a prairie. All memories of his hardy life bared by his body.

"Georges, Charlo." Hélène fanned her sons off the bench. "Bring la famille Desjarlais some supper. Look how thin they are."

Georges and Charlo finished their final mouthfuls before strutting away into the smoke.

"Please. Take seats." Hélène dusted off the bench for me and Nimama to sit. She kicked out chairs for Chapan and Auntie to plop themselves in. Hélène sat beside Nishecabo at the head of the table with her hand on his knee.

"Unbelievable what happened at Duck Lake." Nimama set her hat on the corner of her chair and shuffled under the table. "No way Ottawa will keep this war up."

"Long as Dumont's in charge of Riel's army . . ." Hélène *snapp!*ed her fingers. "Dumont was under Nishecabo's command more than thirty years ago at Grand Coteau—when Gabriel was about Niko's age. Nishecabo used to say even as a kid, Gabriel was the best warrior of all his men. Dumont'll turn Ottawa's boys into mincemeat if they ain't careful. Ain't that right, ninâpem?"

Nishecabo winked at us. Hélène smiled and rustled his knee.

I hoped Nimama and Auntie and Chapan understood what Hélène said. That Gabriel Dumont was a better warrior at my age than grown men. They need to understand I'm old enough to join them on search parties. What if I'm the next Gabriel Dumont? If me and Cousin was born in his time, we'd be famous buffalo hunters and warriors by now too.

All the smoke made it impossible to see across the room. Auntie wanted no part of no gossip. Not after what happened with Laurent. She leaned back to peek around for any sign of young boys with steaming plates of food in hand.

"We talked to Laurent Callahoo outside." Nimama pulled out her tobacco pouch and some papers and tossed them on the table in front of her. She balanced her attention between rolling her cigarette and Hélène. "Is Kate McCannon here tonight? I want to talk to her about my nephew."

"She's south of the Medicine Line at her sister-in-law's on the Great Sioux Reservation." Hélène grabbed her pipe off the table and loaded the bowl with some of Nimama's tobacco. She *shhhhrrripp!*ed a match and sucked the flame into the bowl. "She wants to apologize for not joining our search parties yet. She will. Just coordinating some things. You know? She ever talk to you about her time with the Pussy Posse of the Black Hills?"

Nimama struck her match and brung the flame to her cigarette. "That old gang of hers in Deadwood?"

"I don't mean disrespect, Sara. But I wouldn't call it *hers*. Or a *gang*. The Pussy Posse of the Black Hills is a right powerful organization. They're run by a council of women from all over the Great Sioux Reservation. Kate McCannon's meeting them on Monday for permission to start a provisional chapter here in Lac-aux-Trois-Pistoles."

"What for?"

"Let me answer that with a story. When Custer found gold

in the Black Hills eleven years ago and miners started trespassing on the reservation in Deadwood, they'd have their ways with the town's working girls. So the girls founded the Pussy Posse as a sort of union. They protect vulnerable women and their families. Kate McCannon was another widowed working girl in Deadwood. Then she became the Pussy Posse's Councillor of Justice and Enforcement.

"When Sitting Bull killed Custer, three miners from Deadwood wanted revenge. Them fuckers raided a Sioux camp and murdered Narcisse Little Bull's sister and kidnapped her two girls. Then they fled deep into the Black Hills.

"So Kate McCannon led the Pussy Posse into the Black Hills to find them. They came back a week later with both Narcisse's nieces safe and sound—and three wâpiskwîyâs scalps."

Nimama set her cigarette in the ashtray. Her lungs pushed smoke across the table. "You think the Pussy Posse can find Guille?"

"Kate McCannon thinks so too."

"Just in time!" Auntie shot her hand in the air and waved. She harumphed out her nose. "I thought I'd die if I had to listen to more of that gossip."

Georges and Charlo weaseled through sweaty backs with plates and bowls topped with stew and bannock in each hand. A couple older boys followed behind with even more food. They kept their arms high in the air to not bump the half-drunk people making chit-chat together.

"Oh boy!" I tried not to leak spit onto Charlo's arm as he set me down my massive bowl of moose stew with fried and baked bannock. "Maarsii!"

In the middle of the table for all us to share was a stack of plates, a bowl of smushy potatoes with melted lard, a jar of pickled carrots, smoky moose meat, fried onions and mushrooms, a few slices of pink ham.

I bent my face over the table and inhaled deep as I could. All the steamy scents lined my belly. I could die of deliciousness.

I gripped my spoon and fork in each hand like a sword and shield. I shoveled stew and meat hunks onto my spoon. I stabbed the smushy potatoes with my fork and dunked them in the stew. I was in Heaven. Double tastiness.

Before I even finished my mouthful, I grabbed the greasiest, crunchiest, goldiest, bubbliest piece of fried bannock I ever seen. It didn't have no clue what was about to happen to it. I eyeballed that bannock like a bear eyeballs honey. I dipped it in stew. I chomped it. The stew splashed the roof of my mouth. The bannock collapsed on my tongue. I melted. Honest to goodness. Best bannock I ever tasted.

We was so hungry, we only remembered to thank God for the food after we finished eating and *clank!*ed our cutlery off our plates. After prayer, Nimama figured it was high time to practise jigging with Chapan and Auntie, settling tummies and all. Nimama dragged them to the dance floor with two dozen other moccasined and booted feet. Hélène lifted her skirt and scurried to join everyone.

"I gotta pee," Charlo said to Georges and Nishecabo. "Be right back."

Charlo walked through the maze of bodies toward the back. On the dance floor, all them heels stomped when the fiddler bowed his strings. Me and Georges and Nishecabo watched all the dancers bounce up and down. Their trousers and skirts swirled from the breeze. We watched the dancers slap their soles, toes hopping over heels, grazing their calves—chicken dances with their shoulders not even bouncing.

Then the fiddler hit the final note of the Red River jig. Hélène stood to the side, talking with an anxious woman around her age. Dancers straddled off the dance floor, their legs wiggly as guts.

Nimama spotted Campbell Palmer sipping beer at the bar. He wore moccasins with laces running up his shins, plaid pants, a yellow shirt with nice cotton suspenders. She wandered toward the bar to yack with him.

Chapan waddled back to the table, chatting over her shoulder thinking Nimama followed close behind. Auntie held Chapan's elbow while they walked. Even if Nimama followed, she couldn't hear Chapan over the blaring conversations and the banjo twanging, accordion vibrating, harmonica wailing.

Nimama and Campbell leaned into each other's ears. Both had expressive faces. Angry. Shocked. Confused. Relieved. Music and chatter flooded the saloon.

Chapan twisted around looking for Nimama. She smiled when Auntie pointed to Campbell following Nimama to the table. Chapan spread her arms and embraced the tall man in a big hug—so big Campbell whimpered.

"Campbell Palmer, I didn't know what to think when I heard you were back!" Chapan stepped back to soak the man in. He was handsome: clean dark hair with crunchy curls at the end, thick skin on his cheeks, eyes brown like the sons of Maman Earth herself.

Campbell looked happy to see Chapan too. Like she was an old auntie he missed. "It's been a long time."

"Hasn't it? You should come over for tea. You got a tough job around here. Especially after what happened at Duck Lake. Does your boss know you're here?"

Campbell shrugged. "He has a meeting with the Indian commissioner and police superintendent in Prince Albert this weekend. Things aren't good."

"No." Chapan tapped Campbell's breastbone. "They're not. Come see me for tea when you can. I have a new book you'd enjoy. It's really popular."

Georges stood to shake Campbell's hand. He gripped Campbell's palm like he had to prove he was a fellow man. "Good seeing you again, Campbell."

"Likewise." Campbell shook Georges's hand. Then he patted Nishecabo on the shoulder. "Good seeing you too, sir."

Nishecabo winked at Campbell.

"Listen, I'm going to go find my brother." Georges kissed his papa's cheek and walked to the dance floor to talk with his maman. The woman Hélène chatted with earlier was crying into her hands.

"And I'm getting some beer." Campbell pointed at everyone at the table. "What's everyone want? My treat."

"Just get a pitcher and a stack of glasses." Nimama struck a match against the table and dragged her cigarette. "Bring water if you can too."

Angélique and Lizette and a couple other kids played tag on the stairs. They looked like they was having fun. I wanted to join them. But I wanted to sit with Campbell even more. I wanted to hear him talk with Nimama and Auntie.

Campbell straddled toward the bar. A wobbly man from a nearby faro table rose and put his hand against Campbell's chest. The man's eyes was red as blood. Tobacco spittle dripped from his scraggly moustache. His unbrushed black-and-grey beard forked on his chest.

"Ain't you Constable Campbell fucking Palmer?"

"Who's asking?" Campbell peeled the man's hand off his chest. Behind him at the faro table sat Laurent with the store owners, Narcisse Little Bull and Ned Cunningham.

"Well, Constable Campbell fucking Palmer. Me and you gotta make chit-chat. Should we talk outside? Or you got the nuts to talk right here?"

The angry man stood tall as Campbell. He bumped Campbell with his chest. Breathed heavy into Campbell's face.

"What you say your name was?"

"My name don't fucking matter to a Mountie son of a whore like you." The man spat chaw juice through the gap in his teeth onto Campbell's forehead. "You redcoat wâpiskwîyâs sons of fucking bitches killed my cousin at Duck Lake yesterday."

"Don't fucking call me that!" Campbell winced. He whipped his hand onto his brow and threw the bubbly brown juice onto the floor. "I'm just as Michif as you."

Everyone stood back. They made a big circle around the two men. Chairs and tables screeched as they got dragged out the way.

The Unregistered Indian Band, banjoing and pianoing and accordioning away at their instruments, all stopped at once. They doe-eyed the ring in the middle of the saloon. Dancers on the floor quit their stepping.

"I wouldn't fucking care if you was my auntie's only son." The angry man's voice got deeper with each sentence. Gravelly and hoarse from too many years leaning on the bottle. "That redcoat changes you underneath."

"Pierre! Stop it!" Laurent stood and gave the man a couple slaps and looked him square. "He needs to take care of his family somehow."

"Don't fucking touch me!"

PUNCH!

Pierre grabbed Laurent by the shirt collar and socked his lip. Laurent stumbled. He spat blood and chips of teeth.

"I got a dead cousin because of these Mountie pimps! I got kin following that fucking Riel zealot to Hell! It's fucking hopeless!" Pierre leaned back. He loaded hisself with anger to punch at Campbell, at Laurent, the audience, whoever'd listen. "These Mountie pimps need to go! Riel needs to go! It's all gone to shit! We're right fucked!"

"Come here!" Campbell rolled up his sleeves and threw his suspenders off his shoulders. "Fight me like a man!"

Campbell strutted toward Pierre. They was arm's length from each other.

PUNCH!

Campbell jabbed Pierre's mouth. Pierre stumbled. Then he steadied hisself. Angrier than ever. He loaded his fist at his hip. Then swung his arm overhead at Campbell.

Campbell rolled under his fist. Then he sprung up and clocked Pierre like a gun hammer.

PUNCH!

Pierre's nose broke. Blood flowed into his mouthy beard.

"You son of a whore!"

Pierre swung at Campbell. Campbell stepped aside. Then he clocked Pierre's exposed jaw with a hook.

PUNCH!

Pierre stumbled over his heels and fell hard on the floor. Campbell looked at his fist. The knuckles was split and bloody. He spun around to walk back to the bar.

"Con-sta-ble . . ." Pierre moaned in a nasaly, windless tone. It echoed through the silent hall. He lay flat as frybread on the floor. "Con-sta-ble . . ."

Campbell turned around and walked to Pierre. Pierre mocked him from his back.

"Con-sta-ble . . ."

Campbell lifted Pierre off the floor by the reddened shirt collar. Pierre dangled between Campbell's knees like a pocket watch.

"You know, you ain't the first policeman to beat the shit out of me." Pierre flashed his red smile at Campbell. He was missing more teeth than Laurent and Cousin combined. "But you's the first who's 'just as Michif as me.'"

Campbell drew his fist across his chest like a bow. Then he dropped his entire weight behind his knuckles.

PUNCH!

"Shit!" shouted Campbell. Bones in his hand *burrrak!*ed. He hunched over his busted hand and staggered toward the stairs. Others rushed to Pierre's unconscious aid.

Hélène and Georges met Campbell halfway up the steps. They stood with the woman Hélène chatted with on the dance floor. Her and Hélène both had red, swole, cried-out eyes.

Hélène called out over the mass of dizzy bodies before her through the thick smoke clouds. "Has anyone seen my son, Charlo?" She had a tired voice—too tired for people to quit their mumbling to each other about the brawl they'd seen between Campbell and Pierre.

Georges put his fingers in a ring between his lips.

Tweeeeeooooooooweeeeet!

The floor stopped. Everyone turned to face Hélène.

"Has anyone seen my son, Charles Ducharme?" Hélène petted her belly to soothe herself. The woman beside her sobbed into her hands. Georges rubbed her shoulders. "He's friends with a boy called François Callahoo. Me and François's maman here can't find them anywhere."

"*What!*" hollered Laurent. He pushed his way through the crowd toward the stairwell. Laurent's wife collapsed in his arms.

No matter how drunk, everyone rounded up to search the whole saloon, the whole livery, the whole of Fleury Avenue to find Charlo and François. We joined the herd of families rushing for the barns. Mud sloshed all over our legs. Chapan and Auntie stumbled behind in the stampede.

Dozens of people zipped around the barns getting their saddles ready. People dashed through the snow with torches and lamps. Young families needed to get their kids home safe. Everyone else had to find Charlo and François.

We gathered Huckleberry and hooked up to the cart. People cussed and cried all around us. Nimama hurried me into the back. She whipped the reins. We raced home.

The bunny-hop was supposed to be a good omen. Everything was supposed to get better after Duck Lake. But it's already worser. What did we do wrong to deserve this?

Nimama grabbed the gun from the mantel soon as we got home. Her and Auntie left the cart and Huckleberry for me and Chapan to deal with so they could head out searching on horseback.

After me and Chapan finished putting the cart away and getting Huckleberry into the barn and stepped foot into the house, Chapan lit a braid of sweetgrass. I prayed at the table for Nimama to come home before sunrise like Kate McCannon in Hélène's story. With Cousin and Charlo and François and all the other boys safe. And Odin's scalp too.

CHAPTER 8

ERIK THE RED

PALM SUNDAY, MARCH 29, 1885.

I walked downstairs after sunrise to see Chapan alone at the table with her tea. Maps and pencils was scattered around the tabletop. In the middle was Chapan's smoky smudge bowl.

"Morning, Niko."

I hugged Chapan good morning and pulled a chair beside her. Barney slept on a sheepskin rug by the fireplace. Some of the maps on the table in front of Chapan had scribbles and notes and pencil marks all over.

Chapan fiddled with her wood spoon. Carrot and pea soup bubbled on the stove. She must be expecting Nimama and Auntie to be back for lunch.

"Did Nimama or Auntie come home last night?"

"Not yet." Chapan poured me some tea. Morning light illuminated the steamy plumes fluttering out my cup.

"We ain't going to church today?"

"I'm sure the father understands."

"It ain't Papa Brisson I'm worried about. It's God who worries me. What if He hates us?"

"What do you mean?"

I couldn't look at Chapan. My finger followed lines drawn on the map in front of me.

"The Lord ain't doing this to us," she said. "Odin is."

"How you know? You don't even believe in God."

"So why would I blame Him for what I know a man is responsible for?"

Miss Kitty and Félix speeded down the stairs. Miss Kitty curled up next to Barney by the fireplace. Félix plopped his rumbling body on my lap. His *purr!* vibrated my bones.

"What if it ain't Odin?"

Chapan sighed. She rustled the fur behind Félix's ears. "Do you understand what 'poor' means, Niko?"

"Being broke all the time. Right?"

"Broke is circumstance. Anybody can be broke. Poor ain't just having no money. It's not enough medicine. Not enough horses or land or guns. No friends in good standing with the community. No opportunity. No understanding from people who got enough. The thing that makes poor different is when you're poor, you're stuck. You know?"

Chapan set her spoon on the table. I grabbed it. Felt the soft, splinter-free wood. It amazed me how much work this spoon done over the years to stuff my belly with as much food as Chapan could cook. Even when there ain't much to cook.

"Poor is something that's done to you. That's what makes

poor so unfair. Poor is bad medicine. You understand what I'm saying?"

The homestead was quieter than a cemetery. Chapan hung her head. She rubbed her thumbs against my knuckles.

I crossed my arms at Chapan. "What's this got to do with Odin?"

All the hurt Chapan carried in her wet eyes pressed into me. Four or five tearlets splattered on the table.

"Bad things were happening. The trading post was abandoned. There was disease. I had no idea how bad things could get.

"Then ninâpem died. Oncle Guillaume left for Red River to find work. Me and your kokum were all alone. When we met Odin, we'd never been so hungry. Not like that.

"I need you to know something. Your kokum was my baby. I would do anything to take her back. I'll never forgive myself."

Chapan sniffled. Snot lined the back of her hand. She fought with all her strength not to weep in front of me. But weeping won.

"Odin promised my girl would eat cake off gold plates with him in the United States. I didn't know he was a monster!"

"Chapan?" I held her wet hands and spoke soft. "I don't get what you's trying to say."

"Promise you won't hate me?" Chapan's eyes was bloodshot as they was brown. Her words jumped out her mouth between tears. "Please?"

"Chapan. I love you." I squeezed Chapan's fingers. Like her late husband would've. "What you trying to tell me?"

"Kimama and Auntie can't know I told you. Okay?"

"Told me what?"

"I sold your kokum to Odin."

"*What!*"

"I'm sorry, Niko." Chapan looked at me through all her crying. Her head collapsed onto her chest. She wept into her apron. "Please don't judge me . . ."

I couldn't believe it. I couldn't even move. Not for nothing. I left my body.

My kokum was property. *His* property. Odin's.

"Is that why Odin stole Cousin? Does he think we's all his property too?"

"I don't know . . ." Chapan sighed like it was her dying breath. I never seen her look so old. Her shoulders drooped like lead curtains. "Only he can answer that."

NIMAMA AND AUNTIE CAME HOME ALONE AT LUNCH. THEY SIPPED THEIR SOUPS quiet. Dejected. The search for Charlo and François was fruitless. Worser than fruitless. Every lead was a dead end. It was the quietest lunch we ever ate together.

Once their tummies settled, Nimama and Auntie headed upstairs to take naps before searching again. Me and Chapan sat at the table while she read aloud *Enoch Arden* by Alfred, Lord Tennyson. I sketched lonesome Enoch on his desert island, far from paradise with his beloved Annie.

CHAPTER 9

THE GOSPEL OF JUDAS

SPY WEDNESDAY, APRIL 1, 1885.

It's only Wednesday and it's already the worst Holy Week ever. All we done right is fast. And fasting this year's just normal starving. We ain't got much food to sacrifice in the first place. We ain't even been able to attend no church services this week. Nimama and Auntie been too busy searching for Cousin, and me and Chapan been busy taking care of la bibliothèque. Being grateful for nothing ain't easy as of late. Never mind with Cousin gone and the war so close by.

With the war on top of everything else, it's hard to imagine things getting better without getting worser first. There ain't been no meeting between Riel and the prime minister since the battle at Duck Lake.

Some starving nehiyaw men sieged Battleford on Monday. Scared all the settlers into hiding inside the fort while they looted stores and homes for food and bullets and such. Now lots of Big Bear's and Poundmaker's men's preparing for war with Ottawa too. It's a fucking mess.

Nimama and Auntie wake up every morning tireder than the night before. Today's the first day this week Auntie ate breakfast with us. Auntie left Monday and yesterday mornings before sunrise to search for Cousin alone, not eating all day until supper.

I still can't believe Chapan sold my kokum to Odin. I try not to talk too much at mealtimes in case I vomit out all Chapan's confessions in front of Nimama and Auntie. Chapan needs to know she can trust me. Maybe one day Chapan will say who me and Cousin's papas could be. Or maybe why Oncle tried to kill Odin right before we was born.

"Can I come today?" I asked Nimama at breakfast. Auntie circled her bowl with her spoon. Our porridges and bannock was plainer than plain. No sugar or syrup. No fruit jam. We don't even got much coffee or tea left.

"No."

"Why not?"

"It's too dangerous."

"I ain't afraid of O—"

My face flushed. My gut plummeted from my chest. I damn near didn't catch myself. Nimama stared daggers at me. She knew I knew something I wasn't supposed to.

". . . of whoever stole Cousin. They don't scare me none."

"What were you about to say?"

"I said what I meant."

"No." Nimama threw her spoon into the empty bowl. She folded her arms and leaned back into her chair. "You were about to say someone's name."

"No I wasn't."

"Whose name were you about to say?"

"No one's."

"Don't lie to me, boy."

"I ain't lying."

"Kokum, what did you tell him?" Nimama wagged her finger at Chapan. Her voice punched louder each sentence.

"I didn't tell him anyth—"

"Bullshit."

"*Nimama.*" I stood and pushed Nimama's hand down so she'd stop pointing at Chapan. "Chapan ain't told me nothing."

Chapan shoved her hands into her armpits. She stared sideways into the flames in the hearth. Auntie nibbled her lip nervousful.

Nimama tossed her papers and tobacco pouch on the table. We sat quiet. Tense. Morning sunlight rushed through the windows.

"How about this, Niko." Nimama rolled her cigarette intentful. Never looking away from the paper and tobacco sliding between her fingers. "You can't come search with us. But, if Auntie says yes, we'll go on a trail ride together before me and Auntie head out. Could be good to give kicâpân some time to reflect on things—alone."

"Okay," Auntie said nervous as a whipped workhorse. She set her spoon so soft into her bowl it made no noise.

Chapan breathed slow. Calmed her racing heart. "Good idea."

WE RODE OUT AS THE SUN CLIMBED INTO THE SKY. AUNTIE WAS PLOPPED ON TOP of Viking, spotted and dotted in all his prettiness. We explored animal trails and rode the main road.

My nose tingled from that muskegy, shitty springtime smell. That stench of rotting death being reborn. Made me wish we lived somewhere it was always summer. Like California. That way we could be rich with gold too. Maybe then Chapan wouldn't've never sold my kokum.

A bazillion questions filled my brain. More questions than stars in the nighttime sky. So many I almost puked them all out at once. I couldn't believe how much my family hid from me. Do they think I ain't strong enough to handle the truth? I ain't fragile. I'm human. Just like them.

Odin is my grandpapa. My grandpapa is evil. He bought my kokum. That's my family story. That's where I come from. Nothing I can do but accept it.

We rode silent. Wind whistled through leafless branches. Needles shivered in the pines. The goal of the ride was the lake—a place for us to rest and skip stones from shore where most the ice already melted.

At the lake, Nimama hitched Pony to a tree next to where Auntie hitched Viking. I flung my leg over the saddle and plopped on the ground. Mud splashed everywhere. Nimama walked me to the lakeshore where we grabbed skinny, saucer-like rocks. We hucked them across the water. Nimama was good at skipping rocks. She whipped them with a side-arm swing. Her stones bounced off the water until they smashed into hunks of ice way out in the water. I splashed lots of cold water all over the place, which was fun in its own way. But Nimama didn't think so whenever the water wetted her face.

"Sara?"

Nimama looked ready to whip a stone across the water. But she stopped her throw when Auntie called for her. "Yeah?"

"I found some mushrooms." Auntie's frizzy head nodded back toward the bush. She held a small basket weaved from grasses in her arm. "Can I take Nikosis for a bit? Won't be long."

Nimama whipped a rock across the water. Winnie was slung over her shoulder. The stone *skip-skip-skipp!*ed until it slided on the surface of an ice hunk.

"We'll be fifteen minutes," pleaded Auntie. Her fingers scratched my spine. ". . . I miss being with Guille. You know?"

Nimama looked at Auntie and bulled her nostrils. "Fifteen minutes. Okay?"

I wasn't sure what to think, being alone with Auntie. I loved her and all. But we seldom spent alone time together. I felt strange with her. Uncomfortable.

Auntie took my hand and led me along the lakeshore. Nowhere near the mushrooms under the trees.

"Where we going?"

"There's some fiddleheads up ahead."

"Thought you said mushrooms?"

"Yeah, well, I meant fiddleheads." Auntie tugged me along the shore. She spoke fast like lightning. "Seen them from way over there. Was going to come this way to pee anyway."

Then we arrived at a cluster of crowns that already had tight coiled fiddleheads. I was so excited for Chapan to fry them up with lard and pepper. Maybe with some crushed hazelnuts sprinkled in. And a tiny dash of apple cider vinegar too.

"So I have good news." Auntie dropped a handful into the

basket between us. "Did your maman tell you how we talked to Constable Palmer again on his patrol on Monday?"

"No . . ." I took my hands away from the fiddleheads and sat on my knees to keep my bum off the soggy earth. Auntie kneeled to be closer to me. "What happened?"

"Well, Campbell said he went into the office Sunday morning to file missing persons reports for Charlo and François. But he noticed a folder on the sergeant's desk. Know what was in it?"

"What?"

"Missing persons reports already filled out for both Charlo and François."

"On Sunday morning? Didn't they just get stole Saturday night?"

"Exactly." Auntie laid her hand on my leg. "It makes no sense. But Guille's report was in there too. Same for Michel Morin's and Théo Gervais's reports. Know what else?"

"What?"

"The folder was marked for the Indian commissioner. I think the sergeant forgot the folder on his desk before he went to Prince Albert for their meeting with the police superintendent."

"What's that mean?"

"I don't know. But the police superintendent fought in Duck Lake and lost. And I don't think the Indian commissioner in Regina cares about half-breeds much either. You know?"

I shrugged. Nothing made sense no more.

Auntie held my hands and outhaled steady. "Niko, I think the police are part of what's happening to my son and the other boys disappearing. I think the Indian commissioner is getting the government to pay for it. It may be personal for *us*, but it can't just be nipa—"

I wished Auntie hadn't caught herself. I wanted to talk about Odin. I wanted to know why he was taking the other boys too instead of just me and Cousin. But Auntie can't know I know.

". . . it can't be just *one nâpew* terrorizing us. He has to be financing this somehow."

I looked down at our hands together in my lap. Muddy and cold from plucking ferns. I wiped my thumbs on my thighs. "I thought you said you had good news."

"I do." Auntie placed her pointer finger across her lips like she was shushing me. "But it's a secret. Can you keep a secret for me?"

"What kind of secret?"

"Well, you know how I been searching for Guillaume before you and everyone else wakes up?"

"Uh huh."

"Well, yesterday I wasn't out searching for Guillaume."

"Where'd you go?"

"Promise it's a secret?"

"Uh huh."

"I borrowed your maman's gun and went to the outpost."

"Why?"

"I needed to know about that file on the sergeant's desk. I demanded Wagner tell me what the Indian commissioner needed those missing persons reports for. Know what he says?"

"What?"

Auntie folded her arms and looked shameful at the ground. Like she looked for courage hiding in the muck.

"The sergeant says it's up to me to do the right thing if I want to see Guille again."

I had no words for Auntie. She looked too paranoid. Sad. I'd've hugged her if I wasn't scared to.

"You don't think I'm crazy?" Hell raged over the emptiness in Auntie's eyes. Like a painted portrait of a madwoman. "Do you?"

I couldn't even look at her. I just wanted to sink into Maman Earth and disappear. To hell with picking ferns.

"Good," Auntie replied—even though I didn't say nothing. She looked at the ferns collected in our basket. "That's why I trust you. You know that?"

I didn't say nothing. Just nodded. All I wanted was to go back to Nimama. Real bad.

"Can you promise me something?" I was afraid to see Hell in Auntie's eyes again when she spoke. But they was back to empty. And sad. "Please?"

"Promise you what?"

"Promise this entire conversation is a secret?" Auntie placed her pointer over her lips. "Please?"

"Why?"

"Because no one else will understand. But you understand." Auntie grabbed our basket and extended her hand for me to take. I obliged—afraid of what would happen if I disobeyed. "Don't you, Guille?"

I shrugged. Did my best not to look Auntie back at all. In a couple weeks I gone from my family keeping secrets from me to me keeping secrets from my family.

"Suppose so."

We walked a long way. Auntie held my hand tight. Too

tight. Nothing could take me from her. Couldn't even run away if I was crazy enough to try.

Then the horses came into sight. Nimama whipped rocks against the surface of the lake. I raced over and wrapped my arms around her. I breathed in her smell. All smoky and mediciney and homeful.

Nimama lifted me into the saddle. She planted her foot in the stirrup and swung her leg over Pony's back. With Auntie and Viking behind us, we rode a little ways—not far from where me and Cousin played buffalo hunters before he disappeared.

"Nimama? Can we see the burn scar?"

Nimama and Auntie shrugged. "Why not?"

We bounced up-and-down the trail until we seen the burn scar. A burned-out meadow in the middle of the muddy spring forest.

"What's that?" I pointed to a lump lying beside the post in the middle of the burn scar. It lay like a heavy rock dropped from the stars.

"I don't know," Nimama said suspiciousful. She dismounted and hitched Pony to a tree.

I slipped off the saddle. Auntie took my hand. I took Nimama's. We crossed into the burn scar. My guts twisted. My heart beat crazy. Hairs on my arms stood tall. But I didn't know why.

We toe-over-toed closer to the lump. It looked familiar. Each step another clue.

A space rock? Sleeping deer? Coyote?

Then we seen blood pooled under its mouth and between its legs.

It was Barney.

Throat slit. Nuts sliced off.

Castrated like a coyote pup.

Auntie screamed. I grabbed Nimama by her jacket and cried all over her. Harder than I cried when Cousin got stole. Auntie collapsed over her dog by the post. She held him and wept over his bloody body.

It's not fair! Barney ain't never done nothing wrong. Not even on accident.

CHAPTER 10

BARNEY'S GRAVE

HOLY THURSDAY, APRIL 2, 1885.

We buried Barney in the forest behind the corral. The ground was still froze solid. Chapan burned some brush yesterday to melt snow and thaw Maman Earth so we could dig Barney a proper grave. It's what he deserved.

Our breath fogged our faces in the rosy sunrise. We stood around the grave. Auntie held Barney's body. She bundled him with leaves of tobacco and deer bones and toys in his favourite wool blanket. Didn't matter how heavy he was. She held him tight like she could bring him back to life. Cried over him like he could hear how bad she missed him.

Nimama slipped into the icy hole. Auntie lowered Barney into Nimama's hands. I ran to Auntie. I hugged her and wiped my tears all over the breast of her coat. I couldn't believe Barney was gone. He didn't do nothing wrong. He was a good boy. He didn't deserve to die. Not like that.

Barney was special. No dog was ever going to be like Barney.

Nimama laid Barney down. Gentle as the bundle he was. She lifted herself out the ground and stood to Auntie's other side. She wrapped her arms around me and Auntie both, rubbing each our shoulders. Chapan stood over Barney's grave with a shovelful of dirt.

"Eternal rest grant unto Barney, O Lord, and let perpetual light shine upon him. May he rest in peace."

Me and Chapan finished burying Barney alone. Nimama and Auntie headed into the homestead to wash their faces. They knew to search close by. Odin couldn't be far. It had to be him who murdered Barney. Who else would taunt us like that?

Me and Chapan erected a wood cross headstone for Barney as Nimama and Auntie rode off to kill Odin and bring Cousin home.

When we was done outside, I sat at the table sketching while Chapan cleaned all the bedding for the third time in a week—Nimama and Auntie sweat so much in their sleep every night that the hay they sleep on started growing again. I drew Barney the best I could from memory. Three-legged boy curled up by the fireplace. I drew Barney hundreds of times. This year alone. He was my favourite subject.

But something came over me. Like I lost all the sketching skills I built up my whole life. My drawing was awful.

Fuck up after fuck up after fuck up. Was all I could do. Over and over and over and over. Eyes too wide apart. Mouth too unsmiley. Nose too lopsided. Fur not furry enough. It looked better when it was still a blank page. I worked on it for hours. Every new line looked worser and worser. I was doing Barney's legacy bad. He deserved better!

I couldn't handle it. I got so pissed off I started crying. Little teardrops made the lead run. The pencil tip tore through the wet paper. Through Barney's beautiful dog eyes.

"*God damn it!*"

I tore the page out the sketchbook and whipped it across the room. The pencil hit the window and skidded on the floor. Miss Kitty and Félix sprinted up the stairs. I couldn't do nothing right. Not even draw my own fucking dog.

"Whoa, Niko . . ." Chapan waddled from the laundry tub toward me. Splashlets from her soapy hands dotted the floor. She wiped her fingers on her apron and soothed me. I wrapped my arms around her. I cried for a long time.

I hate the world so fucking much. Why won't God do something? Don't He care?

ME AND CHAPAN PLAYED CRIB AT THE TABLE. NEITHER OF US WAS HAVING FUN. WE wasn't even keeping score. All day I couldn't stop crying. Chapan did her best to keep me feeling okay. But she was just as sad as me.

Hooves *parrup! parrup! parrupp!*ed outside. Wagon wheels screeched and hobbled toward the homestead. I wiped my eyes. Me and Chapan walked to the window.

"Maggie!" Papa Brisson sat in the front wagon seat beside his driver, Narcisse. Étienne and Jean-Baptiste sat in the back seats. "We need to speak to you immediately!"

Me and Chapan opened the door hustled to meet Papa Brisson and Narcisse and Étienne and Jean-Baptiste in their wagon.

"Madame Desjarlais! Where're your girls?" Narcisse pulled back on the reins. He panted through his wispy beard. He was big as the horses drawing the wagon. Wore clothes mixed as his own blood. Métis beaded jacket. Cree shell earrings. Sioux beaded moccasins.

"Sara and Josey are searching for Guille," said Chapan. "What's going on?"

Chapan grabbed my elbow. She walked me toward Papa Brisson and Narcisse. We stopped near Narcisse's horses—two wonderful paint horses with dark eyes solid as Chapan's. The nearer horse lowered his head for me to stroke his nose and scratch his ears.

Narcisse and the boys hopped out the wagon. Étienne and Jean-Baptiste helped Papa Brisson onto the ground.

"Niko, my boy! You're safe!" Papa Brisson hugged me tighter than a bear squeezing honey out a hive.

My insides constricted like a snake. Like Cousin punched me in the gut.

Bad news. It's always bad news.

"What happened to Cousin!" I shoved Papa Brisson away. I needed to know. What could be happening to him?

"We don't know! It's Théodore Gervais—Bella's nephew. He's alive. Narcisse found him."

Narcisse looked all broke up. He stroked his long chin hairs. "Me and my wife heard crying when we was out hunting with some kin of hers. He was lying naked on the grass in one of them burn scars you make."

Narcisse pulled a chaw pouch out his pocket. He dipped his fingers in the bag and whipped out a few grapey, soggy tobacco leaves. He placed the hunk in his cheek.

I wrapped myself around Chapan. I needed her warmth. She was a tree sticky with sap.

Narcisse tried to talk. But his voice kept tripping over its own feet.

"Keep it together, Narcisse." Chapan dug angry hands into my back. "Is the boy okay?"

"He'll be fine. His maman got him. Just bandages that need changing and cleaning. But the poor boy had dry blood all over his ass cheeks. Like he was on his moon-time . . ." Narcisse mopped his eyes. His bumbling lips lost the strength to hold his chaw in his cheek. "I can't fucking dance around it no more, Maggie. The fucking monster who did this castrated the boy!"

Castrated? *Castrated!*

Like a fucking steer!

Like Barney?

A coyote pup?

What if that happens to Cousin? He's supposed to be a buffalo hunter with me. He's supposed to marry Lizette Morin. Become an ancestor. What if it happens to me too?

I SET THE TABLE FOR SUPPER. SOUP BOWLS FOR ALL OF US AND LITTLE PLATES FOR our bannock. I wanted supper to feel a little special. Chapan needed to tell Nimama and Auntie about Théodore—which probably wasn't going to go good. So I wanted every second before Chapan told them to be perfect.

Nimama and Auntie came home after sunset. We gathered for supper. Chapan's pot of potato soup rested on the table. We ladled ourselves the biggest bowls we could, dunking our greasy bannock in the watery soup.

"So I have bad news." Chapan chewed her bannock. She tried acting casual. Like being unstressed could keep Auntie calm when she learns about Théodore. "Mathilde and Narcisse found Bella's nephew. He's going to be okay. He's at home with his family now."

"What do you mean bad news?" Auntie beamed. Like she'd tasted hope for the first time. "That's incredible! Did Théo say anything about Guille?"

"I don't know." The gravity of Chapan's words weighed on her tongue. She spoke solemn. "He was hurt when Mathilde and Narcisse found him."

"I thought you said he'd be okay?" Just as fast as it sparked, the hope in Auntie's eyes flickered. Candle flames fighting through a calm breeze. "What happened?"

"Théo was castrated when they found him."

"Holy fuck." Nimama *clank!*ed her spoon against her bowl.

Auntie's eyes flooded with grief. Her lips bumbled. "What about Guille?"

"I don't kn—"

"What about Guille!"

Auntie stood and smashed her fist against the table. She grabbed her teacup, spun on her heels, threw the cup against the mirror on the wall.

SMASH!

The cup exploded. Tea splattered all over the walls. Ebbed and dripped into the cracks in the shattered mirror.

"*What about Guille!*"

Miss Kitty and Félix raced up the stairs. I wanted to join them. Auntie was going bonkers.

Nimama tried calming her. But Auntie swatted her hands away. Auntie stomped out the door and *slamm!*ed it behind her.

"Go after her," Chapan ordered Nimama. Nimama slipped into her jacket and boots and chased off after Auntie.

Me and Chapan cleaned the porcelain chips off the floor before anyone sliced their feet. We didn't have much to say to each other. Our brains raced with too many thoughts to put them into words.

Nimama brung Auntie home after a half-hour. Maybe longer. Couldn't tell. Time didn't pass normal.

I washed up for bed and said goodnight to everyone before joining Miss Kitty and Félix upstairs. They was already cuddled together on Cousin's bunk. I didn't want to wake them. So I climbed up the ladder and lay in my own bed instead.

I didn't pray for God to strike Odin down. I didn't even pray from Him to give Cousin back. All I prayed for was good dreams. Dreams where Cousin's home and Barney's safe and life is normal again. Just to get away for a night. If God gives me that, I'll never bother Him again.

CHAPTER 11

HUNGER PANGS

HOLY SATURDAY, APRIL 4, 1885.

There was a mass murder at Frog Lake on Thursday. Some starving nehiyaw men stole food and guns and took hostages at the church. Priests. Settlers. Even half-breeds. More than half a dozen people got murdered. Big Bear's furious. It's Hell out there.

By sunrise this morning, Lac-aux-Trois-Pistoles become a ghost town. With the looting of Battleford not long ago and now the murders at Frog Lake and Théo turning up castrated, the whole North-West become bedlam. Lots of families fled to coattail relations all over the prairies to keep themselves and their sons safe. Other families seen their men and boys go down to Batoche to join Dumont's ranks, leaving the women and kids to care for the land and animals.

We was supposed to go to church for Good Friday yesterday. But seeing as all the families who fled and the men who left for Batoche needed food, folks spent yesterday slaughtering all the town's pigs and some of the Gervaises' cattle to supply everyone with salted and smoked meat. Nimama and Auntie volunteered to help. But they wouldn't let me come. Said it was dangerouser than ever now we know what happens to kidnapped boys.

When the slaughtering and smoking and salting was all done, they sent the volunteers home with fresh pork to last the next while. Bacon slabs. Ham roasts. Hocks. We ain't never had so much food before. During Holy Week too.

And Cousin ain't around to eat none of it.

I heard bacon sizzling on a griddle from way upstairs in bed. *Crackl!*ing and *popp!*ing like gunshots. I could only listen to the bacon call me for so long. I followed my nose downstairs and got the surprise of my life when I seen Campbell at the table with Nimama and Auntie and Chapan. They all hunched over their plates of fluffy eggs, thick cut bacon, bannock fried in the bacon fat.

Campbell hung his head low. A stiff bandage was wound around his hand. His purple fingers dangled like tentacles. His suspenders yanked his already sunk shoulders. Black moustache bristles poked out his lip like cat whiskers. He had bloodshot eyes with big bags. He looked awful. Unhandsome even.

"I made food for you too." Chapan passed me an empty plate. I said hi to everyone quick so I could hop into a chair and ladle myself some eggs. I grabbed planks of both soft and crispy bacon. Two crunchy pieces of fried bannock. Some saskatoon berry lard goop. Some maple and pear jams from Québec that Campbell brung over for an Easter present. Before I even finished serving myself up, half my plateful of grub somehow found its way into my belly. I was so hungry I forgot I was nervous to see Campbell again. Forgot to pray too.

"Thanks for breakfast, madame." Campbell wiped his mouth with his bandage.

"I'm happy you're here." Chapan waddled to a bookshelf by the fireplace. She picked a hardcover novel from the stacks and came back to the table. She set the book beside Campbell's plate—*Adventures of Huckleberry Finn*. "If you don't come back and tell me that's the greatest book you ever read, I'll eat Sara's hat."

"Didn't this just come out?" Campbell read the publisher's page.

Nimama rolled a cigarette over her plate. She'd wiped the porcelain so clean, it sparkled. Félix and Miss Kitty snoozed on the bear rug on the floor.

I wanted to ask Campbell something. But I didn't know what to say. I was nervous all over again. I nibbled my bacon slow to give me more time to think. I wanted to sound smart for him. What if my hunch ain't wrong? What if he's my papa?

"Work going good?"

"It's a funny story . . ." Campbell's eyebrows shot up his forehead. His voice sounded unenthusiasticful. He looked embarrassed. "Mind if I have that smoke, Sara?"

Nimama handed her cigarette to Campbell. He placed the

cigarette between his lips. Nimama struck a match and brung the flame to Campbell's mouth. He puffed. She shook out the fire between her fingers.

"I got suspended yesterday. That's why I'm available to join your search party."

"What happened?" Auntie asked defensive. Like she was afraid it got something to do with her intimidating the sergeant into coughing up information about Cousin and them.

Campbell shrugged. He raised his broke, bandaged hand and pointed at it. "Maybe this. I'm not sure. Sergeant never said."

Auntie looked relieved. At least somewhat. Nimama rolled herself a new cigarette.

"How can they suspend you without cause?" asked Chapan. "Doesn't that breach some sort of protocol?"

"I won't push it. They let me keep my pistol. I'm expected back on Monday—in uniform—before the morning meeting."

"Do you need somewhere to stay?"

"I got a room at the saloon." Campbell set his half-smoked cigarette on his plate. He rested his elbows on the table and rustled his hair. "You know, madame. Even before this Riel shit started going on, the hardest part about being Métis and a Mountie has always been being Métis and a Mountie. You know? I joined this force a long time ago because nipapa said Sitting Bull spoke the world of James Morrow Walsh. Called Walsh a man of justice and equality and all that. I thought all other policemen would want to be good men like Walsh. But even before Duck Lake, half the fucking mess hall called me Pope Savage XIII. Now they call Riel the antichrist. They want to scalp Big Bear. I hate this fucking war.

"But my family needs this job. You know?"

Campbell puffed his smoke. The chemicals cooled his brain. He set the cigarette on his plate like a proper ashtray.

"Look, I didn't come here to whine. I came to talk. There's two things before we go find Guille. First is Kate McCannon. She's back from the United States. The council gave her permission. Kate McCannon's okimâw iskwew of the Pussy Posse of Lac-aux-Trois-Pistoles. They have a camp in Loon Lake. They run it a bit like an old buffalo hunt. But with all women leadership. They're looking for the missing boys of Lac-aux-Trois-Pistoles and keeping their families safe. Anyone's welcome to join." Campbell looked around the room. Locking eyes with everyone. Even me. "So that's something to think about."

Auntie crossed her arms and clicked her tongue. She crumpled her napkin on her plate. "What's the other thing you're here for?"

"I'm afraid it's bad news. Hélène's sister came by the saloon this morning. Nishecabo passed away yesterday."

"Oh my goodness." Chapan put her hand over her mouth in shock.

The fire was never supposed to go out inside Nishecabo. Him departing on Good Friday's only fitting. I hope Barney's with Nishecabo in Heaven. Maybe Nishecabo can take Barney duck hunting. Where the guns never jam and the mallards never suspect a thing. Barney would've been a good duck hunting dog. Even with three legs.

Campbell stared vacantful at a woody knot in the centre of the table. He *slurrrp!*ed his coffee. "I'm worried about Georges.

You know? That little coyote wants to be too much like his papa. Told his maman he wanted to head out to the Pussy Posse and find Charlo soon as Nishecabo's in his grave. Poor kid'll get himself killed if he isn't careful."

"We should see them," said Chapan. Nimama eyed the Winchester on the mantel behind Chapan. "Is the wake today?"

"Tomorrow."

"But tomorrow's Easter," said Auntie with a mix of concern and frustration.

"There isn't enough time to have a wake for Nishecabo tonight before the Easter Vigil. And Monday's just too late." Campbell dragged his cigarette and leaned into the table. Smoke leaked from his lips. "Between us, I don't think Hélène and Georges want to spend Easter with Père Brisson. I think they just want to be with people who love them."

"But it's Easter," Auntie hissed. "Hélène shouldn't force us to choose between Easter and Nishecabo."

"It will always be her husband." Chapan wrapped her hand around her other arm. She squeezed like the ghostful hand of her late love was there too. "He'll always come first."

"The Lord won't be going nowhere, Josey." Campbell *tss!*ed his cigarette into a saucy spot on his plate. He patted Auntie's hand reassuringful. "He understands tomorrow's our time to mourn Nishecabo."

"Maybe." Auntie folded her arms. She sounded half-convinced. But scared of retribution.

"Who's riding with the Pussy Posse?" asked Nimama.

"Coco Laframboise's there with her son and their dog; the Callahoos are there with their dog too; Madame Elinore Morin's there with her granddaughter. It's a big camp."

"What kinds of guns they got?"

Campbell wiggled in his seat. He rested his hand above his NWMP-issued Enfield revolver in the holster on his hips.

"I know Kate McCannon's got Corporal San Luis's revolver. And she's always got Li P'chii on her. Then Laurent's got his repeater. If you bring your Winchester, that'll be at least four . . ." Campbell shrugged at Nimama. He wanted her to know there was nothing he could do about their firearm count. "Everyone's guns are in Batoche. It is what it is."

"They got enough food?" asked Auntie.

"Wild game. Canned goods. Madame Morin's the camp cook. She's got a small garden and a chicken coop too. The council in Deadwood loaned Kate McCannon twenty dollars for provisions if they need it. And Mathilde Little Bull rides with the posse full-time—she's one of the okimâwak. I'm sure Narcisse will cut them a discount if they buy anything from their store."

"Know what I think?" Chapan dug her elbows into the table like augers. She pointed at Nimama and Auntie. "I think you should take Niko and join them after the wake tomorrow."

"I can take you." Campbell dangled his arm over the backrest of his chair. "They're camped on the beach not far from the narrows."

"I don't know," Nimama hesitated. She laid her hand against my thigh. "Niko might be safer here."

"Maybe," said Campbell. "But after your dog got castrated—and now Théodore too? What if it's all connected? You know? Then I'm not sure how safe it is here for Nikosis. With the Pussy Posse, he has an armed gang looking out for him."

Nimama wiggled her jaw. Her mouth made weird shapes as she weighed her thoughts.

"It'll be like a buffalo hunt." Campbell winked at me. "Just without the buffalo."

"What about you?" Auntie asked Chapan.

"I'm staying here. Someone's got to look after la bibliothèque."

"I don't know." Nimama rustled my pant leg. "It's a lot to think about."

"We'll find Guille faster together," said Auntie. "Niko'll be safer too."

"What do you think?" Nimama asked me. She twiddled the cigarette butt on her plate. Félix and Miss Kitty snuggled on the rug. Winnie glittered on the mantel.

I was happy Nimama asked my input. It's my safety after all. And I need some excitement in my life.

"You sure you ain't coming?" I didn't want to leave Chapan. Missing her on top of Cousin's a lot for a kid.

"I'll visit Père Brisson and the boys when I can." Chapan set her hand on my other knee—opposite of Nimama. "I'll be safe, Niko. I promise."

"Okay." I thought about it a while. A buffalo hunt could be what I need. "Let's do this."

NIMAMA AND AUNTIE CAME HOME AFTER SIX. NO LUCK FINDING COUSIN. WE DIDN'T talk much at supper. After we finished our soups, Auntie readied herself at the door. She slung Winnie over her shoulder. She headed alone to the church for the Easter Vigil.

Nimama said I had to stay home with her and Chapan. Didn't matter we was missing the Holy Eucharist. Nimama said after Charlo and François disappeared at the saloon, she didn't trust me nowhere but home. Not even the church. But she was going to have to trust me with her and the Pussy Posse in Loon Lake soon.

After me and Nimama packed our clothes and camp gear, we held our own vigil by the fireplace. But we had no way to repent. No way to take Communion.

I hope God won't punish us. Nimama says God understands and forgives us. She says He even appreciates us holding our own vigil at home.

But I doubt it.

CHAPTER 12

LESSONS IN FIREARM SAFETY

EASTER SUNDAY, APRIL 5, 1885. LAC-AUX-TROIS-PISTOLES AND LOON LAKE, DISTRICT OF SASKATCHEWAN.

Me, Nimama, Auntie, and Chapan arrived at the Duchармes' homestead around eleven o'clock. Me and Chapan rode in the Red River cart with Huckleberry pulling. Auntie and Viking rode in front of us. Nimama and Pony followed behind with Winnie slung over her shoulder. We brung all our stuff so me and Nimama and Auntie could swap the cart with Huckleberry and Viking. Then us three would ride out to Loon Lake after the wake and Chapan would do her best to ride Huckleberry home.

The Ducharmes lived in the most typical Métis homestead ever. It's white like ours. But they got a dirt floor instead of wood and no loft upstairs. They ain't got no glass windows neither. They cover their windows with deer hides hammered around the frames from the inside.

Their homestead looked lots like ours and nothing like ours at the same time. They got lots of cabinets and wardrobes to stuff knickknacks into. Moose and elk antlers over the bookcase. Medicines hang-drying in the rolled-open windows. A small stove by the kitchen. Metal crosses and paintings of Jesus and his maman on each wall. They even got a blue flag with a hand and wolf that Nimama whispered was for Riel's war effort.

The Ducharmes' house smelled different than ours too. Leathery and woodsy like Maman Earth's lungs breathed through the ground.

Little plates of cranberry jelly sandwiches, jars of pickled eggs and asparagus, bowls of nuts and seeds lined the kitchen counters. I was so excited for snacks, I caught myself drooling.

Arf! arf!

Georges and Charlo's good boy ran to the door to greet us. He looked like a black coyote excepting the elderful white beard around his muzzle. His tongue dangled out the side of his mouth. We scratched his ears and patted his skull. Auntie bent on one knee to be closer to him. He rubbed his nose into Auntie's arms. Just like Barney used to.

"Bienvenue, mes amies! Et toi aussi, petit Niko," said Hélène through her near-rotted teeth. She welcomed us at the homestead door. Her eyes looked swole from crying. She wore all black. Her greasy reddish-black hair was tied into a perfect bun. No wily half-breed hairs anywhere in sight. She watched her dog snuggle up to Auntie. "Looks like Napoléon's made a new friend."

Georges approached us with his hands in his pockets. He wore his blackest slacks, his blackest shirt, his blackest vest. Wrapped around his waist was his papa's red l'Assomption sash—the sash Nishecabo wore at the bunny-hop.

"We're so sorry for your loss." Nimama and Auntie and Chapan hugged Georges one after another.

"I'm sorry too." I wiped Napoléon's dog dirt off my hand. Then reached to shake Georges's hand.

His lips broke a smile. He shook my hand proud. "Thanks, pal."

Everyone was dressed in their finest clothes: wool vests and jackets, cotton dresses and beaded moccasins. Some wore black like Hélène and Georges. Others wore special occasion clothes: smoked leather jackets and beaded garters and sashes.

Not many people made it to the Ducharmes' for the wake. Most was either gone or at the church for Easter Mass. Campbell stood at the back of the homestead with a couple old-timers—buffalo hunters from Nishecabo's heydays who came to mourn too.

I know lots of old buffalo hunters feel bitter and useless now the buffalo is gone. But I still wish me and Cousin was born at a time when we could ride with the buffalo. I know it don't make no sense. But I'm jealous they know the pain of *losing* the buffalo. Means they know what it was like to have had them in the first place.

Chapan says she ain't never been hungry until the buffalo

started to disappear. Me? I ain't never *not* been hungry. I don't even know what buffalo meat tastes like. Papa Brisson says Communion is the body of Jesus Hisself. What about the body of Maman Earth? I deserve to eat buffalo like my ancestors.

"I have something for you. Come here."

Nimama waved for Georges to follow her to the open window. She unslung Winnie from her shoulder. She mounted the gun to her shoulder and aimed out the window.

Click!

Nimama pushed the lever. The rifle's action opened. Sunlight shined down the empty barrel through the open ejector. Winnie was unloaded.

Georges pulled his hands out his pockets. Nimama handed him her gun. Georges held Winnie gingerful as a pipe. He looked at Nimama astonished. Winnie was Nimama's other baby.

"My kokum smudged her this morning." Nimama reached into her jacket pocket and set a box of bullets on the windowsill. "Take good care of Winnie for me."

"You sure about this?" Georges was fighting tears. "Dumont's men'll give us our guns back when the war ends."

Nimama shrugged. "She's yours until then."

"Thank you, mademoiselle." Georges looked proud with his new gun. He closed the action. Napoléon sat with Georges. He inspected the rifle with his nose.

Hélène met Nimama as she walked back toward us. She put her arm around Nimama's shoulder. "What about you?"

Nimama pointed with her chin at Campbell at the rear of the homestead. "Campbell's taking us to Loon Lake later. He has a revolver. We'll be fine."

Hélène thanked Nimama with a light, meaningful squeeze.

"Suivez-moi." Hélène waved for us to follow her to Nishecabo's deathbed at the back of the homestead. She reached behind her and took Nimama's hand, who took Auntie's hand, who took Chapan's hand, who took my hand. We held hands like we round danced.

Hélène weaseled us through her maze of friends to the back. Everyone stood tall like corn stalks. I recognized Monsieur Xavier Fleury standing at the foot of Nishecabo's deathbed with Campbell and another man I ain't never seen before. Monsieur Fleury's seventy-or-so-year-old shoulders carried more weight than just the grief of a lost friend. His fingers held Nishecabo's blanketed toes. The wool sheened with Monsieur Fleury's tears.

Monsieur Fleury wore his whiskers long. Grey and black hairs surrounded a white mouth like old Napoléon's hairy smile. He dressed sharp. Fine black trousers, black wool jacket, black neckerchief. All black like he'd jumped into a pool of midnight ink. Only his colourful waistbound l'Assomption sash kept the man from being dressed darker than the grim reaper hisself.

At the head of the bed beside Campbell stood the ginormongousest man I ever seen. Like he was half half-breed, half buffalo. He wore overalls with no undershirt and a rugged hat with two long braids and shell earrings. His long duster coat draped to his knees. Wispy chest hairs hid scars from years of getting damn near sliced in half by buffalo horns. I couldn't imagine how much buffalo meat he must have ate when he was my age to get so big and strong.

"Gentlemen." Hélène gestured to the four of us. "This is

Sara and Joséphine Eriksen. You remember Maggie Desjarlais. Last comes Charlo's friend, Niko."

"Taanshii," I smiled. Each man bowed at us. Each looked mournful.

It was in their faces. Sashes. Feathers. Horses. Guns. All that power Nishecabo once had didn't matter no more. Saying goodbye to Nishecabo was like saying goodbye to history hisself.

Our time's over, boys. Ain't nothing never going to be the same.

"Give us a minute?" Hélène said to the men. Monsieur Fleury and his ginormongous friend nodded as they passed into the kitchen to eat sandwiches and socialize with Hélène's relatives.

"Good seeing everyone." Campbell nodded at me and Nimama and Auntie and Chapan. He wore black slacks and a white shirt and black vest with the same moccasins he had at the bunny-hop. His gun was holstered to his hip. "Come get me when you're ready to go to Loon Lake." Campbell then strutted off to the kitchen with Monsieur Fleury and his friend.

Nimama reached into the inside pocket of her tweed jacket. She gave Auntie a hunk of tobacco for Nishecabo.

Auntie stepped with Hélène toward the body that lay on the bed. She gave Nishecabo the tobacco, prayed, and planted a kiss on his cold hand. Then she stepped back to wrap her arms around Hélène. Both women stood vigil over Nishecabo's body as his spirit took their prayers to the next world.

Auntie rubbed Hélène's shoulders. She whispered some words in Hélène's ear that made her giggle and sniffle. She hugged Auntie. Whatever Hélène was feeling, Auntie'd felt it too.

Auntie and Hélène waved for me and Nimama and Chapan to pay our respects to Nishecabo. I stepped nervousful toward the deathbed. I didn't know what to expect. My heart went bonkers. I ain't never seen no dead person before. Last dead body I seen was Barney, bless his soul.

Nishecabo rested on his back. He looked comfortable tucked under his stripey point blanket. His eyes was shut and his beard brushed. He looked like he slept mighty peaceful. So peaceful he ain't even needed to breathe.

WE LEFT AFTER THE LATE LUNCH MADAME DUCHARME AND HER SISTERS AND CHAPAN prepared for us at the wake. Campbell told us to expect about a five-hour ride. By the time dusk fell, we was still an hour away. The bumpy trail brung us deep into the prettiest, stinkiest springtime muskeg. It's amazing—this swampy "land" been filling bellies since them days before smallpox and Frenchmen when people was fed by the breasts of Maman Earth herself.

We bounced along the slender trail. Nimama rode Pony behind Campbell and his horse. Me and Auntie rode in the cart; Viking pulled. All that damn *screech!*ing of them wheels made me wish I was deaf.

Screeeeeeech! screeeeeeech!

Even with all that noise, Nimama and Auntie and Campbell made chit-chat like old times. Talking about this person, that misadventure. Shenanigans they got up to when they was unresponsible kids my age.

We stopped for a break. We wasn't far from Loon Lake. Nimama and them chuckled and wiped tears after laughing hysterical about how they used to rub cranberry jam on the horses' gums and lips to make them look like they was talking.

Campbell smiled wide. He placed an unlit cigarette Nimama rolled for him between his lips. She *shhrripp!*ed a match and leaned over to light Campbell's smoke.

"We had some good times," Campbell puffed. "You know that?"

"Crazy how fast life went by." Nimama shook out the match. The festive moment settled. "I still can't believe you're back. I thought I was seeing a ghost when I seen you at the outpost."

Campbell sucked the cigarette between his fingers. He didn't look comfortable talking about no personal matters. "Never thought I'd be back to be honest with you."

"Is your family still in Fort Edmonton?"

"My parents and brother are, yeah. *We're* in Calgary—well, *were* in Calgary. Here again, I guess."

"What kind of half-breed willingly lives in Calgary?" teased Nimama.

"There's more to me than being Métis. Okay?"

"Is that why you became a fucking Mountie?"

"Sara!" Auntie barked. "Don't answer her."

Nimama looked comfortable with her anger. Like it was fire in her hands. "After the shit we got up to?"

Campbell leaned relaxedful in his saddle. He enjoyed his cigarette like an expensive imported cigar. Him and Nimama stared each other off. "Same thing I told your kokum. My family needs this job. Look, life was good for *us* in Calgary. Now I'm here again. I'm just trying to go back to the way it was."

"Answer my question!" Nimama flexed her jaw at Campbell. Every thought that passed her mind made her more heated. "Why are you a policeman? If you have to be a policeman, why can't you be fucking useful and find my nephew!"

"*Sara!*" yelled Auntie with all her voice. She stood on the cart and looked down at Nimama. "Watch your mouth! We're almost there."

"What do you want me to say?" Campbell drew the last drag of his cigarette. Then he threw the cherry-tipped butt into a shallow puddle beneath him. "I'm taking you to Loon Lake so you can be with the Pussy Posse. They know how to find Guillaume better than them cretins I work with. But you better know I'm risking the career my family depends on by taking you there."

"What family?" Nimama threw her hands up. "I don't care about your job!"

"You should."

Campbell had a cocky look on his face. His hand flittered over his holstered pistol blanketed by the breast of his big coat.

Nimama's eyes followed Campbell's hand through the whole motion. She bared her teeth like a rabid dog. Reached across their horses and grabbed Campbell by his coat collar.

"Don't threaten me!"

Nimama shoved Campbell off his horse. He splashed muck when he *thudd!*ed the ground. Campbell's horse reared high. Auntie handed me the reins and jumped off the cart to grab Pony's and Campbell's horse's reins before they could go crazy and take off.

Nimama swung off her saddle. She marched toward Campbell.

Campbell scrambled backwards on his elbows.

Nimama loomed over Campbell. She grabbed him by the collar. She drew her open palm across her chest.

SLAP!

Nimama whipped her hand against Campbell's cheek. Then she tore open his wool coat and exposed his holster. She planted her knee on Campbell's breastbone. Pinned him to Maman Earth like a tent peg. She reached for the gun in Campbell's holster. Her fingers wrapped around its grip.

Nimama's thumb dragged the gun hammer, cocking Campbell's holstered revolver.

Clllllick!

"Give me the gun."

Campbell quivered under Nimama's knee. He breathed choppy. Shallow. Deliberate. His lungs crushed slow. "I could lose my job if you take my gun."

"I don't want to take it. I want you to give it to me."

Campbell squirmed under Nimama's knee. He thought careful before speaking.

"Take it. Just let me go."

"No. You need to give it to me."

Silence burned through the forest. I could even hear the dying sunlight.

Campbell nodded.

Clllllick!

Nimama uncocked the gun. She removed her hand from Campbell's holster.

Campbell retrieved the revolver with his broke hand. He inspected it mournful. Then he thrusted the gun into Nimama's belly.

Nimama grabbed the gun and dug her knee into Campbell's chest as she pushed herself off him. She slipped the gun into the waistband of her pants, underneath the tail of her tweed jacket. Campbell stared up at Nimama. He pulled hisself onto his elbows.

Nimama grabbed Campbell's horse's reins from Auntie. She towed the white steed toward Campbell. He helped hisself to his feet. His coat was wet and muddy. Nimama threw the horse's reins at Campbell.

"Now get the fuck out of here!"

Campbell rode off into the darkness. Back where we came.

Nimama mounted up. Auntie climbed into the cart and took over the reins. We seen the faintest bit of purple in the sky from the sunset. Bats scattered among the trees. We was almost there.

I spent the rest the ride thinking about the two of them—Nimama and Campbell. Why couldn't Campbell answer Nimama straight? Why did he threaten her? What was he hiding?

CHAPTER 13

THE PUSSY POSSE OF LAC-AUX-TROIS-PISTOLES

We crossed a ridge. A couple wagons and some Red River carts was parked on the beach by the lakeshore. Firelight bounced off tents and even a few teepees. We made it to Loon Lake. The Pussy Posse was not far ahead.

The camp was shaped like a half-moon down on the

beach with the lakeshore cutting the moon in half. Carts and wagons circled the tents and teepees. A fire burned at the centre of camp like a bullseye. From their breath clouds, I seen horses in their halters tied to hitching posts and the highline. We even seen a chicken coop by the chuckwagon and mess tent.

Arf! arf!

Leaves rustled beside us. A tawny dog shot out the bush. She rushed us. Flashed her growly fangs. She flopped like a fish on a line when she reached the end of her rope.

Arf! arf! arf!

"*Whoa!*" Auntie tugged the cart's reins before Viking could spook. The dog nipped at his hooves.

"Hey!" shouted a man's voice from the bush. A gun *click!*ed. "Who's there!"

Nimama reached under the back flap of her tweed jacket and whipped Campbell's pistol out her beltline. She surveyed bushes down the iron sights for whoever shouted at us. "I'll shoot!"

"Josey, Sara, Niko," whistled a chipped-tooth man. He stood straight up from behind a twiggy bush, surrenderful, hands in the air. The barrel of his rifle pointed to the starry sky. He stepped onto the trail with his head high. "It's me: Laurent."

Arf! arf!

Laurent slung his repeater over his shoulder. He ran to calm his dog. Crouched near her and waited until she was tame again. He ruffled her ears. "Good girl."

Laurent stepped toward Viking with his palm open for him. Viking licked the salt off Laurent's hand. "Sorry about Twig here. She's a guard dog at heart. We're on lookout."

"It's fine," Auntie said breathless. Nimama tucked the revolver back into her waistband. "Barney was the same way."

"I heard about his passing. I'm real sorry. I know it ain't much, but my wife lost her horse this winter. Some fool thought she was a cow elk." Laurent chuckled sad and nostalgiaful. "She was damn expensive too. Bought her from a cowboy in Southern Alberta. Man used to be a slave, believe it or not."

"Yeah."

"Hey, listen." Laurent's mournful eyes tracked Auntie's hands like doves. She wiped tearlets off her cheeks. "I want to apologize for what I said at the bunny-hop."

"What do you mean?" asked Auntie with surprise in her voice. She looked anxious as a sinner on her deathbed. Laurent didn't do no wrong at the bunny-hop. It was her who lied.

Laurent stroked Viking's nose while he thought of words to say. He breathed deep. Twig licked her chops and kneeled at the end of her rope.

"I feel terrible I forgot about Guillaume. I ain't stupid. I know why he couldn't come. But I was drunk when I seen you at the bunny-hop and and and I just wasn't thinkin—"

"It's okay," said Auntie fast. She rubbed her face like she was waking from a weird dream. "I understand."

Me and Nimama glanced at each other. We knew it wasn't right for Auntie to take advantage of Laurent. But we needed peace between everyone more than justice.

Auntie outhaled heavy. "Lead us into camp?"

Laurent nodded subtle. He untied his dog from the tree and let her run ahead. *Arf! arf!* Laurent grabbed Pony's and Viking's reins and led us down the mucky trail.

"How're you doing?" asked Auntie after a while. Her voice

sounded sad in ways I suspect only she and Laurent understood as parents of stole children.

"All right, I guess. There's another girl Angélique's age at the camp. So that's good."

"Any news?"

"Yeah. You should prepare yourself." Laurent stopped. He stroked Viking's chin. "Bella says the fucking monster responsible for what happened to her nephew was some old fur trader. Our boys are still with him. But we can't find their camp nowhere."

"What's the fur trader's name?"

"We don't know. Théo hasn't said. He hasn't talked much, truth be told."

When Laurent turned around, Nimama and Auntie sighed in relief. If people find out it's Odin—it's my grandpapa—behind all this, what will they say? Will they blame us?

"Are the other boys okay?" asked Nimama.

"The hostages? I guess—far as hostages go." Laurent cleared his throat and spat into the bush. "Théodore *really* didn't want to talk. Even when they asked. Can't say I blame the kid. Not sure I'd talk about something like that neither."

We rode quiet until we got within shouting distance of the camp. I thought Laurent deserved to know what Auntie told me about the folder on the sergeant's desk. I'm sure Laurent wants to find François as bad as Auntie wants Cousin. Even if he ain't gone bonkers like her.

We was close to the highline at the edge of the half-moon. Twig ran into the camp. Firelight glittered bright enough to make it hard for our eyes to adjust to darkness.

We walked with Laurent to a post where Auntie hitched the cart and Nimama hitched Pony. I hopped off the cart into

Nimama's hands. She planted me on the ground so I wouldn't splash muck all over my moccasins. A couple women who sat at the fire tiptoed toward us.

"It's Laurent." He led us past the highline. I grabbed Nimama's and Auntie's hands and walked with them. Laurent introduced us to the camp. "I'm with Josey and Sara Eriksen and Sara's son, Niko. They've come to join us."

"Josey! Sara!" bellered a few women. They smothered Auntie and Nimama with hugs.

"Niko! It's been so long!" A big breasted woman bent to hug me tighter than any bear could. I always knew Mathilde Little Bull was special. A true saint with a soul of sugar. I always adored the way she seeded the world with love. Her plaid blouse smelled like a charry forest. Her hugs made me feel warm and wanted in ways I'd never say no to. "You must be hungry." Mathilde placed her hand on my belly. "Let's get some grub in you."

Vibrations of a fiddle and plucked guitar strings fluttered through the air. A harmonica wailed. Moonlight reflected off the ripply lake. Rudi, Zacharie Laframboise's dog, gnawed a fat stick by the fire.

"What's for eating?" I asked Mathilde. I rested my hand on my rumbling belly.

"Hope you like wild game. And greens. And soup. And bannock. And canned fruit. And pickled roots." Mathilde's voice grew more and more hurried with excitement the more and more she spoke. "Oh, Nikosis, I'm so happy you and your family are joining us. We'll keep you safe."

Mathilde led me to the fire. Folks sat around the flames, smoking and making chit-chat. Mathilde put two fingers in her mouth and whistled a short *tweeeoooweeet!*

"Nikosis Eriksen needs a bowl of venison soup! He's a hungry boy!" announced Mathilde to eight-or-so firelit faces. Each glowed the moment they heard my name.

Kate McCannon perked right up when she seen me. Her whole face—eyes, hair, lips—was the same shade of brown as pine bark. A wishbone-shaped scar split between her brow, then spilled down her nose bridge onto her cheeks like lashes of war paint under each eye.

Since long before we ever known her, Kate McCannon only wears black. Like every day's a funeral. Every outfit matches her Civil War cavalry hat. And she wears all her own beadwork and embroidery using only black and grey and white beads and threads. She beaded black and white tulips onto the chest and lapels of her black tasselled deerskin jacket. And she embroidered the back and shoulders like a garden beautiful as Eden.

"Niko, my boy!" Kate McCannon approached with wings spread. The tassels dangled like feathers. Li P'chii peeped out one of her gun holsters. San Luis's revolver poked out the other. Shells lined her bandolier. She hugged me and rustled the top of my head. "Looking sharp, young lad."

"It's been a long day for him," Mathilde said. "A good meal should go a long way."

Kate McCannon led me to a cooking fire with a smoking rack scaffolded around it. A massive cauldron of soup bubbled over some coals underneath. Madame Morin grabbed me a wood bowl and spoon, ladled me tons of soup, and gave me a couple pieces of bannock too.

I said the quickest prayer I could, then gulped up my soup like a dying meal. I chomped my hunks of deer meat and nibbled grains of wild rice. I dipped my bannock until it was drippier than a rainy roof. I didn't listen to no one around me talk about nothing. I had importanter business to attend to: an empty belly to fill.

At some point in time Nimama sat beside me at the fire. By the time I noticed, her and Kate McCannon was knee-deep in conversation.

"Laurent damn near shit himself when you brandished that gun at him," Kate McCannon chuckled to Nimama. I spooned the last chunks of venison and rice into my mouth. "Whose gun is that anyway?"

Nimama reached behind her and tapped the revolver grip. "Campbell Palmer's."

"How'd you get that?"

"He gave it to me," Nimama smirked.

"I'm sure." Kate McCannon smiled around the tobacco plugging her cheek. Crackles and swirls in the fire hypnotized her racing mind. She put her hand on Nimama's shoulder. "I'm happy you joined us. You'll be stronger with us. We're already stronger with you."

We sat in the warm light. Nimama wrapped my blanket around me as the night got nightier. Croaking frogs lullabied me halfway between asleep and awake. I didn't even notice Nimama and Auntie left to set up our tent by lantern light. When they came back, I was fast asleep with a big dog snuggled up on either side of me. So Nimama picked me up and carried me to bed.

CHAPTER 14

MÂKWA SÂKÂHIKAN

SUNDAY, APRIL 12, 1885.

It's been a long week. I miss la bibliothèque. It's warm. I get to snuggle with Félix and Miss Kitty. And Chapan's got lots of books to practise reading and papers for drawing on. But at the end of the day, here's got lots more food than home. Madame Morin's always cooking up something for somebody. There's more than a dozen people in the posse total. And not one of us had a hungry night yet.

Being with my friends all week's been great. Helps me forget how bad I miss Cousin. Thing is, when I do miss him, I miss him even worser.

We fish with English-style rods from the lakeshore most

days after we feed the animals breakfast and finish our morning chores. We got two rods to share: the Good Rod and the Broke Rod. The Good Rod is the best in the world. I caught a fat jackfish my first try. But the Broke Rod is so broke, sometimes it snaps like a chicken bone on the back cast. Then on the forward cast, a hook always needles some poor kid's neck. Happened to me twice already.

Seeing as we can't go far if we don't want no trouble, we can't play no buffalo hunters. We fly kites lots. Sometimes we play war in the trees. But we always argue who's Dumont's men and who has to be Ottawa's. Zach plays his fiddle and teaches us how to jig even though he ain't no good teacher at all. And when we play cards or dice, Angélique calls us all sinners and gamblers and storms off with Lizette so they can read scripture together to spite us.

It's fun. But Cousin should be here too.

So far there ain't been no signs of the boys nowhere. No signs of Odin neither. And no word of nothing going on in the war. It's been nice. Kind of boring though. But everyone's safe. And everything's stable. So much so, Narcisse left to look after him and Mathilde's store.

Kate McCannon's still got everyone searching from sunup to sundown. Around the lake, up in burn scars. Private land, wild land. Everywhere.

It all happens in three eight-hour brigades, one or two out at a time with one brigade always at camp no matter what: Morning Brigade leaves at six o'clock in the morning with okimâw Mathilde and returns at two in the afternoon for lunch; Day Brigade leaves with their okimâw at ten to meet the Morning Brigade after breakfast and returns at six for supper; Night Brigade leaves at four in the afternoon with okimâw Kate McCannon to meet the Day Brigade and returns at midnight. Kids stay and take care of camp with Madame Morin. We get three meals a day. But each brigade only gets two: Morning Brigade gets lunch and supper; Day Brigade gets breakfast and supper; and Night Brigade gets breakfast and lunch. Nimama and Auntie ride with the Night Brigade.

The Pussy Posse's got three okimâwak who make up the council. Each okimâw leads her own brigade. Kate McCannon's okimâw of the Night Brigade and okimâw iskwew of the Pussy Posse. Mathilde's okimâw of the Morning Brigade and Kate McCannon's second-in-command as the Sioux Chef of the Pussy Posse. Last comes the okimâw of the Day Brigade. A new okimâw gets elected by secret ballot every Sunday after supper. Anyone can vote excepting Kate McCannon and Mathilde, and any woman sixteen or older can be okimâw of the Day Brigade excepting Madame Morin—she oversees the elections because she can't lead no brigade as camp cook. All voting deadlocks get resolved by Kate McCannon and Mathilde.

This morning, Bella led us in prayer. She's the closest person we got to a preacher. Most devoutest woman from the most pious family in all Lac-aux-Trois-Pistoles. She even gave a short sermon about Job from a Bible borrowed from la bibliothèque.

After our small service, we ate the big Sunday breakfast Madame Morin prepared with Lizette. Fried bannock with berry soup. Unsweetened orange pekoe for the kids and coffee watered down with dandelion root tea for the adults.

Mosquitoes ate us for breakfast as usual too. Slurping our blood through their needles like Papa Brisson drinks tea.

Kate McCannon rode out alone on a six-hour Sunday Brigade after breakfast. Me and Nimama lounged around camp after us kids cleaned all the plates and pots and pans in the mess tent. Me and Nimama lay with our notebooks in front of us. Nimama wrote in her diary as she always does. I tried sketching Barney again. It wasn't perfect. But better than before. He looked happy this time. Like he was having fun with Nishecabo on the other side.

We heard wagon wheels rumble from the trail. Me and Nimama popped out our tent and approached the highline. Narcisse's wagon hobbled toward camp. Hélène and Georges rode behind. Georges slung Winnie over his shoulder. He drove a cart pulled by his horse. Mathilde put her fingers in a ring between her lips.

Twweeeooooweeeet!

Mathilde cupped her mouth and hollered, "Hey! Our friends are hungry!"

Napoléon raced out the cart. *Arf! arf! arf!* He chased Twig and Rudi around the highline before Angélique and Zach caught them and calmed them down.

After getting everything unloaded, we sat around log benches and chairs at the fire for a special supper Madame Morin fixed up for the Ducharmes' scheduled arrival. She brung a couple venison organ roasts whose smells sizzled up my nostrils in steamy and smoky spurts. My lips drooled over the bannock crumble stuffing and jarred cranberry sauce passing in front of me. Napoléon bathed with Twig and Rudi in the heat from the fire, gnawing deer bones.

I sat beside Georges. He wore the same blue shirt and

suspenders as the day Cousin got took. Stared angry into the fire and forked meat into his mouth. Unflinching. Unblinking. Scraping food off the tines with the blades of his teeth.

Shhhhhhiiingk!

Hélène sat with Auntie across the fire. She watched Georges peck at his food with the kind of concern Nimama and Auntie get when me or Cousin is sad.

"You should stay at camp tomorrow." Hélène's voice cut through the popping of water-soaked logs in the fire. "Watch over the transition between brigades while we settle in."

"Ain't got to worry about me." Georges's teeth grated against his fork again. "I'll be with Kate McCannon and the Eriksens on the Night Brigade after lunch tomorrow."

"I'll be staying here all day tomorrow. Just to settle in." Hélène walked over to me and Georges. She brushed me aside so she could be close to her boy.

I walked around the circle to sit in Hélène's now-empty chair beside Auntie. Auntie clapped her hand against my thigh. She smiled cute and sad at me. Like she caught herself thinking I was Guille.

"Maman, I got to go!" Georges smashed his plate against his lap. Metal and ceramic banged together. "Charlo's in danger and I'm sitting around this fire getting fat. I wan—"

"Mon chéri, there's already people—"

"Don't interrupt me!" shouted Georges. "I'm finding my brother." Georges hucked his plate away and huffed off to stare at the lake with Winnie swinging on his back.

Hélène stood to chase after Georges. Either to coddle or reprimand him.

"Let him go," said Auntie.

"I'll talk to him later." Narcisse stood to Hélène's side. He held her in place and sipped his cold dandelion root tea. "He'll be okay."

I SAT WEDGED BETWEEN NIMAMA AND AUNTIE AT THE FIRE AFTER SUPPER. GOLD sunlight mirrored off the ripply lake. Sunday Brigade returned and the whole camp was together. Bella sat on Nimama's other side. They shared a blanket over their legs. Coco Laframboise plucked her guitar strings. Zach bowed his fiddle. Angélique twanged her papa's harmonica.

Kate McCannon stood on a soapbox at the fire. Tobacco plugged her cheek. She cleared her throat to make a speech before Madame Morin announces this week's okimâw of the Day Brigade. I voted for Hélène even though she just got here. She deserves a say in what happens. In particular with all she been through. She'd make a good okimâw.

"Before we get started: I want to extend the warmest condolences on behalf of the Pussy Posse to Hélène and Georges Ducharme. I was between Georges's and Charlo's ages when nipapa passed away. My maman really struggled. Eventually me too. Oncle Nishecabo did whatever he could to fill that void."

Kate McCannon took off her hat. She held it sombre over her bandolier. She spat tobacco. Calm and ready.

"The summer after nipapa died, Oncle Nishecabo said me and him could pick huckleberries and fish for cutthroat trout in the Rocky Mountains instead of going on the summer buffalo hunt. Just us two.

"He bought me my first saddle. Bullets for nipapa's gun. Two fishing rods from Europe. And when mine broke, he gave me his. Only bad part of that trip was knowing it would end. We didn't come home to Red River until after the leaves changed. Lots of stargazing and storytelling at fires like this.

"Oncle Nishecabo was a legend long before I came along. The way nipapa talked about him, I thought Oncle Bo done everything in life. He was already fifty when we left for our trip. One of the last nights we camped creekside together, we was chatting at the fire. I told Oncle Bo that nipapa always said it was a shame he never got to be no father because he would've been a great papa. 'There weren't enough men like Nishecabo Ducharme in the world.' He said that was the sweetest thing he'd ever heard. I just wish nipapa would've told him himself before he died.

"The one thing nipapa had Oncle Bo didn't was a family. When me and him come home from the Rocks, we both knew what we wanted in life. I'm so proud he achieved *everything* he wanted. He deserved you. You deserved him too.

"Georges: Oncle Bo was real excited to be your papa. Same for Charlo too. You two boys were his proudest feathers. I know good as anyone what it's like losing your papa young. It hurts for a long time—in ways you won't understand for a long time neither. But you'll be okay.

"And Hélène: you came into Oncle Bo's life like an angel. You brought lightning to an old man's heart. Oncle Bo never had more than he did when he had his family. He died a rich man because of what you brought him in this world.

"Hélène, Georges: I'm sorry for your loss. All us are. We'll find Charlo soon. I made that promise to Oncle Nishecabo. We won't let him down—or you."

Kate McCannon stepped off the soapbox to hug Hélène and Georges. Hélène wiped her crying eyes on her skirt. Georges kept his lip stiff and shoulders broad.

People stood and waited to hug them one by one. I gave Hélène a good squeeze and Georges a polite handshake. Then I took my seat again beside Nimama and Auntie and Bella.

Madame Morin stood on the soapbox. She was so short, she couldn't help hiding behind the height of the campfire flames. She held a wood crate full of ballots at her waist.

"I want to thank Bella Gervais for her service this past week as okimâw of the Day Brigade. I know how your Sunday sermons bring the posse together. Kate McCannon and Mathilde both say you were a privilege on council. On behalf of us all: maarsii, Bella."

Bella stood and waved. Everyone clapped for her. Kate McCannon and Mathilde shook Bella's hand and returned to their seats.

"I've posted the results on my chuckwagon by the mess tent. This won't come as no surprise. Our results were damn near unanimous. On behalf of the Pussy Posse of Lac-aux-Trois-Pistoles, I humbly declare Hélène Ducharme will be okimâw of the Day Brigade for the week of April 13th to April 20th."

Hélène threw her hand over her mouth. Everyone clapped for her. But she didn't look excited. Or sad. We couldn't tell what she felt excepting pure shock.

Kate McCannon approached Hélène with her fingers wrapped around the grip of the Enfield revolver she stole from San Luis. She took the gun out its holster. Tossed it into the air. The gun somersaulted high above Kate McCannon's head.

Then Kate McCannon caught it by the barrel. "Congratulations, okimâw."

"Je vous remercie." Hélène grabbed the gun honourful with both hands. Her smile swallowed her whole face. Like her lips was connected to her heart strings. "I won't let you down. Any of you."

We congratulated Hélène, then sat around the fire with cups of elderberry tea. Madame Morin reached into the crate and burned the thrice-counted ballots handful by handful. Everyone rolled cigarettes and made chit-chat. Kate McCannon chewed her tobacco.

"Hey, Kate McCannon." Lizette sprung from her seat and marched to the head of the fire. Lizette pointed at the lariat strapped to Kate McCannon's gun belt. "Bet you can't lasso me."

Kate McCannon grinned wildful. She leaned back into her chair and rested her hand on her hip, above both Li P'chii and the lariat. She tipped her hat at Lizette.

"How long's that rope?" asked Lizette.

"Thirty feet. But I'm so good I can lasso you from thirty-one."

"Prove it!"

Kate McCannon and Lizette walked to the beach together. They stopped where the grass meets the pebbles.

"Don't lasso me around my neck. Okay?" Lizette looked down the end of her finger at Kate McCannon.

"Pinky promise." Kate McCannon stuck out her little finger for Lizette to interlock with. "I'm going for your leg. So be careful not to trip."

"Deal." Lizette hooked pinkies with Kate McCannon. Then took off without no warning.

Kate McCannon threw the loop of the lariat overhead. She whirled the rope like a tornado. Lizette raced forward fast as she could. She only had to run thirty-two feet away.

Whoosh! whoosh! whooooosh!

Kate McCannon hurled the lariat forward. Like she was casting the Good Rod into the lake. The loop wrapped around Lizette's ankle. Kate McCannon pulled tight. But Lizette's moccasin slipped through the loop.

"*Woohoo!*"

Lizette spun around. She pointed her fingers victorious at the sky. Camp went crazy. Lizette beamed bright as the North Star.

"Best two out of three." Kate McCannon reeled in her rope. "How about that?"

"Nuh uh." Lizette looked up at Kate McCannon with a wily smirk. "Winner winner chicken dinner. How about that?"

"I like you, Lizette Morin." Kate McCannon smiled around the chaw in her cheek. "Let's do this."

Lizette ran off. Kate McCannon drew her lariat quick like a gunslinger. Loop overhead.

Whoosh! whoosh! whooooosh!

Kate McCannon threw the lariat forward. The loop constricted Lizette's leg. Kate McCannon pulled the lariat taut. Lizette fell flat on her face. Mud splattered her coat. Her leg was pulled tight. Kate McCannon caught her like a runaway calf.

Even though she lost, Lizette looked just as mischieful as before. She slipped the lariat off her leg and marched toward Kate McCannon, chin tall, dripping mud.

"Guess you ain't half bad after all." Lizette whipped mud off her face and stood proud. Back stiff. Arms crossed. Nostrils flared. She dropped Kate McCannon's lariat at her feet.

"You're a goof." Kate McCannon ruffled Lizette's hair. They walked back to the fire together. Lizette sat with her kokum. Kate McCannon looked at us all around the fire. "Who wants to see some tricks?"

"You should see what she can do with a rope on horseback," Bella said to Nimama and Auntie. She leaned so far over our laps, her braids tickled the blanket. She wore colourful clothes decorated with mud. Pockmarks on her nineteen-year-old cheeks made her look distinguished. "Now *that's* special."

"I'm not sure which is Kate McCannon's." Nimama and Auntie looked at the mounts tied to the highline behind us.

"See that grey filly over there?" Bella pointed to a ghost-like horse tied up near the camp kitchen. "That ashy-looking pale horse there. See her?"

"What's her name?"

"Apocalypse."

Nimama snickered. "Where'd Kate McCannon get Apocalypse?"

"Bought her off a cowboy near Calgary. Freedman from the United States, believe it or not."

"John Ware? Bet that's who Laurent bought his horse from."

"Ha! Kate McCannon's *why* Laurent could buy a horse from John Ware."

Kate McCannon made the loop of her lariat wide like a hoop. Then Kate McCannon whirled the lariat to her left. When Kate McCannon's lariat had no more slack, she yanked the rope back toward her body, churning the rope like butter. The loop shot toward Kate McCannon in a spinning vertical ring. She ducked and bounded her feet over the loop as it passed around her.

Over and over Kate McCannon whipped the rope to her left and right, dancing through the ring like it was fire. We clapped along to the beat of Kate McCannon's footwork all night long, sharing stories and songs with world around us.

CHAPTER 15

HER NAME WAS DEATH, AND HELL FOLLOWED WITH HER

SUNDAY, APRIL 26, 1885.

Springtime sunshine's melted most the snow. Even the big dump we got during a storm last week. Maman Earth feels bloated beneath our feet like a grassy sponge. There's soupy sloughs everywhere for all them mosquitoes to make it on and lay eggs. It's awful. I can't decide what's worser: itchy mosquitoes sucking my blood every second, their bellies red like Mountie serges after they needle me good; or the smell of the forest being reborn, all that rotted deadness thawing in the sun.

Ever since the Gervaises bought a small herd of cattle, the past few springs been calving time in Lac-aux-Trois-Pistoles. That meant me and Cousin and all the kids in town got to help the cowboys birth, brand, and castrate them newborn calves. Was always worth it because Bella's maman and aunties cooked up a big supper with scalloped potatoes with butter and cheese, fried mushrooms and onions and fiddleheads, mushy peas, bannock with cranberry jam, wild rice, fresh prairie oysters, circle-shaped beefsteaks sizzled over open flame.

Calving was something me and Cousin looked forward to before Odin took him. We made a right good time of it. Calving's a clear signal to us winter's ending and we got nothing but opportunity ahead of us.

But that ain't the case no more. Ain't nothing the same.

This year it was up to Bella to get her parents' calves born by herself. Most everyone's husbands and brothers and sons left either to fight the war or flee to safety.

Madame Morin cooked up a big supper of jackfish soup, fried bannock, pickled carrots and asparagus to welcome Bella from calving today. Madame Morin even cleaned the oil in her pan to fry prairie oysters if Bella brung the parts. But I ain't sure who got the appetite for prairie oysters nowadays. Not me.

We felt Bella's absence when we didn't get her usual sermons at morning prayer. We all got our roles around here. Even us kids got jobs around camp. We still play and fish lots. Read and draw or play fiddle and harmonica and such too. But only in our free time. Mathilde and Madame Morin make sure we keep camp running and the animals healthy and clean. Me and Lizette's both damn near become lumberjacks with all the wood we've cut together.

But I don't feel like I'm doing nothing important to help find Cousin. I asked Nimama every day this week if I could join her and Auntie on the Night Brigade. Told her there ain't been no sign of danger in all the time we been in Loon Lake. Told her I'm safe long as she has Campbell's gun and I'm riding with her. I even asked if we could join the Sunday Brigade.

She said no.

Every. Time.

Bella descended on camp before sunset. Kate McCannon was out late on Sunday Brigade. This time Georges and Laurent's wife joined. We worried about them. But Bella and Mathilde was in good moods because Bella learned news about the war when she was calving.

We crowded the fire. Swaddled in blankets with bowls of soup. Bella led the suppertime prayer. While we ate, Madame Morin passed around brandy snifters and bottles of Kentucky bourbon Kate McCannon brung up from Deadwood ages ago for special occasions.

I sat sandwiched between Nimama and Auntie. A single blanket covered our legs. I rested my head on Nimama's shoulder. She knows how heavy my thoughts been as of late.

Bella stood on the soapbox at the head of the fire. She swirled the mouthful of whisky in her snifter under her nose and drank. She made a sour face like a dog and set the empty glass on the ground.

"First things first: I talked to Théo and my brother and

sister-in-law while I was at my parents' place this week. He's doing okay. Told us a bit more about his kidnapper. Théo says if we see someone with real bad burn scars on his hands, it might be our guy. He says his kidnapper wore beaded gauntlets to hide his hands. He said the kidnapper had a European name of some sort—Otto or Oskar or something like that. Théo didn't have much else to say. We were lucky to get that out of him."

Nimama's fingers skitted along the burn scars on the side of her neck that washed onto her chest. Scars she burned onto herself when she was my age.

"Second thing: I know every single one of us is touched by this horrible war with Ottawa one way or another. None of us want to be in this camp. We want to be back home with our families. But this camp might be the safest place in Saskatchewan. L-T-P's vulnerable like never before. There's been looting in Green Lake. Fort Pitt too. And just Friday my Oncle Tourond lost his homestead in a battle on his land near Batoche. We're living through war. Don't forget this. This is Hell on Earth.

"But when in our history have we lost? John Macdonald's in *our* house. No one breaks into our home expecting half-breed hospitality. Dumont led a few hundred of our men on Oncle Tourond's land down by Batoche in Fish Creek. Didn't matter the Dominion sent a thousand troops. These are *our* men we're talking about. Our brothers. Our husbands. Our land.

"The boys dug into rifle pits in a coulee on Oncle Tourond's land to stop Ottawa's march on Batoche. Of course they sent all one thousand of those dogs retreating with their tails between their legs. One thousand baby-faced souls humbled by the real sons of Maman Earth.

"This is our home. These are our families. Our friends. Our futures. We know who we are. We know our worth. We know what we deserve.

"iskwewak, *we* are the buffalo hunters. *We* are Maman Earth's caretakers. *We* are the people who own themselves."

Bella surveyed the posse over the flickering tips of the fire. Even people who call Riel a heretic—who say this war with Ottawa ends with everything worser even if Ottawa gives up—know to be grateful for victory. Who don't like victory?

I hope the world goes back to the way it used to be. As unperfect as it was.

"The home we're bringing our boys back to isn't the one they were stolen from. This war's changed things. Forever. Indian life in the North-West will never be the same. But we won't give up hope. We won't give up our fight.

"I'm proud to ride with such a fine group as yourselves. We have what it takes to keep this land safe. And we have what it takes to bring our boys home."

Bella waved for Mathilde to pass her an unopened bottle of bourbon. Bella held the bottle tight in her armpit and yanked the cork out with her hand. Booze shot into the flames.

"iskwewak . . ." Bella thrust the bourbon bottle into the air. Like she was cheersing God. Everyone around the fire raised their snifters too. ". . . the future is red."

Tink! tink!

Everyone tipped their glasses and gulped their whiskies. Bella tilted the bottle back and chugged until she couldn't take the burn no more. She spat a mouthful into the fire. Flames bursted where alcohol splashed. Bella wiped her mouth and made an even sourer face than before.

Bottles of bourbon made their rounds around the fire.

Coco's guitar plucking and Laurent's harmonica harping got sloppier with each glass. Zach brung out his fiddle for the Red River jig. Nimama and Auntie and a few others stood up to dance. A little tipsy, a little topsy. Lizette and a few other kids tried their best to jig like Zach taught them.

Dancing ended after Zach bowed his final note. Conversations grew louder. Coyotes howled at the moon. Nighttime constellations dotted themselves across the sky. Me and Nimama sat together with Bella at the fire. Auntie played with the dogs by the lake. Bella rolled a cigarette with Nimama's tobacco and sealed the paper with her tongue.

"Where's Kate McCannon and them?" I leaned my head back on Nimama's chest and snuggled the blanket up to my chin. Sunday Brigade was supposed to be back hours ago. "We still got to vote for the Day Brigade's next oḳimâw."

"They'll be back," Nimama dismissed. Her words was a tad slurry. But she sounded calm. "We're drinking her bourbon after all."

"That's why I'm worried."

Nimama rubbed my shoulders. I wanted reassurance. But a shoulder rub was good too.

"Promise not to judge me for this?" Bella asked Nimama. Campfire light sparkled off her eyes browner than Chapan's. Her breath smelled like an oaky barrel. She propped an unlit cigarette between her lips.

Nimama brung her whisky to her mouth. "What's on your mind?"

"You know how I said I was nervous about castrating them calves? With all *this* going on?" Bella waved a circle over her head. She lit her cigarette with a burning twig and tossed it like a match into the fire. "I thought calving wasn't going to feel right. You know? After what happened to Théo?"

"Whole world's gone fucking insane."

"Ain't that the truth." Bella puffed her smoke. Innocence burned with her tobacco. "I imagined every scrotum I sliced off was revenge for my nephew."

WE SAT AROUND THE FIRE WELL PAST SUNDOWN. SUNDAY BRIGADE STILL WASN'T back. People wobbled drunkenful to their tents. Vote for next week's okimâw was postponed. Everyone at camp agreed to let Hélène lead Day Brigade again for time being. Me and Nimamą sat together with a few others, watching the flames dance atop the burning logs. Then we heard the *parrup! parrup! parrup!* of horse hooves battering Maman Earth.

A small group of someones rode fast toward camp. Laurent shouldered his rifle. Twig and Rudi and Napoléon raced for the highline.

Arf! arf! arf!

"Hey!" Laurent shouted. "Who goes there!"

Twweeeeeeeeeeeeeeeeoooooooooooooowwweeeeeeeet!

Kate McCannon emerged at the head of her brigade with Georges and Julie Callahoo behind. Sitting sidesaddle behind Georges on his horse's rump was a boy bundled in a blanket. He held Georges's waist tight from behind. The boy looked tired. Like he'd been crying for hours. Georges looked like he'd rode through Hell too.

"Bring me Hélène *now*!" Kate McCannon swung off her

saddle. She marched toward camp with Apocalypse in tow. The dogs hopped around them.

Arf! arf! arf!

"I have Charlo!" yelled Georges to the crowd approaching.

Mathilde raced to slide the blanket-bundled boy off Georges's horse's rump. She shepherded Charlo toward camp. But he couldn't walk no more. He fell to his knees. Napoléon raced to Charlo. He jumped around anxious.

Arf! arf!

Even swaddled in his blanket, I spotted blood stains on Charlo's bum. He cried on his knees. Mathilde rocked him side to side. Napoléon darted with Georges to the Ducharmes' tent to fetch Hélène. Everyone else stood around awkward or ran around scared.

Hélène sprinted out the tent alongside Georges. Charlo lay crying in the cold mud with Mathilde. Hélène's face turned white. Her heart broke. Her knees trembled.

"Charlo!"

Hélène scrambled. Napoléon ran with her. She tripped over herself. Mud splashed her face. Tears cleared streaks on her cheeks. "Charles! Mon fils!"

Hélène collapsed on top of Charlo. Mathilde scurried away so Hélène could hold her baby. Charlo wrapped his fingers into his maman's blouse. Hélène smushed her lips into his forehead. She wept over him.

cried

cried

cried.

CHAPTER 16

THE MOURNING BRIGADE

MONDAY, APRIL 27, 1885.

Hélène didn't leave her tent this morning. No one expected her to. Her and Charlo need each other. People hungover from last night vultured around their spot. Trying to check on Charlo and offer help. But they all got questions. Intrusiveful ones. Georges shooed people away twice before breakfast could start. Kate McCannon had to deliver a speech about giving them time and space. Boy gone through Hell. It's his story. He needs peace.

Everyone knows Charlo got castrated. Just the thought of it makes my parts hurt. How could Odin do this? My own grandpapa. He's the heaviest secret I ever carried. I don't want to carry him no more.

When everyone finds out who Odin is, I hope no one blames us for him. How could I know why he castrates people? I ain't even supposed to know he poisoned my family tree. How could we be responsible for him?

Nimama held me extra tight last night and early this morning. I couldn't stop thinking about what happened to Charlo. I imagined what I'd do if it happened to me.

Even if I could stop thinking, I still wouldn't've slept a wink. Auntie's lungs pumped air all night like she was having a nightmare. Her bedroll stunk with sweat. I wanted to shake Auntie awake and check on her. But I honest to goodness think she was awake the whole time.

We wasn't hungry at breakfast. Wouldn't've mattered if we was. Fact of the matter is camp's low on food. We need groceries. We ain't even got no chickens left. Just animal feed.

Kate McCannon brung the Ducharmes their breakfasts to their tent. We all made sure their plates was the best plates possible. Even if we knew they wasn't going to eat everything.

Me and Nimama sat alone in our tent after breakfast. The Day Brigade rode off with Julie Callahoo as their okimâw to rendezvous with the Morning Brigade on their search for Cousin and Michel and François. Madame Morin got busy cooking lunch with Lizette.

Nimama dug her diary out the crate. She tossed me my sketchbook and a couple pencils. Campbell's gun was hid in the crate too.

I opened to my newest work-in-progress—a wihtikow eating his kids. I didn't want Nimama seeing it and thinking I'm some kind of freak. It's just what I wanted to draw is all.

Nimama finished diarying way before I finished my sketch. It was almost lunch. Day Brigade just headed out and Morning Brigade would be back later. I asked Nimama again if I could come with her and Auntie on Night Brigade even though I already knew her answer.

"Why not? You got Campbell's gun to keep us safe!"

Nimama looked sternful. But a tad sympathetic. Part of her remembered what it was like being a kid living a grown-up life.

"You know what? Do me a favour and maybe we'll have a job for you." Nimama pointed to the path to the outhouses. "Auntie been gone for half an hour. Go check on her."

"That's gross."

"Do you want to help with something more important in the future?"

"Fine."

I dragged my heels out the tent and shuffled past the beach toward the path to the outhouses. Over the past month we reinforced the trail with boards and hung lanterns so nobody trips at night.

I plugged my nose and knocked on the first of two outhouses spaced a few yards apart. "Auntie Josey?"

"No," said a kid's soft voice from inside. I walked to the next outhouse.

"Auntie? You in there?" No answer.

I turned around and walked to Nimama on the beach. I flung my arms in the air. "No idea."

"Damn." Nimama tightened the belt of her riding pants. "I'll look for her."

Auntie taking off without telling nobody been a major problem. This morning she left breakfast to cry in the tent. Wouldn't stop calling me Guille. Spent hours stripping the ends of her hair with her fingernails, mumbling about Cousin, praying God will keep him safe. She was already a loaded gun. Now she might fire on anyone.

Nimama found Auntie crying under a willow. She brung Auntie to join camp at the fire. Auntie rested her heavy head on Nimama's lap.

Mathilde and the Morning Brigade rode in at two o'clock for lunch. Me and the rest the kids handed out bowls of watery jackfish broth and wild rice. Kate McCannon brung lunch to Hélène and Charlo and Georges in their tent. I sat with Nimama and Auntie. Mathilde said a prayer before we ate.

Kate McCannon swaggered back from the Ducharmes' tent as we finished sipping our soups. She stood on the soapbox at the head of the fire and adjusted her hat to shade her eyes.

"Listen up. Mine and Day Brigades heard this spiel at breakfast. But Morning Brigade needs to hear this too. The Ducharmes need their space. Don't go bugging them. Charlo's going to be fine. But we need to give him time. He's never been one to talk. But hopefully in a few days he'll open up to his maman. We just got to be patient.

"The facts ain't changed: Guillaume, Michel, and François are still in danger. You know I want to hang these motherfuckers by their dicks just as bad as you. But the time for revenge isn't now. We need to bring our boys home. We need to keep our home safe."

Kate McCannon waited for her words to press on us. No one gossiped or whispered.

"Next thing: we got a grocery haul to pick up on Thursday. Mathilde's going to Lac-aux-Trois-Pistoles tomorrow to leave orders with her husband and Ned Cunningham at their stores. She'll assemble a small brigade to pick everything up Thursday. If Mathilde selects you for the grocery haul, you're excused all day from your regular brigade.

"That's all I got. Keep your chins up. Won't be long until Guillaume, Michel, and François are safe with us too."

BELLA LED THE SUPPERTIME PRAYER. GEORGES BRUNG CHARLO'S AND HIS MAMAN'S suppers to them in their tent. Our plates was slim pickings: watered-down tea, flat bannock, rabbit and pea stew. I ate supper with Mathilde on a bench at the fire—Auntie and Nimama was out with Kate McCannon on Night Brigade.

"Hey, Niko." Georges's bony hand on my shoulder startled me. He held his supper in his other hand. "Mind if I eat with you and Madame Little Bull?"

"Sure." I shredded a piece off my bannock and dunked it in my stew. "How goes it?"

"All right." Georges took his seat beside me. I sat between Georges and Mathilde. Georges gulped a spoonful of stew. "Charlo and my maman need some alone time. You know?"

"Yeah." I tried talking through my mouthful of bannock. The soggy crumbs stuck to the roof of my mouth. "You doing all right?"

"Yeah," Georges nodded. "Thanks."

Mathilde reached across my lap and laid her hand on

Georges's knee. "So I got a grocery haul to pick up on Thursday. Wouldn't mind if you tagged along to help us out."

"What's the plan?" Georges asked her.

"Was thinking we could ask the Eriksen girls to come with us and we'll take their cart into town after breakfast. Empty the shelves at the Little Bull General Store, then head over to Ned's to do the same. We only need enough for a week or so. Narcisse's bringing feed over Friday."

"Can I come?" I clapped my hands together and begged Mathilde. I didn't even try hiding how excited I was. I know how dangerous it is out there. But I'm uselesser than useless here. "Please please please *please*! I won't be no problem. I'll be with Nimama the whole time. Safest place I can be."

"You okay if we bring Niko?" Mathilde asked Georges. "Monsieur Cunningham could use a hand."

Georges winked at me. "He's all right, I guess."

Mathilde rubbed her chin and clicked her tongue. "How about this: when I talk to kimama, I'll ask her if you can come too. But whatever kimama says is final. Deal?"

"Deal."

I couldn't stop smiling. My cheek muscles locked in place. It was so bad, I couldn't even slurp my soup without dribbling. I hope Nimama lets me ride to Lac-aux-Trois-Pistoles for the grocery haul. I even prayed for it. I hope God won't let me down. I'll be safe. I know I will.

CHAPTER 17

YOU AIN'T NEVER GONNA BELIEVE WHO I SEEN AT THE STORE TODAY!

THURSDAY, APRIL 30, 1885.

"Mesdemoiselles Eriksen?" Through the canvas tent door, we seen a young man's silhouette with a rifle slung over his shoulder. He held two catalogues in his hands. "You awake in there?"

Nimama stretched her arms and squirmed around in the blankets. Her back and neck bones cracked. Her hair, even braided, was wild, frizzled, crunchy, nestlike.

"You can come in." Auntie yawned deep. We sat up in our bedrolls, trying to look half-alive. The clock on the crate in the corner read quarter past eight.

Georges opened the tent door. In the month and a half since Cousin disappeared, Georges's hair grew fast. His reddish black curls hid the tops of his ears.

"How's everyone feeling this morning?"

"Tired," Auntie groaned. "Where's Mathilde?"

"Whole Morning Brigade woke up with diarrhea." Georges kneeled so we could see him better. He fanned our ripe smell from his face absent-mindedful with the catalogues for Cunningham's and the Little Bulls' stores. Then he set the catalogues at Nimama's and Auntie's feet. "I need to make sure you all feel okay before we go anywhere."

"We're all right." Nimama sat up and fisted leftover sleepy out her eyes. "What's going on? Are they okay?"

"Sounds like they refilled their canteens with bad water yesterday. Hoping it ain't nothing serious. You know? How about you, Niko? You okay?"

"I'm fine." I spread my fingers across my tummy. I missed the dry venison snacks Madame Morin made before we ate them all. "Just hungry."

"Porridge is in half an hour. We get the last of the coffee too before the grocery haul."

"We're still going?" Auntie asked. "What about Mathilde?"

"Unless she wants to ride in a soggy diaper, I don't think she's going far," Georges chuckled. His joke even got Auntie cracking a smile. "Just us four today."

"*Four?*" Nimama acted confused. As if she didn't know who Georges meant. "Is Kate McCannon coming?"

"She's leading most everyone who ain't sick on a brigade after breakfast." Georges breathed confident and gestured to me with a crooked smirk. "We just assumed Niko came with the cart. Besides: Monsieur Cunningham's arthritis flared up, so we'll need Niko's help."

"I can help!" I shook Nimama's arm. I wanted to join them so bad. Nimama said yesterday her and Mathilde would decide if I can come this morning and now it's this morning and Nimama ain't said no yet, I already know Mathilde says yes so I have to be allowed to come, *have to*, it's only fair, even Georges says he needs me.

"Yeah, okay," Nimama submitted.

"Guess that's settled." Georges winked at me. "Breakfast tomorrow'll be amazing."

I owed it to Georges for getting me into the Grocery Brigade this afternoon. I was so excited. I need something importanter to do than chores. Me and Lizette can only saw so much wood in a day.

When this is all over, me and Cousin won't never complain about going to town again. I'll even let him win at buffalo hunters next time so he don't have to walk home and risk getting stole. But I ain't letting him win too often. He can't go thinking he's better at buffalo hunters than me.

"What's the plan?" Auntie asked.

Georges tossed one of the two catalogues onto Auntie's lap. It was for the Little Bulls' store. Auntie fluttered through the pages. Some advertisements was circled with pencil lead and Mathilde's regal handwriting in the margins.

"Me and you will head over to the Little Bulls' store; kisîmis and Niko can review our order with Monsieur Cunningham in the meantime." Georges stuck a blade of grass between his teeth like a pipe. "That work?"

"Yeah." Auntie closed the catalogue and tossed it by her clothes in the corner. Desperate as she is to find Cousin, Auntie needs a day off.

Nimama fingered the pages of Cunningham's catalogue at her toes. Her teeth peeled her chapped lips. "That sounds good to you, Nikosis?"

"Yeah!"

I smiled the ginormongousest smile ever since Cousin been gone. I couldn't believe it. I got a mission! I hugged Nimama so tight, she couldn't shake me off. No doubt we was going to find Cousin soon. With full bellies too.

I AIN'T NEVER BEEN SO EXCITED TO RIDE INTO TOWN BEFORE. ME AND NIMAMA RODE Pony alongside Auntie and Viking. Georges drove our Red River cart pulled by his horse, Jérôme. Viking would have to pull the way back. Poor horses going to be exhausted after today.

At first I rode in the cart with Georges. But the *screeeeech!*-ing of the wood wheels got so bad I hopped off and rode with

Nimama the rest the way. Somehow the damn saddle horn squishing my pinger's still better than sitting above two wailing wood wheels.

A breeze carried dust into our eyelashes. Fleury Avenue used to bustle before the war started. Horses and wagons and carts was always stopped on the potholey road or parked at the hitching posts and water troughs in front of each store, the smith, the icehouse. Monsieur Fleury's nephews used to shovel horse poo off the road with their pants rolled up past their knees and their muddy shitkickers clapping their shins. I half expected to see Campbell reading *Huck Finn* on the steps of the saloon. But even he wasn't around.

Lac-aux-Trois-Pistoles's damn near a ghost town now.

We stopped outside Cunningham's store on the west end of Fleury Avenue. Each establishment along the west arm of the lake, from Cunningham's to the Little Bulls' to the saloon and livery at the end of the chubby road, had a pristine view of the water. The forest around us started budding. Geese floated on the shallow waves. Deer munched in the reeds. Birds and squirrels scattered and chirped in the trees.

"Guess this is us." Nimama slided off the saddle and hitched Pony to the post outside Cunningham's store. I hopped off too.

"Me and mademoiselle'll be loading up behind the Little Bulls' if you need us," said Georges. "Otherwise we'll be over in about twenty minutes."

Georges *whipp!*ed the reins. The cart hobbled down Fleury Avenue toward the Little Bulls' store. Auntie and Viking rode at his side.

Nimama grabbed the catalogue out Pony's saddle bag. We walked up the steps to the store. A little *OPEN | OUVERT* sign dangled in the window. In the sunshine, the window looked like a dark, not-quite-see-through mirror.

Nimama pushed the handle and leaned into the door with her shoulder. It swung on its hinges. My eyes flashed as they adjusted to the shaded interior. Cunningham waited behind the counter at the far end of the store. His orange cat lay on the counter by the register.

"You can leave the door open, Sara. I like having a draft in here." Cunningham waved for me and Nimama to come in. "This place is humid as Hell."

Me and Nimama said hi to Cunningham and approached the counter. His cat sniffed the catalogue in Nimama's hands before rubbing his whiskers against Nimama's wrist.

"Taanshii, Asiniy." Nimama's fingers massaged along the cat's back. Asiniy leaped off the counter and into his bed on a bare shelf behind Cunningham.

"How you two doing? We pray for Guille every night."

"We're okay." Nimama whiffled through pages of the catalogue. "Looking forward for this all to go back to normal. You know? How're you?"

"Ankle's swole like lame horse. But that's life." Cunningham gestured to his leg and shrugged. He pointed with the knob of his cane to the sacks of flour and salt, bottles of vinegar, boxes of soap, cans of vegetables that lay half-organized in the corner of the store. He removed a pencil from behind his ear and retrieved a notebook and another catalogue from by the register. "Picking up for the Pussy Posse?"

"Mind if we go over our order?"

"I'm going to look around," I said to Nimama. "Let me know when you need me."

I walked to the front of the store and looked at the shelves near the door and window. They was stocked all right considering how slow business must be since everyone left town. A few cans of candy, tobacco, laudanum syrups. But no guns or bullets.

I wondered how much money everything in this store cost. I wished we could buy it all. Cans of fruit in syrup, jars of jams, bags of seeds. Seeing so much food made me hungry. I wanted to eat everything. I was in a hungry boy's Heaven and Hell at once.

As Nimama reviewed the order with Cunningham—Nimama and Cunningham huddled over the catalogue on the counter, fingers pointing at different sections—the breeze waved the *OPEN / OUVERT* sign in the window. We heard the *clupclupclupclupclupclupp!*ing of trotting horses outside. Policemen's voices floated into the store with the dust from Fleury Avenue.

"I've seen this horse before," said a man outside.

"All bay horses look the same," squeaked his high-pitched corporal.

I knew them voices. Wagner and San Luis. But the number of horses sounded like they wasn't alone.

I dived away from the shelves in full view of the open door. I shuffled on my elbows and hid under the windowsill, out of the men's sight outside.

Nimama owled her head from Cunningham at the counter to the open door behind her. The police had to be close. Long as they didn't come inside, I was safe.

I squished my spine flat against the short wall underneath the window. I couldn't guess how many policemen there was. I just prayed Campbell wasn't with them.

Nimama flapped open the back of her tweed jacket. She wrangled her fingers around the grip of the revolver tucked in her waistband. She pulled the gun out and set the butt on the counter with the muzzle pointed at Cunningham. She breathed calm. Her thumb dragged the gun hammer.

Clllllick!

"Say a fucking word about Nikosis and I'll polish this barrel with your throat."

Cunningham swallowed his fear.

"I'm not too interested in the horse," said a third man's pipey voice outside. It was deep and bird-like with a slick and delicate tone. Tinge of a funny accent too. "But I like this saddle."

Nimama recognized that dangerous voice outside on Fleury Avenue. She shoved the catalogue off the counter. Pages feathered through the air. She sprinted to me and dived onto the floor, sliding under the windowsill beside me, closest to the open door.

Gun cocked, Nimama pointed the muzzle at the ceiling.

Men outside slided off their saddles. Their boots pounded the ground.

"Hold our horses, Corporal San Luis," Wagner ordered.

Sunlight sparkled in the dusty air. Cunningham's face glowed like the moon at the other end of the store.

I heard Pony neigh delightful-like while someone petted her neck.

"Taanshii, sweetheart," said the foreign voice to Pony. We heard leathers tug like someone was playing with her saddle and bridle. "I'm enamoured with your wonderful saddle."

Nimama looked the scaredest I ever seen. I had to be

brave for her. Quiet and strong. Hard as it was. Whoever was out there terrified Nimama. Enough to freeze her loving bones.

Cunningham hobbled around the counter. Every few steps he stabbed his cane into the wood floor and shuffled his feet.

Bomp!

Shff-shff.

Bomp!

Shff-shff.

"Can I help you, sirs?" Cunningham leaned heavy into his cane. He was careful not to look at me or Nimama.

"Mister Cunningham?" said the man who scared Nimama. Boots and spurs hit the stairs on the porch outside. "I take it you're the proprietor?"

"I own the place if that's what you're asking." Cunningham stood in the middle of the door frame. His big body blocked the men's views inside. "Sorry, gentlemen. I'm afraid I'll need a note from your wives before you blow the family budget inside."

"Ha. Very funny," said Wagner sarcasticful. Outside a match struck a matchbook. Sulfur wafted through the store. Then it was overpowered by clouds of supreme cigar smoke.

"Whose mare is this?" said the third man.

"Mine. And unfortunately I'm closing to take her to the horse doctor." Cunningham grabbed the doorknob behind him and tried stepping outside. The door started closing behind him. "We're already late for our appointment at the livery."

A beaded gauntlet pushed open the door before Cunningham could close it. Cunningham was trapped in the door frame by the men outside.

"Not so fast," said the third man. My heart raced. He had to be Odin. Who else could it be? "I'd like to hear more about your saddle."

Another cloud of sweet smoke flooded the room. I looked around for an escape should hell raise in a firefight.

"It's a fine saddle. I haven't met many men in the North-West who can afford a Mexican roping saddle like yours."

Nimama was ready to fire on Odin and Wagner should they breach through Cunningham into the store. She breathed in through her nostrils, outhaled through pursed lips.

In slow. Out slow.

In slow . . . out slow . . .

in slow . . . out . . .

in . . . out . . .

"I'm sorry, sirs. But the store is closed. Come back later."

Cunningham tried closing the door behind him again. But Odin's gauntlet shoved the door back open.

"I need to know where you got that saddle."

"Bought it, asshole. Now if you'll excuse me—"

"I'm not sure you understand, dear nitôtem: *I* bought that saddle. Many years ago. It was a gift for sweet nîwa's mother. I'm shocked it would leave Madame Desjarlais's possession."

Cunningham swallowed. He flashed his teeth at the man on the other side of the door frame. "Shame she had to sell it."

"I'm not convinced she did sell it." Odin sounded cold enough to freeze spring in place. "I know what dear Maggie's willing to sell when she's desperate."

Two gauntlets grabbed Cunningham by the collar and tossed him back into the store. His cane knocked half a dozen cans of corn off the shelf.

Nimama aimed for Odin to pop his head through the doorway so she could splatter his brains against the wall.

CRACK!

"Holy shit!" shouted San Luis from outside. A bullet *ping!*ed the trail and ricocheted away. All the horses outside the store spooked and screamed. Odin and Wagner hustled off the porch and into the road to collect their horses. "Two of 'em! By the other store!"

I peeked over the windowsill. Georges and Auntie was on their horses beside each other in the middle of Fleury Avenue. Cut free from the cart, Jérôme looked anxious to charge. Viking chomped at his bit too. Georges mounted the rifle to his shoulder and aimed for the sky.

"*Go!*" Auntie hollered.

CRACK!

Georges and Auntie charged. They stampeded down Fleury Avenue.

Parrup! parrup! parrup! parrup!

"*Whoa!*" San Luis's horse reared high like a boxer, spooked by the gunshot. San Luis sailed off the saddle. He *thudd!*ed the trail hard. The reins of Odin's and Wagner's horses flung in the air. They reared and roared like mustangs.

Georges and Auntie closed in on Odin and Wagner. The men ducked for cover. Odin in his blue capote and brown Stetson hid against the façade of the store; Wagner turtled at the edge of the road.

Georges *click-click!*ed the rifle lever. A spent casing sprung out the ejector. He mounted the gun to his shoulder and aimed for Odin. Like a real life buffalo hunter.

CRACK!

"*Augh!*"

The muzzle flashed when Georges passed Odin. Odin clasped his gauntlet over his arm. The bullet grazed him and ricocheted away.

Pony screamed and kicked scared. She yanked hard on the reins tied to the post near Odin, desperate to free herself.

Galloping alongside Georges at the same time he shot at Odin, Auntie yanked Viking's reins and dug her heel into his body. They slided sideways, shooting tidal waves of dirt into the policemen's faces across the road.

Auntie spun around in the dust cloud and raced back eastward up Fleury Avenue. Viking galloped with all his might. He was taking Auntie past the livery and saloon, past the church and rectory, past the whole townsite—home to la bibliothèque where Chapan was all alone with Huckleberry and Miss Kitty and Félix.

Georges kept galloping forward down the trail back toward Loon Lake—toward camp where everyone in the posse waited like sitting ducks.

Odin chased after his horse. He caught its reins, jammed his boot into the stirrup, and threw his leg over the saddle without missing a beat. He raced off in the same direction as Georges.

"We're after the girl!" shouted Wagner to San Luis.

The men got hold of their horses circling in the dust. They mounted and took off after Auntie.

Cunningham slammed the door. He bent over with his hands on his knees and panted like an old dog in the July sun. Asiniy came out his secret hidey hole in the shelves.

Nimama helped me to my feet and led me to the door. We stopped. Breathed in. She pulled the door open. All was clear.

"Pony!"

I smooched Pony's nose soon as I seen her. I was so scared for her. She was safe. But her eyes was still wide and fluttery and full of fear.

Nimama picked me up and swung me onto the front of the saddle before unhitching Pony from the post. Then Nimama hopped into the saddle behind me.

We raced home. Me and Nimama had to make a fast effort to find Auntie before the policemen could hurt her and Chapan. Then we could all go back together to Loon Lake.

Please, God! Please look out for us!

We passed the stores, the livery and saloon, the church and rectory. Pony took us toward la bibliothèque fast as she could.

Thick smoke haunted the trail. The closer we was to home, the more ash Pony coughed out her overworked lungs.

We turned the corner off the main trail to face la bibliothèque. No trees stood in our way. I pulled my shirt up over my nose to protect me from the ash. Heat from the fire scorched my forehead.

La bibliothèque was on fire.

Orange flames tore through the white paint on the homestead. The roof burned out and crushed itself. Ash flew out open window frames where circus glass used to be. The fire burped blackened pages from all Chapan's books, manuscripts, maps, letters out its open mouth. Just the chimney and stove stood. The fire inhaled cool air around us into its flaming lungs.

Our only saving grace was the barn wasn't on fire. Them doors was even forced open. My home burning down wasn't no accident.

We scoured the lot, hollering for Auntie and Chapan. The animals too. Checked everywhere inside the barn. But there was no sign of nothing. Not even the police. We felt heat from the fire everywhere we rode.

Huckleberry, Miss Kitty, Félix. All gone.

Auntie and Chapan. Gone.

My home.

Odin and Wagner and San Luis stole it all. I have nothing. My home is Hell.

I couldn't stop crying. I cried so much I wished I was God so my tears could've rained on the homestead. I would've put out the fire before all was lost.

What the hell is God's problem? He's worser at being God than anyone. All He does is punish punish punish! I hate Him!

I felt jealous of the fire. I, too, wanted to make the world burn.

CHAPTER 18

UNTO DUST THOU SHALT RETURN

We raced for camp. Pony panted heavy after trudging swampy trail damn near twenty miles back to Loon Lake. It was around suppertime. Loon Lake never felt so far away. But we ain't never got there quicker before neither.

Arf! arf!

Twig barked excitedful for us. She ran onto the trail. We was a few hundred yards from camp. Laurent was on the other end of the lariat leashed around Twig's neck. He slung his repeater over his shoulder. He held Twig's rope with one hand and rested the other on his achy belly.

"Praise Mary. What happened? Kate McCannon and her brigade just got back for supper. Then Georges stormed in saying you and Niko got trapped at the store and Josey's gone?"

Nimama sniffled. She rubbed her hand up-and-down the side of my arm. Her tears splashed my cowlick. She inhaled a shallow, choppy breath. "Is she or my kokum here?"

"No . . ."

"What about the police?"

"Only Georges. . . ." Laurent sounded confused and concerned at the same time. He stepped closer to me and Nimama. Pony licked the salt off his palm. "What's going on?"

"Was he followed by a man on a horse?"

"No," Laurent assured.

"Are you sure?"

"Yes!" insisted Laurent. "Sara, what's going on?"

"Our homestead! The police torched it!"

Laurent looked eastward up the trail behind us. His eyes followed the black tube of smoke cracking the robin's egg sky. The fire took Laurent's words from him too.

I did my best not to cry no more. I had to be the strongest boy on the planet for Nimama. I cried enough already. All I had to contend with was that ginormongous hunk of spikey heartache lodged in my throat.

Laurent took Twig off the lariat and let her run ahead. He took Pony's reins and led us to camp. Sweat steamed at the edges of her saddle blanket.

We dismounted at the hitching posts. Hélène and Georges met us at the edge of camp. Hélène wrapped her bullish body in her husband's old blanket; Georges jogged toward us with Winnie slung tight against his back.

"Where's Joséphine?" Hélène looked us over worryful. "Isn't she with you?"

"See that smoke over there?" Nimama wiped her wet eyes with the veiny side of her hand. "That's our homestead. Me and Niko went there to look for Josey after the standoff. But her and Kokum are gone. Everything is gone. I can't take this shit any longer."

"A real man wouldn't've missed his shot." Georges spoke fast. Embarrassed and scared. His cheeks looked dusty and pale. He buried his head in his hands. "It's all my fault!"

"What the hell's going on?" Kate McCannon joined us at the highline. Li P'chii and San Luis's stole revolver swayed in her gun belt. "Where's Josey?"

"Her and Kokum are missing!" Nimama's voice cracked like a whip. Mathilde waddled toward the highline slow with her hand on her belly. "They trapped us at Cunningham's. Georges and Josey scared them off. But they followed Josey home. They burned it down!"

Nimama flung the tail of her jacket up and gripped the revolver in her waistband. Georges unslung Winnie off his shoulder.

Kate McCannon glided her hands down her flanks until her palms found the grips of the guns in her belt. She drummed her fingers on Li P'chii's oak grip. It was engraved with a buffalo maman and her calf.

Kate McCannon pulled Li P'chii out its holster. She popped the sawed-off open at the hinge. Inspected each shell before reloading them into their barrels.

Then she plucked the revolver out its holster. She tossed

the revolver in the air. It somersaulted above her head. Kate McCannon caught it by the barrel with her free hand. She gestured for Hélène to take it.

"What's this for?" Hélène wrapped her fingers around the pistol grip. Her eyes bounced between Mathilde and Kate McCannon. "I'm not an okimâw this week."

Every one of the posse's guns—Laurent's rifle, Georges's borrowed rifle, Nimama's stole pistol, Kate McCannon's sawed-off shotgun, the stole police pistol issued every week to the okimâw of the Day Brigade—was ready for Kate McCannon's orders.

"This is the last ride," said Mathilde calmful. Her and Laurent soothed their tummy aches with their hands. "Laurent and I can look after camp. Sara, Georges: take both my horses—Pony and Jérôme have run enough today. You go to the fort and end this."

"What's the plan?" asked Hélène. She fiddled with the revolver in shameful excitement.

"The four of us are seizing the fort while those pimps are in bed." Kate McCannon spoke harsh and aggressive. Like shotgun blasts. "I want their guns. I want their ammo. I want their food. I want Josey Eriksen and Marguerite Desjarlais safe as stones. And I want that Sergeant fucking Wagner hostage. And we're going to make him take us all the way to our boys and that fur trader motherfucker who stole them. We end this our way."

"Hey!" I tugged Kate McCannon's arm. "What about me?"

Kate McCannon grinned at me like I was a horse she was offering an apple to. She took off her hat and bent eye to eye with me.

"We need you here with okimâw Mathilde."

"I want to find Cousin!"

"Us too. That's why—"

"I want Cousin! I want Auntie! I want Chapan! Michel and François too! I ain't staying here. You need me!"

Kate McCannon nodded submittingful and stood tall. "Me and the okimâwak will give you a special job soon. Okay?"

"Fine."

I didn't feel fine though. No job's importanter than getting Cousin. Everyone's crazy if they think I ain't man enough to get Cousin and Michel and François back. Auntie and Chapan too. I ain't afraid to do it. I'm braver than a buffalo hunter.

I'll save Cousin. Even if it means bending the rules a tad.

AT THE FIRE, KATE McCANNON ANNOUNCED TO EVERYONE THE PLAN TO TAKE OVER the fort from the police. We sat nervous with the fire cackling in front of us. Bella led us all in prayer.

We amened. Then Nimama, Hélène, and Georges thundered off with Kate McCannon.

I waddled to the mess tent to help clean the dishware. The dogs hung around for extra scraps. The adults shared cigarettes and made chit-chat by the fire under the rosy sunset. Time crawled by real slow—thank goodness because I needed extra time to think of a plan for sneaking into Kate McCannon's brigade.

"This water's gross." Angélique scrubbed a pot in a giant tub of used-to-be-soapy water. Her tongue squirmed out her lips. She tried not to hurl. "Uck! I hate this."

I was handing more dried bowls to Zach to put away when I seen Laurent stroking his horse's nose and feeding him grass from his palm at the highline. His horse is the ginormongousest horse in the world. Blacker than night too.

It gave me an idea.

"You ever ride kipapa's horse?" I asked Angélique. I tried sounding conversational and such while I rubbed my rag on drippy spoons.

"Chickadee? All the time." Angélique pinched her nostrils over the mucky water. Her and Lizette scrubbed a pot and cutlery in the mucky tub. "Blech! This is so gross."

"What's Chickadee like bareback?" I handed more cutlery to Zach to put away.

"Real bumpy. Gotta hold his mane for dear life. But he's a gentle giant."

"Your papa must take good care of Chickadee. He's a beauty."

"Oh, nipapa spoils him," Angélique's hands splashed out the nasty water. "Chickadee spooks easy though. When you fall off, you're in the air for two whole seconds. I kid you not."

"Mounting him don't look easy," I said. Lizette passed me the pot to dry. The inside shined like the day it was boughten. But it was scratchy like it was already a hundred years old.

"Nipapa taught Chickadee to kneel." Angélique turned away from the mucky tub and bent over to pat Maman Earth like she done a good deed. "You tap the ground in front of him like this until he plops down."

"Interesting . . ."

I did my best not to smirk. My idea was perfect.

"Oh no . . ." I spread my fingers across my tummy and acted like I needed to race to the outhouse. "Don't wait for me."

I dropped my rag in Zach's hands and sprinted around the mess tent out of sight to the back of Madame Morin's chuckwagon. There must have been a dozen crates on the ground. All full of doohickeys and whatchamacallits. I rifled through them, looking for a good knife to slice the rope around Chickadee's neck that connected him to the highline.

"Bingo!" I found Madame Morin's collection of slicing and paring knives in a holder in a box. I took the one I knew would be hardest to notice missing.

I creeped to me and Nimama's tent with the knife tucked into my sleeve. Most everyone was making chit-chat with each other around the fire. Laurent brushed Chickadee's neck and whispered to him at the highline.

I arrived at the tent. Peeped inside the crate where Nimama keeps her journal and canteen and my sketchbook and such. The gun was gone. I looked over my shoulders and tucked the knife under her journal in the crate. Then I hustled out the tent and walked back toward the highline to check if Laurent was done with Chickadee.

"Hey, Niko." I damn near jumped out my skin. Laurent scared me half to death when he snuck up behind me. "You okay?"

"Uhh . . ." I craned my neck up to see Laurent. My heart ain't even calmed yet. He stood tall like a statue. I spread my fingers across my tummy while I thought of a believable lie for him.

"You got a bellyache? I seen you walking slow from your tent."

"Yeah . . ." I put both hands on my tummy and grimaced. Even hunched over a tad. "Oof . . . I must've ate something rotten. Pain comes and goes. You know?"

"Oh, I know." Laurent patted his own tummy. "I'll let everyone know you're feeling sick. Just take it easy tonight. You'll be fine by morning."

My plan was sealed. I wish I didn't have to steal Laurent's horse. But there ain't no other way. The ends justify the means.

CHAPTER 19

BOOM!

I got to our tent and grabbed the knife I hid in the crate. Then I hustled to the highline to steal Chickadee. I could hear Zach bowing his fiddle at the fire. His maman plucked soulful guitary undertones. Chickadee pulled his lips back and ripped grass with his tall teeth. A loose rope hung from a knot on the highline to his halter.

"Taanshii, Chickadee." I brushed my hand along his halter and stuck my other palm out for him to lick the salt. I stroked the white stripe on his black nose.

Just like Angélique showed me, I patted the ground like Maman Earth done good.

"C'mon, Chickadee."

Chickadee rocked forward and tucked his hooves under his chest. His front knees buckled under his barrel. Then he plopped his backend on his hind knees.

"Good boy." I stroked his nose splotch and scratched his twitchy ears while he lay tilted in the dirt. Then I hurled my leg over his back and cut the rope connecting his halter to the highline.

I tucked the knife back into my sleeve and wrapped my fingers around Chickadee's mane. Then I flung my hips into his withers to make him stand. Chickadee lifted hisself on four legs like he was carried by an angel puppeteer.

I heard fiddling and guitar picking and everyone dancing and clapping along. Angélique harped her papa's harmonica. Coyotes howled their songs too. No one at the fire paid me no attention. They was all busy dancing to rhythms and melodies and beats.

Me and Chickadee creeped into the bush until we couldn't hear no more music. We had to catch up to Kate McCannon and Nimama and them. I peeked behind for followers sneaking up on me. Didn't hear or see anybody.

Me and Chickadee rode down the trail for hours. Through Fleury Avenue and past the livery, the church and rectory, the trail to la bibliothèque. We could even smell the smoke of the homestead. But we had to keep moving. We had an attack to join.

It was dark. We rode until the trail washed under the shallow ford in the river. All the snow and ice was gone. Hoofprints and wheel ruts speckled the mud leading into the water.

I whirled Chickadee's mane over each my hands and pulled my chest into his neck so I could squeeze myself into place. Chickadee ploughed the crest of the swole river. The old wagon trail continued into the forest on the other side.

We clopped along the trail after crossing the river. Careful not to move too slow, but not too fast neither. We didn't want to make no noise and startle someone.

Thirty-odd yards ahead I seen the backside outline of the nearest of the four riders: a young man with a gun slung over his shoulder. Had to be Georges.

I figured Hélène rode in front of Georges. Nimama and Kate McCannon rode further ahead.

CRACK!

A gun flashed from the forest. Hélène's mare squealed. She buckled into her front hooves. Her vertebrae *crack!*ed while her body rolled over her neck. The bullet entered the base of her skull. Hélène soared off the saddle into a branchy bush.

The gunshot spooked Chickadee. He dashed forward. I dropped the knife and clung to Chickadee's mane tight as I could. He bounded up the trail where Georges was.

Then Chickadee seen Hélène's horse lay dying ahead. He dug into the ground to stop. Threw his weight onto his hind hooves and reared. Screaming. I couldn't hold on. I drifted high through the air a long time. Long enough to say my final prayers.

I *thudd!*ed the ground back first. The collision booted the air out my lungs.

"*Niko!*" Nimama leaped off her saddle ahead. She scrambled toward me from up the trail by Kate McCannon. Only Hélène's dead horse lay between us.

Georges rode up beside me. He shouldered the repeater and scoped the bush.

I found enough strength to rock myself onto my hands and knees. I tried sucking air. But my chest felt half-crushed.

CRACK!

I was hunched over with my body pressed snug against Georges's horse's ankle when wet splattered my back and neck. Winnie knocked my shoulder when it fell to the ground. I heard Georges gargle like he had whisky in his throat.

I wiped blood off my neck and looked up. Georges clutched his Adam's apple with both hands. Blood seeped through his fingers. He tilted off the saddle.

"*Georges!*"

The horrors of Hell burned through Hélène's voice.

"Niko! Look out!" Nimama was pressed tight against Hélène's dead horse on the trail for cover. She pointed to Georges. His body tipped further and further off his horse.

Georges's bloody hands cupped the bullet hole at the bottom of his throat. I covered the back of my head and hoped his body wouldn't hit me. He *thudd!*ed the ground. His boot twisted and got trapped in the stirrup.

Scared and spooked, Georges's horse raced up the trail. He dragged Georges over the dirt. Blood streaks in the dust followed behind them.

The horse screamed and skidded on the mucky grass. It collapsed on its side and crushed Georges beneath him. Georges's boot came untrapped from the stirrup. He lay dead in the dirt. The horse rolled to its hooves and ran into the forest without no direction.

"*Mon fils!*"

Hélène scrambled out the bush for her son. Her legs buckled. She collapsed face first into Georges's blood-drenched armpit. Her cries echoed through his hollow body.

I lay crumpled on my knees and elbows. I opened my lungs and breathed the best I could. Winnie lay in the mud beside me.

From my hands and knees, I moved the best I could toward Nimama. But I was still winded from the fall.

Corporal San Luis emerged from the forest behind me. He hustled to steal me.

Twwwweeeeeeeeeeeoooooooowwweeeet!

Kate McCannon spurred Apocalypse and barrelled down the trail toward San Luis. She whirled her lariat. Before San Luis could grab me, Kate McCannon threw the loop over his helmet and around his neck. He dug his fingers underneath. Apocalypse slided to a stop.

The lariat clung taut and yanked San Luis onto his ass—hard enough to choke him red, but soft enough not to break his neck. His helmet tumbled onto the ground.

Nimama collected me off the trail and helped me limp to cover behind Hélène's horse.

Kate McCannon sprung off her saddle. She whipped Li P'chii out its holster. She raised the gun high over her shoulder.

Thwack!

San Luis's face whipped sideways. Blood splattered out his lips. His cheekbone caved and his eyeball wasn't right. His limbs stiffened when he buckled into the ground. Out cold.

Kate McCannon struck San Luis across the cheek so hard, she hurled Li P'chii on accident. It landed not far from where Georges dropped Winnie when he got shot.

"Stop right there."

Clllllick!

Two other policemen in spiked white helmets popped out the bushes. They aimed their Winchester '76s at Kate McCannon. She raised her hands above her head and stepped away from San Luis. His neck already had deep bruising where the lariat was.

I recognized the Mounties. They was the two men in buffalo coats who watched us cross the fort to the sergeant's office when we tried reporting Cousin missing.

The Mounties approached the guns in the dirt. One walked toward Winnie; the other Li P'chii. They slung their rifles over their shoulders and collected our best guns off the ground.

"Ain't this that sawn-off you wanted, sarge?" hollered the bushy sideburned Mountie brandishing Li P'chii to someone in the bushes.

"Precisely, Constable Lyght," said a voice smooth as snakeskin. Two sets of feet scuttled over springy branches toward the trail. Wagner emerged from the trees with his arm around Auntie's neck. Like a human shield. His sidearm was holstered. But he held a blade against Auntie's cheek. The steel flashed moonlight.

Lyght rubbed his sooty gloves all over the custom designs in Li P'chii's woodwork. He pointed the gun at Kate McCannon's head.

"Nice gun, *bitch*."

"My name is Kate McCannon."

"*Ahhhhh!*" screamed Auntie.

A thin line of blood rolled down Auntie's face from the blade of Wagner's knife. He edged their way onto the trail beside the two constables.

Tweeeeooweet! whistled Wagner. "Hey! Campbell! Get out here."

Campbell Palmer emerged from the bush. His helmet was scuffed and the spike broke. He had stubbly cheeks. A button or two was missing from his serge. His lips sagged.

"Take this knife from me." With his arm still around Auntie's neck, Wagner handed his blade to Campbell. "Cut Corporal San Luis loose."

Campbell's eyes couldn't lift themselves off the ground. He brushed past Kate McCannon. Reached under the loop of the lariat and cut San Luis loose. San Luis groaned as he came conscious. His cheek bled into his serge. His eyeball bulged. Apocalypse ran into the forest to join our other horses.

"I'd like to see that gun." Wagner waved his fingers for Constable Lyght to give him Li P'chii. Wagner pressed the barrels into Auntie's bloody cheek.

"As you can see, Kate McCannon, I have something—err, perhaps I should say, some*one*—you may want. And you have someone *we* want." Wagner fiddled his finger over the trigger guard. Auntie mopped her teary and blood-smeared face with the backs of her hands. "I propose an exchange: Joséphine Eriksen for Nikosis Eriksen."

Nimama pulled the pistol from her waistline. Cocked the hammer. She aimed at the policemen. I plugged my ears in case she fired.

Hélène hid behind a thick tree across the trail for cover. Georges's body lay on the dirt. His blood streaked across Hélène's face. Like war paint. She aimed at the men up the road. Her thumb dragged the hammer. The chamber was loaded with a mother's wrath.

"Constables Lyght, Vale: get the boy." Wagner nodded at me with his chin. Lyght and Vale took their first steps up the trail. Campbell was froze still.

Kate McCannon brung her fists to her chin.

Nimama pulled the trigger.

CRACK!

The bang rung loud in my ears. Blood splattered across Lyght's crotch. He dropped his gun and collapsed into the dirt with his arm between his legs. He squirmed like a pig in shit.

"*Auughhh!*" Lyght placed his hand through the bullet hole in the front of his trousers. "*Bitch shot my prick off!*"

Nimama cocked the gun again. She shifted her aim to Vale. He couldn't mount his rifle to his shaky shoulder. Campbell dived behind a fallen tree.

Wagner let Auntie go and shoved her forward. She collapsed into Kate McCannon's arms. Kate McCannon shielded Auntie with her body.

The shot never came. Wagner turned his back to Auntie and Kate McCannon. He marched toward Lyght. *Cllllick!*ed one of Li P'chii's hammers. He stared Lyght point blank down the barrels. Lyght's eyes flashed wide. He knew Wagner was sending him to meet his maker.

BOOM!

Lyght's white helmet blew apart in a red cloud. His body sprawled like a spider web.

"*Holy shit!*" Campbell and Vale quaked in Wagner's violence. They threw their hands over their faces.

Auntie screamed. She sprung from under Kate McCannon and sprinted for cover with me and Nimama. Kate

McCannon stood with her hands up surrenderful. Wagner aimed at her and dragged the second hammer.

Clllllick!

"All right, Kate McCannon. Let's settle this like *civilized* people. I've still got one shot left."

"Why'd you kill him!"

"*Me?* Constable Lyght was executed with *your* gun. The evidence is incriminating. And look at poor Corporal San Luis. He'll be lucky if he keeps his eye. I can only imagine how many men Ottawa will send me to arrest you. Until then, you better leave us alone, Pussy Posse. Ottawa will win this war. And Odin will have his boys."

"Arrest me. Right now."

"Now? Oh, we don't want you *now*. This cat and mouse game is business." Wagner filed his fangs with his tongue. "But you can stay on the lam forever if you give us the boy."

"Go fuck yourself."

Wagner looked to Campbell and the other constable over his shoulder. Both men stood like cowards. Their guns was too shaky to shoot. San Luis groaned on his knees with his head in his hands. What was left of Lyght was splayed out on the trail.

Nimama and Hélène aimed their guns steady at Wagner. Hélène's tears streaked through the blood under her eyes.

"We'll be in touch." Wagner uncocked Li P'chii and slided the gun into his waistband. He collected Lyght's rifle off the ground and nodded at Vale to drag his body away. Campbell assisted San Luis. Auntie ran into the forest to collect our horses. "Now get the fuck out of here."

Without never turning away from Wagner, Kate McCannon

walked backwards up the trail to meet me and Nimama. Auntie emerged from the forest riding Chickadee leading Apocalypse and the two horses Nimama and Georges borrowed from Mathilde.

Hélène cried into Georges's body in the middle of the trail.

Nimama helped me mount our horse. She tried to shield my eyes from Georges. But it made no difference. I couldn't stop staring. He didn't look peaceful at all. Nothing like his papa.

Hélène slided her elbows under Georges's underarms. She dragged him toward Georges's horse so she could place his body on its rump.

"Stop there, madame," called Wagner from a distance. He stood alone on the trail with a rifle slung over his shoulder. "He's part of the crime scene."

"This is my son!"

"We will collect his corpse. You can retrieve it from the outpost next week. Now leave."

"*Please!*"

Hélène cradled Georges's body. She held him like he was her most sacred bundle. Her crying broke the hardest parts of me.

Kate McCannon walked to Hélène and set her hand on Hélène's shoulder. They rested Georges's body next to the trail. Made him look as rested as Nishecabo as they could.

Kate McCannon helped Hélène swing her legs into Georges's saddle. Hélène held the horn tight. Kate McCannon mounted Apocalypse.

We rode back the direction we came. Wagner disappeared with the other policemen. We knew they was spying on us. Like wounded cougars.

We wasn't safe until we forded the river. I leaned back and rested my head against Nimama's chest once we was on the other side. We was hours away.

WE ARRIVED AT CAMP UNDER MOONLIGHT. COYOTES HOWLED LOUD AND ANGRY. THE central fire burned out. People gathered in Kate McCannon's lodge. They barked at each other like wild dogs.

I didn't care. Not tonight. I hustled straight for the tent. My brain felt heavy. I crashed headfirst into the bedroll. Asleep before I even hit the ground. Like a boxer crumbling from a knockout blow.

NIMAMA WOKE ME WHEN SHE CAME TO BED. IT WAS CLOSE TO SUNRISE. HER CHILLY body soaked through her pyjamas. She felt warm and cold at once like January sunshine.

I closed my eyes. Tried imagining wild buffalo, wild horses, wild roses on the prairie. Whatever would drift me back into the dream world.

But all I could see was Georges's dead eyes keeping me awake.

Nimama's hand drifted onto my shoulder. She massaged her thumb over the tissues.

"Everything's going to be okay. I've got you."

I rolled into her arms and rested my head on her chest. I could feel against my cheek the scars on her neck and her bosom where she tried to burn off her young breasts when she was my age.

But I felt safe there. Like the day I was born. When Nimama was the only world I knew.

I cried and cried and cried until I fell back asleep.

CHAPTER 20

REVELATION

FRIDAY, MAY 1, 1885.

The tent door was open. Chapan's long silhouette casted over me. She sat cross-legged at the mouth of the tent.

"Chapan!"

I couldn't believe my eyes. I jumped into her body and hugged her tight as I could. I ain't never been so happy to see someone.

"Oh, Nikosis!" Chapan dug her face into my shoulder and breathed deep. I must've stunk. But she didn't care. She rubbed my shoulders like old times. "I missed you so much."

"How'd you get here?" I wrung the sleepy out my eyes and looked around the tent. Nimama and Auntie was gone. "You okay?"

"I'm fine. I got here with Viking last night after the fire at la bibliothèque."

"Georges got killed yesterday! I took Chickadee and damn near got stole by police too."

"Yesterday was a bad day." Chapan's normal smile hung a heavy frown. She pressed her sleeve into her eye sockets to soak up the tears. They was puffy and red. Like she stared into the rising sun too long. She sniffled as she spoke. "I have more bad news . . ."

"What happened?"

"Auntie hurt herself last night . . ." Chapan looked longingful over the lake. The morning was beautiful and calm. "I think yesterday was too much for her. You know?"

I felt terrible. This can't all be my fault. Can it?

God damn . . .

I shuffled next to Chapan. She rested her forehead against mine. Ducks quacked excitedful in the distance. Songbirds serenaded each other from the trees. Bees bumbled among blooming flowers by the shore.

"You know, kikâwiy was born in a hunting camp kind of like this. I delivered her. She cried and cried and cried. kohkôm was so exhausted. I thought they'd sleep forever.

"In the morning when everyone else was out doing their business, I had nothing to do. So I watched kohkôm snooze with baby kikâwiy in her arms. I was proud of kohkôm. You know? She'd gone through so much so young. And she still had the two most beautiful baby girls I ever seen. I should have never let her go.

"I always says you, kikâwiy, and kohkôm got ninâpem's eyes. Bright blue eyes like Rocky Mountain lakes. I'd never met a half-breed with blue eyes like his before. So I married him and now half my family looks just like the guy. Sometimes I think when him and my son died, part of them came back as you and Guille."

Silence weighed on us like angel wings. I squeezed Chapan's hands. "Is Auntie okay?"

"Why don't we go check on her together?"

Me and Chapan crawled out the tent. She led me toward Mathilde's teepee. I didn't notice until we stepped on the stony beach I was barefoot. Still had on the clothes I fell asleep in too.

Angry voices bursted from Kate McCannon's lodge. Lizette and Angélique sat with Twig and their families at the fire. Laurent glanced at me while eating his porridge. Guilt filled my belly like a cancer. I hope he ain't too mad about me lying and stealing Chickadee. I'd take it all back if I could.

Bella's horse was saddled up at the highline. Jérôme was yoked to the Ducharmes' cart, ready to go; next to them was Coco and Zach's horse yoked to their cart too. Charlo and Napoléon lounged in the grass with Bella and Coco and Zach and Rudi. They stared daggers into me.

Just our family's tent, Kate McCannon's lodge, Mathilde's lodge, the Callahoos' tent, and Madame Morin's mess tent and chuckwagon was still in place like normal times—the okimâwak and the rest of us who still got stole sons.

Chapan led me to Mathilde's teepee. We ducked inside. Auntie sat cross-legged with a dime novel in her hands. Stitches on her cheek jutted out where Wagner cut her. Gauze was wound along her whole forearm. Blood slashed through like blades of crimson grass.

"Auntie!"

I damn near tackled Auntie when I seen her. I was so worried. She ain't even had time to toss her book away when my arms swept over her. I felt the pages crush between our chests.

Auntie was slow to hug me. Then she squeezed tight. Inhaled me like I smelled as homeful to her as Nimama does to me. Like I was Cousin.

The walls of Mathilde's lodge was bare. The top of her tiny dresser next to her bedroll was decorated with a herd of hand-carved buffalo figurines.

"What happened?" I glanced at Auntie's gauzed arm.

"I didn't mean to lead the police home . . ." Auntie lifted my chin gentle. Her eyes was sunk deep as the day Cousin got stole. Chapan sat on her knees with me and Auntie. "We need to tell you about what happened at la bibliothèque."

"Me and Nimama seen it! They burned it down!"

"No, Niko." Chapan breathed deep and deliberate. "Me and Auntie did."

"*What!*"

"I don't trust the police with our home. I don't trust them with our belongings. I don't trust them with our medicines or our bundles, our Bibles, our stories. I'd rather lose it all to Maman Earth and start over with nothing than give them anything more.

"A long time ago, people all around Lac-aux-Trois-Pistoles trusted me to keep our stories alive. They trusted me to keep them safe. And I have. But you and Guille are all that matter. What good are our stories if I have no one to give them to?"

"What about the cats! And Huckleberry!"

"The cats will be fine; Huckleberry is at the livery." Chapan squeezed my hand. My skin glowed under her fingers. "We treated you like glass your whole life. Now look what you've seen."

I had to trust Chapan. Auntie had to too. But Chapan got to trust herself most.

"Want to hear something funny?" Auntie rubbed my shoulder soft. Her lips cracked a reflective smile. "When I seen you, I almost called you Guille. Wouldn't that've been something?"

I didn't know what to say. I walked to the figurines on Mathilde's dresser. More than a dozen bulls, cows, calves decorated the top like a prairie. I held a calf in my hand. About the size of my fist. Its curly coat felt rough under my fingertips.

More shouting erupted from Kate McCannon's teepee. Hélène sounded mad as hell. Nimama yelled defensive. Kate McCannon and Mathilde tried to calm them. But Hélène got madder. Poor Charlo got to be hearing this all too with Bella, Coco, and Zach.

"Why they arguing in there?" I set the figurine back in its spot and looked over at Auntie. Whatever life was in her eyes faded. She receded into herself.

"It's nothing," Chapan lied. The yelling got louder. Auntie rocked scareder and scareder. "Why don't we—"

"*If it weren't for the lot of you, my boys—*" yelled Hélène.

"*We got nothing to do wi—*" defended Nimama.

Twwweeeeeeeeeeeeeeeeeeeeeeeeeet!

Kate McCannon's whistle rung out like a gunshot. Silence echoed after.

It called me like a dinner bell. I stepped outside and marched across camp toward Kate McCannon's lodge.

"Nikosis!" hissed Chapan from inside Mathilde's teepee behind me. I owled my head around. She waved angry for me to return. "Get back here!"

"No." I spoke with confidence I couldn't explain. "No one talks to Nimama like that."

I barged inside Kate McCannon's teepee. Nimama and Hélène stood angry across from each other. Kate McCannon and Mathilde was at their sides.

"Bon-jour, Ni-ko-sis." Hélène's tongue spat each syllable like she tasted bloodlust. Her blouse was sweaty and stained red from her son. Her hair hung loose and blunted at the shoulder like she chopped off her braid in the moonlight. "How lovely of you to join us."

Nimama glared at Hélène. She set her hand on my shoulder and gestured outside. "Niko, go back—"

"Let him stay," barked Hélène. The revolver Kate McCannon issued her yesterday jutted out the waistband of her skirt. "He needs to learn conseque—"

"*Stop it!*" Mathilde put her hands between Nimama and Hélène. "What happened yest—"

"Bullshit!" Hélène peeled Mathilde's hand off her chest. "They're the reason Odin—"

"*Don't talk to us that way!*" I screamed at Hélène.

Our secret was out. I couldn't believe what was happening—Hélène'd been so loving and homeful. All that made her beautiful turned on us. She blamed us for Odin.

"Nikosis, come here." Nimama tugged at my arm. But I swatted her away.

I stepped forward to confront Hélène. "We ain't responsible for Od—"

"You and your cute little family's responsible for *everyth*—"

Twwweeeeeeeeeeeeet! whistled Kate McCannon. She pushed against Hélène before she came unhinged. "What the hell's gotten into you?"

"You're so lucky you can never know." Hélène pulled the revolver out her waistband. She grabbed its barrel and thrust the grip into Kate McCannon's breast. "We're done here. Me and my boy're going home."

"Hélène! Wait!"

Hélène marched out the teepee door. Kate McCannon chased after her and grasped at her arms. Hélène spun on her heels like she wanted to throw fists at Kate McCannon.

"Fuck you."

Kate McCannon stopped at the edge of camp. Hélène joined her small caravan with Charlo and Bella and Coco and Zach. Napoléon hopped into the back of their cart. Coco and Zach readied up with Rudi too. Bella threw her leg over her saddle.

Hélène *whipp!*ed the reins. Hers and Coco's carts *screech!*ed forward up the trail toward Lac-aux-Trois-Pistoles. Bella followed in the rear.

Kate McCannon watched them go. She hucked her hat onto Maman Earth hard as she could. Then she stomped on it.

KATE McCANNON LEFT FOR A SOLO BRIGADE. NIMAMA AND CHAPAN WAS ALONE with Auntie in Mathilde's teepee. Mathilde sat on a chair at the edge of camp with her knitting. She waited anxious for Narcisse and Ned Cunningham to arrive with our Red River cart and the groceries we left behind yesterday. Madame

Morin used up the last of the flour and canned cranberries for bannock and sauce for breakfast.

I sat alone in the tent. My latest sketch was almost done—a man in a straightjacket in an asylum somewhere. He had beautiful eyes. Crazy like Auntie's. Dead like Georges's.

When I went to toss my sketchbook in the crate with Nimama's journal, I noticed Nimama's unloaded gun staring at me. Calling to me.

I wrapped my fingers around the grip and pulled the gun out the crate. Aimed out the open tent door. I imagined Odin on his knees in front of me. Bruised. Battered. Bloody. Begging for God to save his soul before I blasted him to Hell.

Please, Niko! Please! I'm your grandfather! Tears washed down Odin's cheeks. Salty, guilt-riddled tears. Useless tears. *Please! Don't kill me!*

You think I give a damn about you? My thumb *clllllick!*ed the hammer. Wrath devoured my soul. I was God. *I'm just here to finish the job.*

Pow!

I imagined the gun recoiling in my hand. The flash. The bang. The smoke leaking out the muzzle.

Odin was defeated. Soulless. Dead.

"You in there, Niko?"

I heard Auntie's voice before I seen her. Then I noticed I cocked the gun in real life. I tried uncocking it before Auntie could see me. But the hammer was stuck. It wouldn't budge. My heart speeded like a racehorse. There was nothing I could do. I hid the revolver behind my back right when Auntie squatted at the tent door. Fresh gauze was wound around her forearm.

"Want to come pick mushrooms by the narrows with me and Viking?"

"Okay." I nodded fast and hoped Auntie would look away. "One second."

Auntie turned her back to the tent. I had to squeeze the trigger to uncock the hammer. I pointed the gun to the corner and closed my eyes. Nimama, please tell me you unloaded it!

Click!

The hammer slapped the empty cylinder. I wiped my forehead and calmed my heart.

In slow . . . out slow . . .

I slipped the gun under Nimama's journal in the crate. Auntie didn't see nothing.

"Okay. I'm ready."

Me and Auntie rode Viking together a couple miles along the shore to the narrows. We dismounted and hiked up to some black morels Auntie knew about at the top of a knoll. Viking roamed the base of the hill, chomping grass. We tossed mushrooms into little baskets and watched ducks swim across the lake.

Crack!

(. . . crack . . . crack . . .)

"Hear that?" asked Auntie, unfazed. The ducks *quack quack!*ed and flew into the sky. We'd picked chubby mushrooms a while by the time the gunshot rang out. "Sounds like Laurent shot something."

"I hope it's a big meaty moose."

"Wouldn't that be nice?" Auntie waited for me. "Want to know something?"

"What?"

"The sergeant gave me this when they apprehended me." Auntie pulled a folded piece of paper out a pocket from her blouse. She unfolded the paper and handed me a drawing Cousin done of a ginormongous spruce tree. A fire burned in the background. Four silhouettes with guns was lined up beside the tree. The paper was crunchy with dried tears. "They said they'd take me to my son if I surrendered . . ."

I handed Auntie back Cousin's drawing. She folded the paper and tucked it into her pocket.

"I want my son!" Auntie imploded on top of her basket. She tugged her blouse to her hairline. Her voice was muffled by fabric and horror. "I want Guille!"

ME AND AUNTIE WAS ALONE ON THE HILL A LONG TIME TOGETHER. HER EYES WAS bloodshot and swole. We took our time before we returned to camp with the baskets full of mushrooms. Angélique played her papa's harmonica with Twig at the fire. Madame Morin busied herself with cooking venison stew for supper. Mathilde knitted in her chair at the edge of camp.

Then the thunder of a single horse's hooves *clop-clop! clop-clop! clop-clopp!*ed the trail.

Twweeeeeeeeeoooooowwweeet!

Narcisse pulled his mount to a stop. He jogged to camp without even tying up his horse. Mathilde ran to him. "Hey! I need Laurent and Elinore!"

"What's happening?" Mathilde ran to her husband anxiousful. "Where's Ned?"

"We found their boys! We found Michel and François."

"What!" shouted Mathilde. Chaos started to ripple through the camp. "Where are they?"

"Ned'll be here with them and Kate McCannon in a minute."

Angélique tossed her papa's harmonica into the grass and ran to fetch her maman and papa. Twig *arf!! arf!*ed behind. Chapan searched for Madame Morin and Lizette.

"What the hell is happening?" Laurent and Julie hustled to meet Narcisse at the foot of the trail. Madame Morin and Lizette followed behind. "We heard you found François and Michel?"

"Kate McCannon got him and Michel bandaged up good. Don't worry."

"Huh? What the fuck does that mean?" Laurent spoke fast. He smacked his fist against his opposite palm. "Where are they?"

"They'll be here soon." Narcisse squeezed Laurent's shoulder. "They're going to be fine."

"I don't understand," said Madame Morin. Everyone gathered with her by the edge of camp. "Are they hurt?"

Narcisse cleared his throat. He swallowed thorny courage and looked Madame Morin square in the eye. Then Laurent. He didn't want to shake them out their denial. But he had to.

"I'm sorry to tell you. They got castrated . . ."

Madame Morin wept into Chapan's shoulder. Lizette and Angélique consoled each other too. Laurent's head fell to his chest. He crumbled to his knees and hammered the ground hard as he could. His knuckles stamped the dirt with blood.

Punch! punch! punch!

punchpunchpunchpunch!

"*My boy! My son!*"

Maman Earth muffled Laurent's cries. Julie rested her hands on her husband's shoulders. She crouched over him and rubbed his back. Narcisse squatted to be closer to Laurent too.

"We'll get through this, brother." Narcisse choked on his own tears. "Don't you worry."

I ain't never seen grown men cry like that. Not even at Nishecabo's wake.

CHAPTER 21

REAL PEOPLE

There wasn't no prayer at supper. We didn't want to waste our breath on words God will just ignore. Everyone knows He don't listen no more.

Even though Cunningham brung our cart full of groceries when he arrived with Kate McCannon and Michel and François, we didn't eat much at supper. Mathilde and Narcisse cooked so Madame Morin and Lizette could be with Michel. Doughy bannock and peppery venison with gravy. Strips of deer meat hung on the smoking rack over the cooking fire.

Most everyone ate in their tents. Chapan was on a walk with Auntie. Nimama needed alone time in our tent too. So just me, Kate McCannon, and Cunningham sat by the fire.

"What a fucking disaster." Kate McCannon pulled her tobacco pouch out her pocket and stuffed a few leaves inside her cheek. Her greasy plate rested on the grass under her chair.

"The Pussy Posse done a lot of good." Cunningham mopped gravy with his last hunk of bannock. "Think about it. All them families who left are safe now. That counts for something."

"Don't bullshit me, Ned." Kate McCannon cast her crumply hat behind her and shook her head. "I got Georges killed last night; Charlo and two other boys got castrated. My job was to keep this community safe and I fucking failed."

"We still got to find Cousin," I said firmful. We need him back worser than ever.

"We will." Kate McCannon watched the fire like she was seeing her own nakedness in the mirror for the first time. The flames looked wet in her eyes' reflections. "You got my word."

Madame Morin and Laurent snuck up behind us with Mathilde and Narcisse. They all looked sad and exhausted.

"Mind if you, me, Narcisse, Elinore, and Laurent have a chat in your lodge?" asked Mathilde.

Kate McCannon waved for them to follow. I tugged Laurent's sleeve before he passed me. I asked him to wait. I knew he was disappointed in me. I took a breath to calm my heart. I had to apologize. I just wish it wasn't so damn hard.

"Sorry for lying and stealing Chickadee. Was trying to help is all."

Laurent outhaled heavy. He wiped his palm with his sash. The knuckles was split and bruised. He reached to shake my hand. "I respect the hell out of that. Find Guille safe. Okay?"

"We will." I shook his hand firm. I hoped I wasn't telling him no lie.

Laurent looked over at Mathilde, Narcisse, and Madame

Morin waiting outside Kate McCannon's lodge. He nodded soft at them. They ducked one by one into Kate McCannon's teepee. Laurent turned his attention back to me.

"I suppose no one's told you this is our last night?" he asked.

"What you mean?"

Laurent rested his hand on my shoulder and sighed. "My family, the Morins, the Little Bulls. We're all going home tomorrow after breakfast. We've got to take care of François and Michel where they're safe so they can recover. You know?"

I turned my head to the side so Laurent couldn't see my eyes fill with tears. I didn't want him to know my heart was breaking. I know Laurent's got to take care of his boy. But what about Cousin? What about us?

Laurent heard me sniffle real loud. I didn't want to cry in front of him. But it was too hard not to.

Laurent tugged close me into his body and hugged me. I pulled him tight and rubbed my wet eyes against him. As mad as I felt, I never wanted him to leave. Laurent's been more of a papa to me than anyone. Even Papa Brisson.

"I need you to do me a favour, Nikosis."

"What is it?"

"You need to be nâpew of the Pussy Posse now. Okay?"

"What you mean?" I sniffled and wiped my cheek.

"When I'm gone, you'll be the only man in camp. You'll have a special type of responsibility not even the okimâwak have. You have to be someone everyone here can trust. Even yourself. Can you do that for me?"

I wiped my last tears and outhaled steady. I wasn't going to let Laurent down. "Yeah."

"Good."

Laurent pulled me close for one more hug. "You're going to be okay."

"I know."

Laurent patted my back. Then he readied to go over to Kate McCannon's lodge. "François was saying he wanted to chat with you and your maman in your tent. He'll be by in a few minutes if you wait for him."

"Okay."

Laurent walked to Kate McCannon's lodge. I spun around and zipped to me and Nimama's tent.

"Can I come in?" I asked. When Nimama said yes, I pulled open the tent door.

Nimama lay on her side and wrote in her leatherbound journal in the lantern light. She laced her journal shut and tossed it aside. "How you doing?"

"Fine." I ducked inside and shuffled into place beside Nimama. I lay my head on top her thighs. She plucked dead grass from between my wily, overgrown hairs. "Laurent says François wants to come to talk to us."

"About what?"

"Didn't say," I shrugged. I missed Cousin. "I wish Hélène didn't have to be so mean."

"Me too," sighed Nimama. My hairs flapped like feathers on a duck. "What she been through would break the best of us."

I watched an ant, blacker than a hunk of coal, muscle its way toward the tent from outside. The ant held a veiny springtime leaf between its pincers. He marched through the wispy grass with his quarry.

Then a gust blew the leaf away. The ant clung to the leaf like a dying soul clings to its body.

"Be careful who you trust your stories with, boys," I remember Nimama saying to me and Cousin at the table one freezy February morning. It was so cold we could see our breaths even with the fireplace burning. We played cards and sipped tea with her and Auntie and Chapan. Nimama rolled a cigarette. "Stories are trust and trust is a gift."

Cousin blinked a couple times. "I don't understand. Is trust, like, a book or something?"

"Let's pretend it is." Nimama set her fresh rolled cigarette on her saucer and waved for Chapan to pass her a dime novel lying beside her playing cards. "Let's pretend your trust is this book right here. Okay?"

"My trust is this book. Right." Cousin dropped his cards in front of him and reached across the table. Nimama propped the book between Cousin's hands. He fingered the wore and used pages.

"Now let's pretend you want to share your book with me. One day you get brave and say, 'I'm going to give Auntie Sara my book!' So you give me your book."

Cousin gave the book back to Nimama. She opened its front cover and flipped through the first few pages.

"This is a great story." Nimama smiled at Cousin. Her fingers massaged the paper. "Thank you for trusting me with your story."

"You're welcome." Cousin smiled that classic, mad-cat grin he got. "I'm glad you like it."

Rrrrrrrrrip!

Nimama tore out a page from the book. She crumpled it into a ball and tossed it between me and Cousin's heads.

Rrrrrip!

"What're you doing?" Chapan reached across the table to

protect the book from Nimama. Nimama swatted Chapan's hand and pulled the book closer to her chest. She scratched out more pages and tossed them at the ceiling.

Rip! rip! rip!

"Why you tearing my book apart?" Cousin's gold eyes zipped like moths batting the glass of a lantern. He must've surveyed each freckle on Nimama's face four times over. "We said it was a gift. Remember?"

Nimama threw the book across the homestead. Pages poofed when the book nailed the staircase. Like a duck's feathers after getting blasted by shotgun pellets. Poor Félix and Miss Kitty scrambled upstairs together in a cloud of fluttering paper and pattering footsteps.

Arf! arf!

Barney stood. Twisted in a couple circles. Waited for any of us to stir at the table. When we all sat stiller than statues, Barney spun again, then lay back down in front of the fireplace.

"That book on the floor? It's your gift to me. But it's still *your* trust. I broke your trust."

"Why?" Cousin looked at Nimama. Then me. Like he thought I could see inside her brain and read her thoughts. I shrugged and made my best hell-if-I-know face for him.

"Hmm." Nimama scrunched her face. "Guille, would you kindly grab me the book?"

"Okay." Cousin slided his chair back. Then Nimama interrupted him.

"Wait." Nimama's eyes batted around Cousin's face like blue butterflies trapped in a jar. "Why don't you ask Niko to help you get all those pages off the floor."

"Uhh . . ." Cousin looked to Auntie and Chapan for answers. They both shrugged just as hell-if-we-know at Cousin as I did. "Want to help me get my story off the floor?"

"Uhh . . . okay." I slided my chair back when Nimama interrupted again.

"So you trust Nikosis with your story?"

"Uhh . . ." Cousin looked at me again. My jaw hung open. I nodded. "I trust him. Yeah."

Nimama said to me, "You're not going to harm Guillaume's book like I did. Will you?"

"No. Got no reason to." But Nimama had no reason to harm Cousin's book neither.

Nimama grabbed her cigarette off the saucer. She *shhhhrrripp!*ed a match against the table and cupped the flame to her lips. Smoke petered out her mouth. The room smelled like fresh tobacco and gunpowder. She said to Cousin from under her brow, "Are you sure you trust Nikosis to be right by you?"

"Yeah . . ." Cousin looked hollow. "What you mean?"

"You trusted me with your book when you gave it to me. You had no more control over your story once I had it. I broke that trust. You trust Niko not to break your trust?"

"To not tear up the pages?"

"Exactly. You trust him not to abuse it like I did?"

"Yeah."

"That's good. Niko's a good person." Nimama rested her cigarette on the saucer next to her teacup. She brung the cup to her lips and *slurrrp!*ed a scorchy mouthful. "Would you kindly ask Niko to grab that book?"

"Can you grab my book for me?"

I swept off the seat and marched to the book and picked up all the exploded pages. I dropped the book and stacks of pages on the table in front of Nimama. On top her playing cards even.

She set her teacup on the saucer. She took the cigarette from its spot. Smoke and cold air bulled out her nostrils like snow.

"Why'd you give me Guillaume's book?"

"Uhh . . ." I looked to Cousin for answers. He had none. "You wanted it."

"But it's Guille's story. Right?"

"Nimama?" I couldn't look up no more. I looked for all sorts of patterns in the grainy tabletop. Seen nothing but chaos. "Ain't this all pretend?"

I didn't have no clue what Nimama was doing. I'd grown used to Nimama's ways of being strong-willed and such. But even this was weird.

"Guillaume, did you want Nikosis to give me your book?"

Cousin shook his head.

I became tiny as an ant. I ain't had no clue what was going on. I thought I did nothing wrong. How was I supposed to know it was still Cousin's? He gave Nimama the book. She started all this.

"So why do I have his book?" Nimama asked me. She set her cigarette against the saucer and shuffled some tore-out pages and placed them tidy on the book cover.

"Cousin gave it to you."

"Does Guille's story *belong* to me?"

Words trickled out my mouth like the last droplets of piss. "It's a gift though."

Nimama reached for her teacup.

Slurrrrrrp!

Auntie's clock *tick! tock!*ed on the mantel beside Winnie. Nimama set down her cup.

"*Give it to me!*" Cousin dived across the table for the book. Cups chattered. Tea splattered on the playing cards and extinguished Nimama's cigarette. He yanked at Nimama's hands hard as he could, desperate to get that book out her grip.

Rrrrrrrrip!

Cousin wide-eyed the mess of shredded paper in his fingers. Nimama still held the bulk of the tore book.

"That's mine!" Cousin fell to his seat. He breathed loud and messy through bared teeth.

On each side of Nimama, Auntie and Chapan looked shocked into silence.

Nimama wrapped her arms around the book like she was its protector. "This is all pretend. This book isn't *really* your trust. Not in real life." Nimama plopped the dime novel on the table—an old copy of *Malaeska: The Indian Wife of the White Hunter*. "It's just a book."

"Why'd you tear it up?"

"You trusted me." Nimama blinked sadful. "I couldn't let that go unpunished."

"I'm your nephew!"

"Did you *really* trust me?" Nimama put the book under her elbow. "I didn't stop hurting your book when you asked. I took advantage of you. Being your auntie doesn't make me good."

Cousin flexed his jaw muscles. Then his body sinkholed into itself. He blinked out the anger in his eyes and cupped his hands on his lap.

"No one said I had a choice *not* to trust you."

"You wanted to trust me with the book. Didn't you?"

"nisîmis, please . . ." Auntie whispered awful quiet.

"That was wrong of me. Wasn't it? You couldn't trust me. But you had to." Nimama fanned smoke and steam away from her words. She looked at Cousin with a strange blend of innocence and fear. "Right now, in pretend life where I destroyed your book, my heart knows I'm a bad person. Your heart knows I'm a bad person. But I'll do whatever it takes to convince you I still deserve your trust. I'll move mountains to make you think I'm the hero *and* the victim."

Nimama waved for Cousin to give her his hands. He hesitated. Eventually he held Nimama's fingers. Nimama's thumbs massaged circles onto his skin.

"I still don't understand what to do when I get took advantage of," said Cousin.

"Trust *yourself* to be real people. If you're real people, you'll be okay."

"Real people? I don't get what you mean."

"Let's pretend it's real life and you're in danger. You're all alone. Can't be with your maman, not Niko, not Chapan, not me. No one. Who you trust to be there for you?"

"No one?"

"You know, me and your maman's papa taught us something when we were kids. Love and trust ain't the same thing. Trust is something that *belongs* to *you*. You can't control who has your heart. But you can control who has your trust. Trust is the easiest thing you have to hurt. Especially by someone you love. Real people trust no one more than themselves. That's why real people are always okay."

"Auntie Sara?" Cousin brung his hands back into his lap. "Am I real people?"

Nimama outhaled a long, breathy, thinky sigh. "Niko, what do you think? Is Guille real people?"

"I trust Cousin. He's real people."

Nimama turned to Chapan. "Kokum, what about you? Is Guille real people?"

Bundled in her thickest moose fur-lined coat, Chapan nodded. "Absolutely, Guillaume is real people."

"And you, nimis? You trust your son to be real people?"

"Of course." Auntie looked warm like she carried a buffalo horn of fire in her hands. She smiled at Cousin and reached across the table to squeeze his arm. "My boy's good."

"I think so too. Sounds to me like you're real people." Nimama removed her hat, brushed her hand over her hair, then set it back on. "I think you can trust yourself to be all right. No matter what."

"Yeah." Cousin beamed like Barney used to whenever we had moose bones to toss for him. "Real people."

"Am I real people?" I felt silly to ask. Pathetic even.

"What do you think? Do you think you're real people?"

I looked to Cousin, to Auntie, to Chapan. They all waited for me.

"I know I'm real people." I batted my chest like a buffalo hunter.

"Yeah!" Cousin batted hisself on the chest like my mirror. "Me too!"

"Me too, boys." Nimama made the proudest smile I ever seen her make. She stood and batted herself in the chest. "We're real people!"

I wish I knew then Cousin was going to disappear. I miss him so much.

He got to be okay. He's real people.

"EXCUSE ME. MADEMOISELLE ERIKSEN?" FRANÇOIS IN HIS WHITE PYJAMAS HID behind the tent door. He had red speckles on his bum like Nimama's moontime underwear. "Can I come in?"

"Of course." Nimama crossed her legs and sat attentionful. She wiped sweat off her face and smudged lead on her nose bridge on accident. "What you need?"

I lifted myself off Nimama's leg and leaned back against a box. François ducked into the tent. His face crumpled as he lowered hisself onto his bum.

"We have water." Nimama dug for her canteen behind me. Water splashed inside. She unscrewed the cap, sniffed, then handed it to François. "It's from yesterday."

François whirled his magpie talons around the canteen and tipped the opening into his mouth. Half the water ran down his chin from the corners of his lips. Then he handed me the canteen and scrubbed his face dry with the collar of his pyjamas. It was damn near empty.

"I appreciate it, Mademoiselle Eriksen." His rosy cheeks looked embarrassed.

"Just call me Sara."

"I think me and Michel's families going home tomorrow. Madame Little Bull too."

I owled my head so François couldn't see me frown. I get why him and Michel and their families need to go. But that don't stop me from being sad. What about Cousin?

"Home's good for you." Nimama outhaled heavy through her nose. "Is Guille okay?"

"I don't know. O-Od-Od . . ." François didn't want to cry in front of us. But his tears didn't care. He wrapped his arms around Nimama and squeezed her like a snake. He smeared his eyes against Nimama's blouse. She was the blanket he used to hide from the world. No amount of crying could empty his well.

"I hope he fucking dies, Mademoiselle Sara! I hope you fucking kill him! He's a fucking monster! A fucking monster! I fucking hate him! I fucking hate him! I hope you fucking kill him!"

Nimama held François's head close to her heart. She was his nest. They cried a long time.

"It's okay . . ." Nimama soothed. They swayed like two trees tangled in an empty forest. "We're safe here."

"He's a monster." François wiped his face using his pyjama shirt. "Ain't he, Mademoiselle Sara?"

"The worst kind." Nimama dabbed her eyes and cheeks with her sleeve.

"I'm sorry for crying like that. It's just—"

"It's okay." Nimama petted François's cheek with her thumb. A trail of lead streaked across. "We missed you."

"Nipapa says even Chickadee missed me." François wrung leftover tears out his puffy eyes. He looked at me and chuckled. "I hear Chickadee sure likes you, Niko!"

"Oh no . . ." I rolled my eyes deep into the back of my skull. I was so embarrassed. How did word spread so fast?

"That's pretty funny." François sniffled and smiled at the same time. "Nipapa says he ain't never training no more horses to kneel again."

Nimama winked at François. She smudged lead under his other eye. "How you doing?"

"I'm okay. I got something important to tell you, mademoiselle."

"What is it?"

"Guillaume ain't alone with Odin. Wyatt's there too."

"Who's Wyatt?" asked Nimama.

"Another boy Odin stole before everyone else. He's only eight. He don't talk much. He ain't from here." François scrubbed his face with his sleeve. He looked sad at the tears smeared on the fabric. "Promise you'll find him and Guille?"

Nimama rubbed François's back. "Promise."

François glanced over his shoulder. Cunningham puffed his pipe alone by the fire. "Mademoiselle Sara, I want to talk alone with Niko."

Nimama placed her hat on her head. Me and François watched her approach Cunningham at the fire. He handed Nimama some tobacco for a cigarette.

I slipped my feet under my bum and sat on my heels. François put his hand on my arm.

"I know how you and Guille's related to Odin."

I wanted to bury myself. The shame will never go away. I never asked to be Odin's grandson. It ain't fair!

I hate Odin! I want his blood on my hands. Not in my veins.

"It's okay, Niko. You ain't like him. He's bad."

I looked up at François. He didn't look angry or afraid of me.

"It ain't your fault what happened," I said to him. "You didn't deserve it."

"He said I did."

"Well, I hope you didn't believe him." I tapped François's breastbone to get to his heart. He looked like he already felt all the sad in the world to feel. "Nimama taught me to listen to what's in there when people say bad things to me."

François looked half sad, half confused.

"Want to know what I think about you?" I scooted to be closer to François. "I think you's real people."

"What's real people?"

"You don't know what real people is?" I leaned back, raised one eyebrow, and one-overed him. When I determined he was ready to learn, I nodded. "I'll tell you. Real people is people you trust to be good. No matter what. Even to themselves. I got to trust you to look after a friend of mine—a boy called François Callahoo. He's good. I wouldn't trust you none if you wasn't real people. But I trust you a lot."

A couple seconds passed. François draped his arms over me. His weight felt welcome on my shoulders. "Thanks."

CHAPTER 22

NIKOSIS ERIKSEN, OKIMÂSIS

SATURDAY, MAY 2, 1885. LOON LAKE AND LAC-AUX-TROIS-PISTOLES, DISTRICT OF SASKATCHEWAN.

I wished breakfast would never end. I wasn't ready for everyone to leave. Not with Cousin still out there. Wyatt too.

Madame Morin and the Little Bulls used as much of the groceries as they could. Porridge with sugar and maple syrup from Québec. Fluffy bannock with canned jam. Omelettes with sautéed wild mushrooms. Fresh orange pekoe for the kids and coffee with a splash of moonshine for the adults. They even made deer pemmican with dried blueberries, syrup, and the last of the smoked venison.

We ate together at the fire. Twig begged for scraps. People told stories about their families, their friends. Cunningham and Narcisse compared their suppliers' prices. Madame Morin shared groceries and recipes with Chapan and Julie and Mathilde. Nimama rolled cigarettes with Laurent. Angélique and Lizette quizzed each other on scripture. François and Michel even sipped their teas by the lakeshore with me and watched loons on the water.

It was like times should be. Excepting everyone but us and Kate McCannon was riding home after. Mathilde and Narcisse took her lodge down and yoked their horses to their wagon. Chickadee was ready by the Callahoos' cart. Cunningham even agreed to take Kate McCannon's wagon and teepee home to Tom, leaving just her and Apocalypse with us.

Soon as me, Lizette, and Angélique scrubbed dry the last cast iron pan, we took down the mess tent and chicken coop and loaded Madame Morin's chuckwagon too. Everyone's horses was ready to go. We lined up at the fire to hug everyone goodbye.

I tried not to cry. I didn't want them knowing how I feel like they's abandoning us.

Lizette was the last to hug me. She squeezed like she wanted Cousin to feel through me. "Make sure you find Guille. Okay?"

"Promise."

Whiptch!

The Little Bulls' and Callahoos' and Morins' and Cunningham's wagons and carts lunged forward. The kids all waved goodbye as their rides lumbered along.

Soon as they turned out of sight, there was no stopping my tears. Grief pulled me under like a wave.

"What about Cousin!" I yelled at Kate McCannon. I couldn't even see her through all my crying. I chopped the air with my finger like a meat cleaver. "How could you let this happen? You gave me your word!"

"Niko! Don't—" Nimama reached to grab me. But I swatted her hand away.

"*What about Cousin!*"

Kate McCannon rested her hands on her flanks and stared at her toes. I couldn't stand her avoiding me.

I shook my head and stormed off to the tent. Then I tied shut the door so I could cry alone. I wanted to pack everything into a big pile and set it all on fire. Instead I screamed loud as I could into the folded pyjamas I used as my pillow.

"HEY, NIKO?" NIMAMA ASKED FROM OUTSIDE OUR CLOSED TENT. IT'D BEEN AN HOUR or so since I blew up at Kate McCannon. "Can I come in?"

"One second." I shuffled to the tent door and untied the knot locking it shut. The fabric flung open like curtains.

Nimama slided inside and sat beside me. She wrapped her arm over my shoulders. "You doing okay?"

"What if I'm not?"

Nimama had no response. Her hand massaged the back of my neck.

My brain flooded with memories of Miss Kitty and Félix. Drunk on fantasies of me and Cousin playing buffalo hunters, riding home to Barney barking at us like we was the full moon.

I imagined me and Cousin crashing through the front door to a hot-cooked meal with greasy bannock and elderberry tea. We all sat at the table together. Miss Kitty jumped on his lap and Félix on mine. I could taste the drippy duck with fried onions and wild rice. Dandelion, carrot, strawberry salad. A bitter sip of Auntie's favourite wine.

I could smell home. The dusty pages of the dime novel Auntie read at the table. The fresh-lit cigarette Nimama puffed. The scorched duck fat from the cast iron pan whose smoke Chapan fanned out the window.

"Sara? Can we join you and Niko?" Chapan and Auntie asked from outside. They shuffled into the tent. We sat in a circle like a compass. Chapan asked Nimama, "Have you told him the plan?"

"I don't know if I trust the father with him."

"The Ghostkeeper boys are there too." Chapan rested her hand on Nimama's forearm. "Kate McCannon wouldn't've agreed if she thought Niko would be in danger there."

Nimama looked at me and asked, "You trust Père Brisson. Don't you?"

"What you mean?"

"Would you feel safe staying with him at the rectory?"

Icicles shivered down my spine. Little hairs all over my body rushed in waves. I thought I'd go my whole life without never worrying about if I trust Papa Brisson.

"We want you to stay with Père Brisson so we can take Guille back," said Chapan.

I wanted to ride with Nimama and Auntie and Chapan. I want to be the one who finds Cousin. Who defeats Odin.

But I don't want to make things worser again. Or end up dead like Georges. Or like Charlo neither.

But staying with Papa Brisson?

"Can't I stay with Kate McCannon?"

"She's coming with us." Chapan looked scared and vulnerable. But confident in a damn near divine way. "We can change the plan if you don't trust Père Brisson."

"It's your choice," said Nimama.

"I thought you and Kate McCannon didn't trust the father?"

"She trusts you'll be *safe* with him. Just a couple days."

It was a weird way to answer a question. I asked Chapan and Auntie, "What about you?"

They glanced at each other. Waited a long time. Then nodded. "We trust Kate McCannon's judgment. It's the church. The Ghostkeeper boys are probably the safest kids in L-T-P."

"You?" I asked Nimama.

"You're real people." Nimama tapped her finger against my breastbone. Looking into her eyes was like looking into my own. "I trust *your* judgment."

I gave myself time to think. Then I nodded. "Let's do this."

WE PACKED OUR CAMP AND LOADED THE CART. CHAPAN SAT IN THE BACK WHILE Auntie drove. Me and Nimama rode Pony together. Kate McCannon led us through the swampy trail toward Lac-aux-Trois-Pistoles. The damn cart *screech!*ed the whole ways, as always.

We was just breaching the west arm of Fleury Avenue. Gold suppertime sunlight glittered off the lake. Birds sung from the trees. Frogs croaked from the wetlands. The trail still had streaks from outside Cunningham's store where

Auntie and Georges charged. The walls of the fort stood tall across the lake. The rectory was just ahead.

"This is where I let you go." Kate McCannon pulled the reins to halt Apocalypse. She stuck out her arm for me and Nimama to stop beside her. "You sure you want to go through with this, Niko?"

Kate McCannon rubbed Apocalypse along the mane. Pony needed a good scratch too. So I rubbed her mane until she shook her bridle and *hububububb!*ed her lips relaxedful.

"You and Pony got something special between you two." Kate McCannon rested her hands on her saddle horn. Two lariats was strapped to either side of the horn. White embroidered flowers decorated the leather. Excepting the embroidery, Apocalypse's saddle looked an awful lot like ours. Way better quality though. Newer too.

"Cousin and Viking get along good too," I said. Kate McCannon can't forget what's at stake. "I'm sure Wyatt's got hisself a loyal horse at home."

Kate McCannon nodded. She rested her hand on the grip of her revolver.

"You know, Niko, I was about your age when nipapa passed away. On a buffalo hunt too. I wanted to be just like him. You know? Thought I'd be as good a maman as he was papa. Was all I ever wanted to be.

"I was seventeen when I married a Civil War vet. Miscarried myself his God damn baby a few months later. When I miscarried myself the second time, I made sure I'd never miscarry again. My husband didn't like me much after that.

"I don't know if that war made him a dog or just never killed the dog in him . . ." Kate McCannon placed a finger on either side of her crooked nose, along the edges of her wishbone-shaped scar, and glided her fingertips down the bridge over the lashes under each eye. "... but I had two black eyes and a broke nose the night I took nipapa's hatchet to his skull."

Kate McCannon pulled the revolver out her holster. She tossed the revolver into the air. It somersaulted between us. She caught the revolver by the barrel. The grip faced me.

"Each okimâw needs their own gun. Your maman's got Campbell's revolver because her brigade's in charge of finding Guille and Wyatt. But the okimâw of *your* brigade still needs a gun. Your brigade's in charge of keeping *you* safe. The Ghostkeeper boys too. You've earned this revolver, okimâsis Nikosis."

I looked down at the gun in front of me—the one Kate McCannon used to issue to the new okimâw. The one Hélène gave up. Its grip poked the wool of my jacket.

I closed my eyes slow and outhaled slower.

"Keep it." I shook my head and palmed the gun away from my belly. "You need it to find Cousin and Wyatt. We'll be safe."

Kate McCannon nibbled the tobacco in her cheek and spat the juices behind her. Time slugged by. She twirled the gun around her finger and stabbed it into the holster. "In that case, I got a request, okimâsis Nikosis."

"What is it?"

"Mind if I sit in on your meeting the priest?"

"Permission granted, okimâw Kate McCannon."

CHAPTER 23

WINCHESTER REPEATING ARMS MODEL 1873

We passed through Fleury Avenue. Town was dead. No Constable Palmer patrolling or reading his book. No one parked at the stores. No piles of horse poo on the road. Nothing.

Kate McCannon dismounted and hitched our horses and Viking and the cart to the post by the trees near the church.

Then she helped Auntie and Chapan off the cart. Me and Nimama dismounted too. We walked along the boardwalk and stood outside the rectory. Setting sunlight reflected off the windows. Chapan *ring-ring!*ed the doorbell.

"It's Maggie, Sara, and Josey. We're with Niko."

The bolt unlatched. Étienne opened the door. Papa Brisson's tiny calico cat slipped through our legs outside. Étienne's eyes popped when he seen Kate McCannon behind us. She laid her finger across her lips and mouthed a *hushhh . . .* for Étienne.

Jean-Baptiste entered the foyer from the kitchen behind Étienne looking confused. Étienne mouthed for Jean-Baptiste to keep Kate McCannon a secret.

"Is Père Brisson home?" Chapan asked Étienne.

"*Why's she here!*" hissed Étienne. He nodded to Kate McCannon behind us.

"Is that you, Maggie?" echoed Papa Brisson from the top floor. "Open the door, Étienne."

Étienne shook his head and stepped aside to let us inside the sun-warmed foyer. He closed the door behind us. Papa Brisson's shoes clopped down each stair.

Kate McCannon removed her hat. She swaggered around the foyer and admired the paintings on the wall. Her boot heels knocked the floor. Papa Brisson spotted her when he reached the foot of the staircase.

"You!" Papa Brisson hovered into the foyer in his black cassock. His heavy cross dangled from his neck. "You're not welcome here!"

Kate McCannon ignored him. She stopped in front of a beautiful, blurry pastoral painting of a fine dressed man reading a newspaper in his big, lush garden. Her fingers floated over the short, deliberate brushstrokes. The aggressive, moving shadows. Like the leaves blew in a breeze. She stepped backwards away from the painting. Admired it from afar.

"I ever tell you what I love about Monet, father? Up close, everything looks simple. Basic, bold palate. Any of our boys could do it. But from back here, it's like a colourized photograph that moves. Realer than real. The way it is and the way we experience it all at once. You know?

"Me and Tom got a Marie Bracquemond watercolour at home. It's his favourite. Funny story how it came into our hands actually. Had to patriate it from Tom's old fence in Chicago."

"You need to leave, Kate McCannon."

"We will soon, father." Kate McCannon brushed the breast of her jacket over the holster on her hips. The pistol grip held the jacket in place. "But we could really go for a cup of coffee first."

"Mes fils." Papa Brisson licked his lips nervousful and swallowed. His forehead sweated. His handless sleeve waved for Étienne to enter the kitchen. "Our guests need coffee and tea."

Jean-Baptiste shepherded us into the dining room. He shimmied around the table pulling mahogany chairs for each of us, all cushioned with sheepskin pillows. I wiggled into the chair beside Nimama. Chapan and Auntie sat beside me. Kate McCannon took her seat at the foot of the table nearest Nimama. The revolver poked out the holster. She tossed her hat on the table. Papa Brisson sat opposite Kate McCannon at the head of the table nearest Auntie.

Jean-Baptiste lit the candles and brung blue china cups

and stirring spoons and saucers for us all. Then he gave us each a raisin biscuit with a plate and dull knife to spread some of the glossy butter from the dish in the middle of the table. Beside the butter was a pepper grinder and salt shaker and a tall jar of honey with a long wood dipper sticking out.

Jean-Baptiste sat across the table from me, Nimama, Auntie, and Chapan. Étienne brung a coffee pot in one hand and a teapot in the other. One by one, Étienne poured us each our hot drinks—coffee for the girls and tea for us boys. Then he sat beside Jean-Baptiste.

Kate McCannon brung her coffee to her lips and *slurrrp!*ed. Steam drifted over her wishbone scar.

"Incredible coffee, Étienne." Kate McCannon cheersed the air to thank her hosts and sipped another mouthful. "Best cup I've had in years."

Étienne nodded sheepish and smiled. I blew waves into my tea. The hot water felt soft on my tongue.

"I'm grateful we can share the Church's resources with you." Papa Brisson swallowed anxiousful. Jean-Baptiste brung a buttered biscuit to Papa Brisson's teeth. Crumbs tumbled onto his cassock and rained over Jesus's crown on his pendant. "I take it you require something from us."

Auntie twirled her cup in circles on the saucer. The bottom scraped the porcelain underneath. "We need a favour."

"You need to take Niko," pleaded Chapan. "Just for a couple days."

"Please, father." Auntie reached to tug Papa Brisson's sleeve. "I can't wait anymore. I need to bring my son home."

Papa Brisson sighed. He looked around the dining room. At the paintings of Mary and her son. Of Jesus's crucifixion. He looked at Étienne and Jean-Baptiste sitting innocent beside him. At Nimama and Kate McCannon boring their eyes into him. At me.

"We need this from you."

Papa Brisson nodded to Kate McCannon across the table. "Do you approve of this?"

Kate McCannon lounged deep in her chair. Her stare held Papa Brisson hostage. One hand dangled over the back of her chair like a lure. Her other hand's fingernails drummed against the steamy coffee cup.

Brrrrink! brrrrink! brrrrink!

"Please, father," begged Chapan. "We wouldn't ask unless we were desperate."

Papa Brisson outhaled heavy. The candles flickered in his breath.

Kate McCannon *slurrrp!*ed the rest of her coffee. She set the empty cup down soft on a saucer and *tsahh!*ed. "Damn good coffee. I'll give you that, father."

Papa Brisson nodded subtle. He waved his sleeve for Jean-Baptiste to stand. "If you may, Jean-Baptiste: fetch Mademoiselle Eriksen the Soixante-Treize."

"Yes, father." Jean-Baptiste's chair clawed the floor. He skitted from the table and skipped up the stairs. His pointy heels echoed each step he took above us.

Jean-Baptiste bounded into the dining room with a Winchester Model 1873 repeating rifle aimed at the ceiling. The gun Jean-Baptiste held looked no different than Nimama's. Exact same model and everything. Only difference was Papa Brisson's Winchester got a different polish on it. No wear or tear neither.

"You need this more than us." Papa Brisson waved for Jean-Baptiste to give the gun to Nimama. He shook his handless sleeves in the air. "I have no use for the rector's gun."

Jean-Baptiste handed the rifle to Nimama. She thanked him and pointed the barrel out the window behind her. She pushed on the lever and opened the gun's action to peek for any bullets in the chamber. All clear, she *click!*ed the lever shut.

"Some alone time with Nikosis," said Nimama.

"Mes fils: to the kitchen." Papa Brisson waved his cassock sleeves upward. Him and the boys rose from their seats. "La famille Desjarlais needs to be together."

"Père Brisson." Kate McCannon replaced her hat on her head. She stuffed tobacco into her cheek. "Let this be the last we ever see each other."

"It is." Papa Brisson nodded subtle. "Rest assured."

Papa Brisson led Étienne and Jean-Baptiste into the kitchen. Nimama rested the rifle against the windowsill. Kate McCannon stood and waved for Chapan and Auntie to stand too. It was time for goodbyes. I slided off my chair and gave Chapan a big hug.

"We'll see you again soon." Chapan pecked my cheek and stepped aside so I could hug Auntie.

"Be good, sweet boy." Auntie ruffled my wily hair and pecked my cheek. I held her tight enough for Cousin too.

"Take good care of the Ghostkeepers," said Kate McCannon.

"We'll be fine. Find Cousin. Wyatt too."

"Gave you my word, okimâsis." Kate McCannon shook my hand firm. Then she waved for Auntie and Chapan to follow her into the foyer.

Nimama motioned for me to sit closer to her. I plopped myself on her thigh and wrapped my arms around her.

"Don't go anywhere alone with anyone. Okay? Promise me you'll be safe."

"I'll be fine—"

"*Promise me.*"

"I promise." I squeezed Nimama tight. Who knows next time I'll hug her. "Promise you'll find Cousin?"

"Promise." Nimama's heart hammered against me. She inhaled me with the dust on my clothes. Her tears dripped into my hair. "kisâkihitin nikosis."

"kisâkihitin nikâwiy."

CHAPTER 24

FATHER, HALLOWED BE THY NAME

SUNDAY, MAY 3, 1885.

Service was unlike any I ever been to before. Ain't never seen the church so lonesome. A few old people with their daughters and granddaughters sat near the stove. A couple sonless Nakoda and nehiyaw families sat there too. Even seen a young family of blondies at the back. Excepting me and the Ghostkeepers, the only other boy was a baby who suckled his maman's empty breast to quit his crying.

I sat in the front pew with Étienne to one side, Jean-

Baptiste the other. My clothes was in the laundry, so Étienne lent me his nicest white shirt. Even the collar was starchy. He also lent me a pair of pressed slacks and cotton suspenders. And his fancy new black vest too.

"Dear friends." Papa Brisson's voice rolled off the vaulted roof. "I spent all week preparing a sermon about dear Job. But yesterday changed things. Yesterday God welcomed more men into His kingdom following a bloody conflict at Cut Knife Hill. We must thank God for sparing Christian and Indian souls alike yesterday. Despite the bloodshed, may we show gratitude an historic massacre was averted from under His holy eyes by merciful Poundmaker.

"As well, we shall pray for one of our own. Georges Ducharme has joined his father in paradise. May God have mercy on his young soul. We must pray for his grieving mother.

"We shall pray for the grieving families of all God's children. Sons, brothers, and fathers will be laid to rest in the coming days. We shall pray Poundmaker and more of his people find salvation in Jesus Christ. May all Christian souls, Indian and European alike, be welcomed to His kingdom as brothers. And may there be gentleness and forgiveness for the lost.

"The worst is yet to come, friends. We've already been through so much. Our faith will be tested again. But we must endure. We have no choice."

AFTER SERVICE, ME, ÉTIENNE, AND JEAN-BAPTISTE TUGGED WEEDS OUT THE GARden. Marie the calico cat hopped around us, pawing after butterflies. A ladybug creeped around the leafy tops of the carrots. I reached my finger for her to cross. Her eeny-weeny legs tickled my fingerprint. I brung my finger to my face to see her better. Then she popped her wings out her shell and flew away.

Budding trees clapped in the breeze. Squirrels chirped. Geese honked. I missed Cousin more than ever. I missed how much that boy would do anything to make this quietness disappear. Then I wouldn't be alone with my dark thoughts.

ME AND THE BOYS PREPARED A NICE SUNDAY SUPPER. PERFECT MIX OF CRUNCHY, steamy, meaty, soupy. Étienne and Jean-Baptiste had tons of ingredients to cook with because the Church stocked Papa Brisson so good. I ain't done much cooking in my time. So my job was to toss the tomato and carrot salad and stir the goose stew. Étienne put his ear to his bread and knocked the crust. Jean-Baptiste smushed boiled peas and butter in a bowl with a wood spoon.

My second job was to set the table with fancy foodware: ceramic plates of a bazillion sizes with blue flowery patterns, forks and knives of different thicknesses and sliceynesses, glasses tall and short, bowls with tall lips and short swoops. So much just for eating.

I didn't know if Papa Brisson used cutlery when I got to his spot at the head of the table. So I dropped two forks, two knives, and two spoons in a pile beside his big plate. I put the bowls and glasses in a line in front of him so he could slurp his foods through some cow parsnip or something. I don't know. I didn't have no clue what I was doing. It was all so much.

I set the salad on the table and walked up the first few steps of the stairwell to peep onto the upper level. Papa Brisson sat at his desk at the top of the staircase. He used his forearms to clamp open a ledger. He trapped a drippy pen between his lips. "Papa Brisson?"

"Oui, mon fils." Papa Brisson spat the pen onto the ledger and closed it.

"C'est servi." I shot back down the stairs into the dining room.

Étienne brung over the bread platter and bowl of mushy peas. He set them in the centre of the table beside the pepper grinder, salt shaker, butter dish. Jean-Baptiste followed behind carrying the stew to the table. Étienne threw a folded cloth down as a trivet.

"A blessing, mes fils." Papa Brisson's ginormongous body passed through the door frame. He dragged his chair back with his forearms. He plopped onto the wool cushion. "What have we here?"

"Goose stew, mushy peas, tomato and carrot salad, and fresh bread." Jean-Baptiste pointed to each dish with his wood spoon. He dropped the spoon into the peas bowl, then took his seat beside Papa Brisson.

"This is quite the arrangement, Niko." Papa Brisson evaluated the sculpture of glassware, silverware, porcelainware in front of him and smiled. "Well then. Let us pray."

Papa Brisson set his elbows on the table and lifted his

forearms to be held. Étienne sat to one side of Papa Brisson and Jean-Baptiste to the other. Both covered Papa Brisson's wrists with their palms. I held Étienne's hand.

Papa Brisson and the boys bowed their heads in submission. Like chumps. The Lord ain't looking out for none of us no more. Why thank God if His damn plan is for me to get castrated by my own blood? I'm better off without Him. Chapan and Kate McCannon don't even believe in Him.

A real papa would protect me from Odin. Wouldn't he? Even Jesus had Joseph to be his papa on Earth to protect him. Is that why Campbell won't protect me? Ain't I good enough to be his son?

A man wearing a blue capote and Stetson hat appeared behind Papa Brisson. He stretched a barbed wire garrote between beaded gauntlets.

"*Papa Brisson!*"

The man wrapped the wire around Papa Brisson's throat. He planted his boot into the back of the chair and pulled on the garrote like reins on a race wagon. Wood spindles clambered on the floor. The man's hat tumbled off his head.

"*Father!*"

Me and the boys scrambled out our chairs. We shuffled on our butts and heels along the floor to the wall at the back of the dining room. What the hell was happening?

Barbs on the wire sliced through Papa Brisson's neck. Blood flooded his collar and rained onto his pendant. He slapped his empty cassock sleeves against his throat. His forearms sliced on the spikey wire around his neck. His phantom fingers dug under the barbed wire.

Papa Brisson turned blue. He stopped slicing his wrists on the wire.

The man unwhirled the garrote from around Papa Brisson's bloody neck. Papa Brisson's hulky body tipped. Cabinets rattled when Papa Brisson *thunk!*ed the floorboards. Breathless.

The man in the blue capote tossed the garrote onto the table. Tugged his beaded gauntlets and lobbed them by the garrote. His burn scarred fingers untied his sash and flipped open the breast of his capote. Dried blood stained the arm where Georges's bullet grazed him. Li P'chii sparkled in a holster.

Odin looks just like Cousin. Same smile. Handsome like Cousin too. Only difference is all Odin's wrinkles and their colouring. Odin's hair and scruffy moustache is orange and greyish like smoky fire. Skin pale as moon. But Cousin's dark like Auntie. Cousin and Odin got the same gold catlike eyes though. Eriksen Eyes.

If Odin was a half-breed boy, him and Cousin would've looked exact same. But Odin ain't no half-breed boy. Odin is a monster.

CHAPTER 25

YOU FUCKING MONSTER, I WANT YOUR BLOOD!

Blood puddled under Papa Brisson's cheek. Odin ripped Li P'chii out its holster. Our spines quivered against the back wall.

Odin directed us with the muzzle of the gun. He herded us out the rectory and across the boardwalk to the church. Three police horses was hitched out front. A few yards from the horses was two pintos pulling a police wagon with a jail cell in the rear.

"Open the door, dear Nikosis." We stood in front of the church. Odin pointed to the door handle with Li P'chii.

My heart battered inside my throat. I squeezed the door handle with both thumbs and bumped my shoulder against the door until it swung open. Odin directed us into the nave. His spurs rattled through the hollow church.

Inside was dark. Early evening sunlight beamed colourful blocks through stained glass windows. The only other light was the flames flickering in the stove in the centre of the aisle.

Wagner sat cross-kneed in a pew near the stove. His legs dangled in the aisle. Stained glass made his pale face glow purple. I recognized Winnie slung over his shoulder by her varnish.

San Luis sat next to Wagner. Bloody bandages covered half San Luis's face. His eye too. His skull was too swole to wear his helmet. He even still had red rope lines across his throat.

Behind them both stood Constable Vale with his snakey brown eyes and little eyelids.

Campbell stood next to Vale. He looked like shit in his tattered serge. He was unarmed. All the policemen excepting him had repeating rifles slung over their shoulders. Wagner and Vale carried sidearms too.

"Nikosis!"

Sitting on his butt with his wrists cuffed to the altar, Cousin yanked and yanked, trying to tear hisself free. His eyes glimmered gold like he found a wallet full of deeds.

"It's you it's you it's you!"

A younger boy cuffed to the altar beside Cousin beamed too.

I forgot all bad things in this world when I seen Cousin. I wanted to punch his arm for making me miss him so damn much. I wanted to tell him about the bunny-hop brawl and the Good and Broke Rods and the other kids I became friends with in the Pussy Posse and all the animals I got to meet. I wanted to tell him everything that happened while he been gone.

Guess we got all the time in the world now.

"Stay with me." Odin pressed the double barrels into my back. The gun metal chilled my bones through my vest. My bladder muscles couldn't hold my pee in no more. It felt warm and embarrassing on my lap.

"Hey!" chuckled Wagner. He bumped San Luis's elbow. "Son of a bitch gone and pissed himself!"

Odin lifted the gun away from my back to Wagner in the pew. He marched down the aisle. San Luis and Campbell and Vale scrambled out Odin's way. Wagner scrambled backwards along the pew.

"Say a fucking word about *any* of my dear babes . . ." Odin planted Li P'chii against Wagner's skull. ". . . and I will *torture* you. You hear me, you little wart on a whore's cunt? I'll make your slut mother wish she aborted you."

Smack!

Odin bumped the gun against Wagner's forehead.

"*Augh!*" screamed Wagner into his hands. "Jesus!"

Campbell and Vale stood froze with San Luis against the pew. Odin walked into the aisle. He brandished Li P'chii like a sword. He looked over his shoulder at Cousin and the younger boy cuffed to the altar.

"Corporal San Luis, Constable Palmer: bring Guillaume

and Wyatt back to the cell. Constable Vale: take the priest's boarders. I've got Nikosis."

Odin strutted toward me and Étienne and Jean-Baptiste tucked near the back beside the door. Odin's spurs rattled against the wood. He hooked his eyes into me.

My skin tingled from my forearms to my forehead. I slowed my breathing. Calmed my heart from tackling its way out my chest.

"You have nîwa's and nitânis's eyes, dear nikosis." Odin bent to be level with me. He extended his hand for me to shake. It looked like it'd once been tarred, feathered, flamed. "How I've longed to meet you, my dear son."

dear nikosis

my dear son

Odin shattered the glass I see fatherhood through. The sandy illusion slipped through my fingers. Papa. Grandpapa. How could I not know?

I exist because Odin is a monster.

I should've been there for Nimama. I should've protected her. I should've stopped Odin before he could molest her. Even if it means I'd never be born.

But I was born. Now I have a duty.

ᑭᑯᓯᐢ

God, answer me one prayer: take me to Nimama's childhood. To when Odin hurt her. Take me so I can kiss her wounds. So I can promise her I'm coming to make everything okay. So I can tell her, "kisâkihitin, Nimama. I can't wait to be kikosis."

Odin dragged me by my shirt collar and flung open the church door. Early-evening sunlight stunned my eyes as we emerged from the dark church. Odin lugged me through the dirt to the wagon. He stormed to the rear, unlocked the door, and tossed me into the cell in the back. My knees bonked the floorboards. A point blanket and a milk pail was already inside.

I wrapped my fingers around two bars and pulled my face into the gap to watch Étienne and Jean-Baptiste tremble out the church with their hands above their heads. Tears ran down their faces. Vale aimed his rifle at the boys' backs. Even with the gun on his shoulder, he looked scared. Shaky. Odin opened the cell door for Étienne and Jean-Baptiste to crawl inside.

Campbell emerged from the church carrying Wyatt in his arms. Wyatt cried into Campbell's shoulder. Campbell consoled him as they approached the cell. "Everything's going to be okay, nikosis."

Odin opened the cell door. Campbell carried Wyatt inside and set him down. Wyatt begged for Campbell not to leave him.

"*Nipapa! No! Please!*"

My heart broke for Wyatt. He looked just like Campbell must've when he was eight. Cropped, curly black hair. Plaid shirt. Dusty trousers. Tall moccasins laced up his shins. Beaded with a cross surrounded by wildflowers. Beautiful gifts from his kokum. I could tell.

For Campbell, everything's about Wyatt.

But for Odin, it's me and Cousin. Nimama and Auntie too.

Difference is we ain't safe with Odin. Not like Wyatt with his papa.

"You'll see me in the morning." Campbell held Wyatt's cuffed hands. He fought tears of his own. "We'll be okay."

The church doors *crash!*ed open. Planks slammed. Stained glass windows rattled.

"Stop fussing, you fucking savage!" San Luis yanked Cousin out the church by the handcuffs. Cousin whipped his skinny body like a fish on the end of a fishing line. San Luis grappled him in the church door frame.

San Luis tossed Cousin onto the trail. Cousin's shirt was half tore off, dangling only by a single sleeve trapped on his wrist. He scuttled his butt along the dirt.

Huuuuuck! Thpew!

Cousin spat gob onto San Luis's bandaged face. "Ha! Now you look pretty!"

"You son of a bitch!" San Luis's fangs flashed red sunlight. He pulled his blade out his belt. "I'll cut your face like we cut your slut mother's!"

"Stop him!" barked Odin. He smacked Vale's ribcage and galloped off toward San Luis.

CRACK!

Vale pointed his rifle's barrel skyward. Horses tethered to the post kicked their legs crazyful. Our wagon jostled up-and-down like the horses driving couldn't decide to run left, right, back, or forward. Campbell fell out the cell through the open door.

Vale clambered up the ladder to the driver's seat. He plopped on the bench and tugged the reins and called for the horses to calm before they raced to Nowhereville with us in the back. I squeezed the metal bars to balance myself the best the rocking wagon would let me.

Odin sprinted toward San Luis.

Near the church, San Luis grabbed Cousin by the handcuffs. Cousin mashed his moccasins against San Luis's shins.

Odin bounded through the dust to San Luis. He raised Li P'chii high like a hatchet.

Thwack!

Odin clipped San Luis across his chin. San Luis's jaw slopped sideways. He dropped Cousin and collapsed to his belly. The knife flipped in the air before clanging the trail.

Cousin scuttled away. San Luis clawed hisself toward the knife. He dragged his stomach against the trail, drooling blood.

Odin marched beside him. He booted San Luis's exposed jaw. San Luis's head whipped like leather.

"You mustn't have understood what I said to poor Sergeant Wagner . . ." Odin's long, sunsetting shadow blanketed San Luis. Odin stepped over him like an A-frame. He gripped the shoulder of San Luis's serge and threw him to his back.

San Luis gurgled. His broke jaw hung open like a treasure chest.

"Say *any*thing about *any* of my dear babes . . ."

Clllllick!

Odin lowered the gun into San Luis's gaping mouth.

BOOM!

San Luis lay dead in the road. The upper half of his head splattered on the dirt.

Our horses shook the wagon. I fell flat on my back and banged my skull. Vale tugged the reins with all his might until the horses was calm.

Odin dragged Cousin by the handcuffs all the way to the cell. Cousin didn't put up no fight. San Luis's blood streaked across Odin's open blue capote. Odin holstered Li P'chii and opened the cell door. He tossed Cousin inside and keyed the lock.

"Move." Odin marched to the ladder at the driver's seat of the wagon. Vale shuffled off the bench and joined Campbell loitering on the trail.

"Constable Palmer: collect my hat and gauntlets from the rectory. They're in the dining room with the father. When you're done, do like Wagner did to la bibliothèque and burn this all down. A tragedy the father shall die in a horrific fire like that poor old Desjarlais hag."

I bit my tongue. Odin had no idea about Chapan. Police lied to him about the fire.

"As for you, Constable Vale: check on poor Sergeant Wagner. I fear I may have knocked too much sense into him. When he comes to, both of you can assist Constable Palmer burning this down. I expect the three of you at camp before sunrise. Don't forget my hat and gauntlets."

Campbell and Vale nodded sheepishful up at Odin. Wyatt scrambled across the cell and rammed his hand through the bars. He reached with all his might for Campbell.

"*Nipapa! Don't leave! Please!*"

Campbell kissed his fingertips and touched Wyatt's outstretched hand. He looked fragile through his dammed eyes. "I'll see you in the morning, son."

Odin *whipp!*ed the reins. We rumbled forward. The wagon bounced loud on the trail.

A long time passed. It was getting dark. Just the brightest stars shined above. All five of us shared the ginormongous point blanket. Étienne and Wyatt fell asleep next to each other. Jean-Baptiste rested his eyes too.

"How you doing?" I asked Cousin.

He blinked slow. Breathed deep. Outhaled purposeful.

in . . . out . . . in. . . .

"Buffalo hunters ain't afraid of nothing." Cousin smacked his chest. Like a real buffalo hunter. "I feel it in my blood."

I peeked at Odin driving above us. "You feel him in our blood?"

Cousin peeked at Odin too. He looked back at me and smacked his chest again. "Real people. Me and you. Remember?"

"Yeah." I let them words sink into me. He was right. "Real people."

CHAPTER 26

BUFFALO HUNTERS

MONDAY, MAY 4, 1885. MIDDLE OF NOWHERE, DISTRICT OF SASKATCHEWAN.

We was in an old burn scar in the middle of nowhere. Tents and structures of Odin's camp was on fire. The forest around us burned too. A red sunrise raged over the treetops. Wagner and Vale threw handfuls of paperwork into a flaming barrel in the centre of camp. Stitches poked out Wagner's bruisy and swole forehead.

Us five boys all lay on our backs in the middle of the floor of the wagoncell. Our bodies reached wall-to-wall, covered by the ginormongous blanket.

"Constable Palmer: my hat and gauntlets."

Campbell mounted his horse and trotted up to Odin in the driver's seat of the wagon. Campbell tossed Odin his hat and gauntlets. He eyed the scars that covered Odin's hands while he slipped them into his green, blue, white, pink flowery beaded mitts.

"Dear nîwa made me these gauntlets. She taught me to survive the North-West. During the Sioux Wars, dear nîwa and I had a ranch in Dakota Territory. Trading was dangerous then. My trips were long. My girls were young. I came home late one evening. I crawled into bed with dear nîwa without even taking off my boots.

"Couldn't've slept more than a couple hours when my youngest shook me awake. 'Nipapa! The house is on fire!' The door was boarded from the outside." Odin removed one gauntlet, flexed his fist so the knuckles cracked, then slipped his hand back inside. "nîwa left us to burn inside. But I saved my girls.

"I had land. I had livestock. I had family. I had everything." Odin glared at us over his shoulder. His eyes shuffled from me to Cousin. "I'm entitled to what's left of mine. Aren't I?"

"What about Wyatt?"

Silence followed. Wyatt sniffled into the blanket and left a snotty streak where he rubbed his nose. Campbell quivered under Odin's heavy glare.

Smoke slugged through the air. The horses shook their heads and jangled their reins.

Twwwweeeeeeeeeeeeeeeeeeeeeeoooooooooooooooow-weeeeeeeeeeeeeeeet!

I recognized that whistle. I whipped the blanket off and

jutted my face between the cell bars. Across the burn scar I spotted the figure of a ghost-like rider in the fiery bushes.

"Wagner, Vale: investigate." Odin directed the policemen to cross the burn scar and meet whoever approached. "You too, Palmer."

The three men loped across the smoldering camp to meet the rider at the edge of the burn scar. Wagner drew Winnie on the rider. Vale mounted his rifle to his shoulder too.

"I ain't armed." The rider raised her hands above her head. Her and her horse cast a long silhouette across the burn scar. "I just came to make chit-chat."

"It's Kate McCannon!" called Wagner to Odin.

"Bring her over."

The policemen escorted Kate McCannon across the smoky burn scar toward us and Odin. The closer she got, the clearer I could see the black beads and embroidery on her jacket.

"Stop there." Odin extended his hand to halt them and their horses fifteen feet from the wagon. He pulled each of his gauntlets off and set them on his lap. Apocalypse was saddled and painted like a warhorse—red handprint on her shoulder, yellow stripes on her nose, black circles around her eyes and nostrils, blue lightning bolts on her legs, white hail marks on her hindquarters, a feather in her mane.

Kate McCannon dismounted and walked to the foot of the driver's seat. The shadow cast by the brim of her hat covered her face. She didn't wear her bandolier or gun belt with shotgun shells and holsters. Instead she sported a normal leather belt with a flashy Civil War buckle.

Odin looked down at her like she was shallow water at

the bottom of a cliff. He tucked the breast of the capote behind the grip of Li P'chii.

"You're in quite some trouble with the law, Kate McCannon. This gun of yours has killed two Mounted Policemen point blank. And now you're a suspect in two fatal arson attacks. A jury of your 'peers' will hang you."

"Let them. I came to talk."

"No. You came to take my boys from me."

Kate McCannon spat into the dirt. She tucked her thumbs under her Union buckle.

"I'm not afraid to kill you." Odin plucked Li P'chii out its holster. He needled his finger into the trigger guard and *click!*ed a hammer.

"Like you said: that double barrel's already killed *two* policemen." Kate McCannon waved to the repeating rifles on the policemen's shoulders and the Enfield revolvers in their holsters. "I know you haven't reloaded. None of your boys got shotguns. Why would you have shells?"

Odin's eyes flashed like muzzles. He lifted his back off the cell and uncrossed his knees.

"There's fire all around us." Kate McCannon whirled her hand above her head. "The trail in front of you leads to the main road along the Beaver River. But if my people hear so much as one gunshot, they'll ambush you on that trail if they don't storm up it.

"Leave the kids with me and take off. Send these fine men of the law back to the fort while they're still masculated."

"You said you were alone," said Odin.

"I said I was unarmed. I ain't never said nothing about being alone."

Odin sat quiet on the bench. Smoke haunted the burn scar from all edges.

The wagon horses whipped their shoulders. Their reins and bridles clanged. They neighed smoky air.

"If you leave now, you got a half-hour to get away scot-free." Kate McCannon peeped her watch before tucking it back inside her pocket. "Leave the boys behind. I promise you: no one's coming after you if we have our boys back.

"Odin, we know our land. You should leave it."

"Let's bring her to the outpost." Wagner sat giddy in his saddle. He reeled his neck around his shoulders. "Hear she ain't got a gag reflex."

Kate McCannon clenched her fists. She breathed angry and spat into the dirt.

Vale leaned over Apocalypse beside him. He unstrapped a lariat from the horn, careful not to spook Apocalypse while he tugged on the buckles.

"You're under arrest, *bitch*."

Vale lassoed Kate McCannon's torso. The loop pinned her arms to sides and clung taut. With his horse's help, he pulled the rope tight enough to drag her off her feet.

"*Kate McCannon!*" I stretched my hand through the cell bars.

Wagner hopped off his horse. Kate McCannon squirmed at the end of Vale's lariat. Wagner planted his knee into her back and hogtied her hands and feet like a runaway calf.

"Get the hell out of here. Cut the boys and get their bounties. And send us our bit after you're paid," Wagner hissed to Odin. "Forget this whore. She'll hang after she sees a judge."

"Fuck you!" shouted Kate McCannon. Wagner smushed

her face into the soggy earth. The flaming camp around them cackled.

No one came flooding up the trail to Kate McCannon's rescue. It was hopeless.

"Constable Palmer, follow behind us. Constable Vale, Sergeant Wagner: I'll see you're paid discreetly soon. May we next cross paths in Hell. *Yup!*"

Whiptch!

Odin lashed the reins. The wagon kicked forward. I couldn't see Campbell behind us through the smoke. The rumbling wagon wheels and the thundering hooves was so loud, I couldn't hear nothing. Not even my dark thoughts.

CHAPTER 27

ELLES BRÛLENT DU BOIS

Crack!

(…crack…crack…crack…)

"Easy!" Odin tugged the reins. The horses slowed to a trot. There wasn't supposed to be no gunshots. Odin listened for more echoes behind us.

Crack!

(…crack…crack…crack…)

I looked out the back of the wagon. Trail dust disappeared into smoke behind Campbell following us. Something bad was going down in that burn scar.

Jean-Baptiste petted Étienne's back while he wept into

the blanket. Wyatt squinted to see his papa trotting through the smoke. Cousin stared longingful into the forest.

Crack!

(...crack...crack...crack...)

Crack!

(...crack...crack...crack...)

Crack!

(...crack...crack...crack...)

"Come on, nitôtemak!" Odin lashed the reins. The horses speeded into a gallop. Echoes grew fainter each step. We bumped along the root-riddled trail.

The closer we rode to the river, the thicker the smoke grew. Each cloud got blacker than the last. Odin whipped all his arm strength down the length of the reins against the horses. Their lungs wilted in the smoke.

Crack!

(...crack...crack...crack...)

Crack!

(...crack...crack...)

Crack! Crack!

Crackcrackcrack!

Crack! Crack!

Crack-crack-crack!

Crackcrackcrack-crack-crack!

Crackcrackcrackcrack!

Crack!

Crack! Crack! Crack!

Crack-crack-crack-crack!

Crack! Crack!

Crack!

Crack! Crack!

Crack!

(... crack ... crack ... crack ...)

(... crack ... crack ...)

(... crack ...)

(... crack ...)

(... crack ...)

"Whoooa!"

The river appeared at the end of the trail. Odin stomped both his boots onto the dashboard and heaved on the reins. His hat flew off like a ladybug.

The horses skidded into the T-intersection where the trail met the main road alongside the river. They dug their hooves into the trail. Their butts slided along the dirt. The wagon drifted sideways. As the wagon swung, Cousin and Wyatt and Étienne and Jean-Baptiste slided into my corner and pinned me to the bottom of the pile. We fishtailed toward the riverbank.

"Ahhhhhhhhh!"

Time slowed to a stop. The wagon tilted sideways. Leaned. Two wheels.

Bonk! bonk! bonk! CRACK!

One of the wheels flew off when the wagon slammed down. The wagon crumpled to the rear corner. We catapulted against the cell bars. Étienne cut his head on the flailing pail. He pressed the blanket around his wound to stop the bleeding.

Odin flew off the bench onto the trail beneath him. He ripped off his gauntlets and whipped them at the dirt. His middle finger bent sideways past his pinky. Odin wrapped his other fist around his finger. He pushed.

Crick!

"Urrrrgh . . ." Odin moaned. He leaned back relievingful on the grass.

The road was pinned on one side by the thirsty Beaver River and thick brush to the other. The main road was just wide enough for two wagons to pass without crashing.

"Boys!" We heard Campbell before we seen him. He rode up beside the wagon with wide eyes. Anxious to see his son. "Wyatt! Are you all right?"

Wyatt waved at Campbell while his other hand nursed his forehead. "I'm okay."

"How're the rest of you, boys?"

"Fine," I said. Étienne and Jean-Baptiste turned their backs to Campbell.

Campbell rode toward Odin. "What about you? You all right?"

Odin lifted hisself to his feet. He brushed dead leaves and ash off his capote. "I'm fine."

"What're we going to do about the wagon?"

Odin eyed the two horses leaning crooked with the broke wagon pulling them sideways while putting his gauntlets back on his hands. Then he eyed the five of us in the cell. "There aren't enough horses. I can't afford to abandon the orphans."

"Afford?" Campbell swung off his horse and hitched him to a wagoncell bar. "What the hell does that mean?"

Odin grabbed Campbell by his collar and tossed him onto his ass. Odin picked Campbell up by his loose serge. Odin drew his fist across his chest and socked Campbell's mouth with his beaded gauntlet.

PUNCH!

Beads exploded off Odin's gauntlet. Campbell rolled to

his side and wiped blood and beads off his lip. Odin loomed over Campbell.

"I'll geld you too if I have to."

"Nipapa!" Wyatt rammed his arms through the bars and cried for Campbell.

Clop-clop! clop-clop! clop-clop!

Loping down the trail from the burn scar, Vale's hot red serge cut through the smoke like a candle flame. He rode a painted filly pale as the smoke around her.

"Odin! Campbell!"

Vale tugged Apocalypse's reins and hopped off her black Mexican roping saddle. His serge was ripped and muddy. Nose broke and bloody. His helmet was missing. Rifle too. Just the revolver in his holster was in place.

"What the hell happened back there?" Odin hustled to meet Vale. Campbell nursed his split lip in the background.

"They ambushed us!" Vale panted like a dog. "Came out the fucking woodwork!"

"Where's Wagner?"

"I don't know! You don't know what they tried to do to me!"

Odin shook his head. He grabbed Apocalypse's reins and hitched her to the wagoncell beside Campbell's horse. He eyed Vale like meat for sale. "Where's your rifle?"

"Fucking harlots stole it!"

"What did I say about insulting my family?" Odin pulled Li P'chii out his holster. He cocked a hammer aggressive and aimed square at Vale's head. "Do you *really* think I was stupid enough not to reload this gun?"

Vale threw his shaky hands up in surrender. Blood leaked out his nostril. "No, sir."

"Then show some respect!"

Odin raised Li P'chii high overhead. He feigned like he was going to tomahawk Vale. Vale whimpered and flinched. Odin laughed. He uncocked and reholstered the gun.

"Come here, Constable Palmer. I need your help." Odin pulled a blade out a sheath on his ankle. He approached Campbell and handed him the knife. "We're in luck. Go cut free the horses. All of the boys are coming with us.

"Constable Vale: follow me." Odin sauntered to the rear of the wagoncell. Vale puttered behind. Odin keyed the lock and opened the door. "Get Guillaume."

Vale climbed into the cell. He marched to Cousin.

"Get your hands off me!"

Vale swatted Cousin's legs. He crawled on top of Cousin's chest and smushed his face against the floorboards. He grabbed Cousin by the handcuffs and pinned Cousin's wrists over his head. Cousin wriggled like a jackfish. Vale wanted Cousin to tire hisself out. But Cousin wouldn't stop kicking.

Vale pulled his revolver out his holster and *clllllick!*ed the hammer. He pressed the barrel tight against Cousin's temple.

Cousin froze still. Threw his hands up. Vale grabbed him by the cuffs and dragged him out the cell. Cousin's shirt dangled from a single sleeve. Vale tore Cousin's ripped shirt off his wrist. Odin cuffed him outside next to the horses. Cousin shivered like he'd chatter his teeth to dust. Vale reholstered his revolver.

Odin gave his gauntlets to Vale and entered the cell. He stomped toward me. I held my knees tight against my chest and moused into the corner. Wyatt and Étienne and Jean-Baptiste scrambled away.

Odin grabbed my ankles and yanked me straight. He sat on my outstretched knees.

"Be still." Odin gathered both my wrists with one of his hands and pinned them over my head to the wagon floor. His hand tugged at my suspenders. He fiddled with the clasps.

"Let me go!" I screamed. I tried throwing him off and kicking him away.

My suspenders unwhirled around my shoulders. The leather drooped from Odin's hand like a dead snake. He tied my wrists together with the suspenders and lugged me out the cell toward Apocalypse. He lifted me into her saddle and dallied the suspenders on my wrists around the horn. Then he took his gauntlets back from Vale.

Campbell came out from in front of the wagon towing two pintos, freed from their yokes and harnesses with only their bridles. Him and Vale hitched the horses with the others to the cell. Wyatt and Étienne and Jean-Baptiste tucked the blanket to their noses. I looked down Apocalypse's side at Cousin shivering below.

"Constable Vale, get Guillaume and yourself a horse. I'm taking Apocalypse."

Odin uncuffed Cousin from the cell and hoisted him onto one of the bareback pintos. Then Vale unhitched the horse from the cell and hopped on behind Cousin. They stepped aside and waited.

"Come here, Constable Palmer." Odin pointed at Wyatt in the cell. "Get your son."

Campbell nodded shameful. He crawled into the cell and squatted at the door. He waved for Wyatt to approach. Wyatt ran fast and hugged him.

"Nipapa!"

"We're going to be okay, nikosis."

Campbell held Wyatt tight. Then they spun for the door.

I hung my head. I still wore Étienne's shoes. Them beaded moccasins I love so much got to be lost in the fire at the rectory.

There ain't nothing I can do. Ain't no dodging my God-given destiny. I did my best.

Campbell led Wyatt out the cell. He helped Wyatt into the saddle of his horse hitched beside me and Apocalypse.

"Hey, Guillaume's shivering here." Vale nodded to Cousin in his lap. "Odin!"

Odin ignored Vale.

"I said Guillau—"

"I heard you the first time!" barked Odin. He untied his sash and shook off his capote. He carried it in his angry hands for Vale. He threw his capote into Vale's face and walked away. The sash lay on the muddy trail. "Make him wear this."

Odin unhitched Apocalypse from the wagon and jammed his boot into the stirrup. He swung onto the saddle. Odin took up all the good space like Nimama used to when we rode Pony together.

We waited for Campbell. In front of Vale, Cousin slipped into Odin's blue, blood-stained capote. Wyatt cried as he waited for his papa to join him.

"The orphans, Constable Palmer."

Campbell glared at Odin and approached Apocalypse. He unbuckled one of Kate McCannon's lariats from the saddle and walked toward the second wagon horse hitched to the cell. Campbell cut her reins and bridle. Then he slipped the loop of the lariat over the horse's head and led her to the rear. Étienne and Jean-Baptiste waited anxious inside.

"Étienne, Jean-Baptiste: get on the horse."

Étienne and Jean-Baptiste both nodded fearful. They scurried out the cell. Étienne wrapped the blanket around his shoulders.

Campbell interlocked his fingers and made a step ladder for Jean-Baptiste and Étienne to mount the horse. Étienne sat behind Jean-Baptiste and wrapped his arms around his older brother's waist. Jean-Baptiste held the horse's mane. Campbell handled the end of the lariat so he could lead them from his own horse.

At last, Campbell unhitched his horse from the cell and mounted behind Wyatt. Odin patted Apocalypse soft and lovingful. Campbell and Vale nodded.

"Let's go!"

The four horses loped down the road. Me and Odin was at the front. Cousin and Vale followed next. Wyatt and Campbell rode behind them, leading Étienne and Jean-Baptiste's horse at the back.

We turned a bend in the trail. Odin pulled the reins to slow Apocalypse. Twenty yards away, a bunch of logs was laid deliberate across the trail. They raged fire. The tallest flames flickered higher than the horses stood.

"It's a fucking trap," said Vale. "We have to turn around."

We spun our horses. A ginormongous pine tree tipped slow onto the trail behind us. Its needles raged fire.

Creeeeeeeeaak!

Whoosh!

The flaming tree collapsed across the trail. Sparks and ash exploded everywhere.

Étienne and Jean-Baptiste's horse reared high. Batted the air with her hooves. The boys slided off her back and *thudd!*ed the ground. The riderless horse ran up the deer path in front of us into the bush terrified, dragging her rope behind her. We was pinned between the flaming barricade and tree and the river behind us.

Out the corner my eye, I spotted Chapan scuttle through the burning bushes. She held a buffalo horn of gunpowder, and another full of fire.

"I thought Wagner burned the witch!"

Odin whipped Li P'chii out the holster. He cocked the hammers and pulled the triggers.

The gun *click!*ed empty in his hand. Twice.

"Fuck!" Odin hurled the useless gun at Campbell. Campbell ducked. Li P'chii sailed past Campbell and Wyatt and slammed into Vale's face before tumbling onto the ground.

A deep gash split into Vale's skin. He wiped his cheek. His eyes popped when he seen all the blood on the back of his hand. "You son of a bitch."

Vale plucked his revolver out his holster and aimed at me and Odin. His thumb cocked the hammer. Cousin plugged his ears and twisted away. Odin shoved me against Apocalypse's neck and shielded me from the gun.

Click!

Click!

The hammer of Vale's revolver slapped spent casings in the cylinder.

Click! click! click! click!

"Motherfucker!" Vale threw his gun at Odin. It swooshed over us and skidded along the trail until it stopped at the base of the flaming barricade pinning the road.

Then a revolvered figure rode up behind the fiery barricade wearing Odin's hat. Her silhouette flashed through the flames.

"I want my son!"

Auntie aimed her revolver at the sky.

CRACK!

The horses reared high. Even Apocalypse startled. Campbell and Vale and Odin tugged the reins to settle them. Étienne and Jean-Baptiste ran into the bush after Chapan.

"Follow me!" Campbell yelled to Vale. They zipped up the deer path Étienne and Jean-Baptiste's horse escaped to. Campbell and Wyatt led the way with Vale and Cousin racing behind him. The horses snaked around bushes and thistles. They hurdled over fallen trees and growth-stunted bushes.

"Come back here!" Odin kicked Apocalypse and chased into the bush after them.

We galloped up the path. I spotted someone hiding in the smoke way up in a tree canopy ahead. Kate McCannon waited overhead on a thick branch. Her bark-colour skin and black and leather clothes camouflaged with trees and the smoke around her. She whirled a lariat anchored to the branch she sat on.

Campbell and Wyatt raced safe under her.

Behind them, Cousin bounced in Vale's lap. Vale focused on Campbell and Wyatt and the path ahead.

"Guille! Duck!"

Kate McCannon whipped the lariat soon as Vale rode beneath her. Cousin grabbed his horse's mane and forced his whole body onto its neck. Kate McCannon rung the rope around Vale's throat, locking him in place.

Vale slided off the horse's rump. He dangled like a grandfather clock. His tongue flapped around his lips. His legs thrashed air. His face shined red.

Gluck! gluck!

"There's a burn scar ahead!" shouted Kate McCannon. She pointed up the path. "Go!"

Cousin heeled his moccasins into his horse. The tail of his blue capote fluttered in the smoke. He raced behind Campbell and Wyatt for the burn scar.

"We got you, Niko!" hollered Kate McCannon from the treetops.

We dodged Vale's swinging body. The bloody sun rose in front of us. Apocalypse wheezed. Odin spurred her hard.

"Come on, sweetheart!"

Twenty-odd yards ahead, Cousin veered out of sight when he reached the opening of the burn scar behind Campbell and Wyatt.

Odin slowed Apocalypse to a walk. We entered the ginormongousest burn scar I ever seen. A lonesome spruce stood tall in the centre. The rising sun cast hazy silhouettes of four rifled riders lined up facing us to one side of the spruce tree. Campbell and Wyatt and Cousin rode slow toward them.

"Everything's going to be okay, Niko," said the rider closest to the tree. "We got you."

"Nimama! Nimama!"

I exploded into tears. I tried tearing my hands from the saddle horn to reach for her. Not even God could stop her.

Nimama sucked her cigarette. Her freckles glowed in the warm tobacco light.

Campbell and Wyatt and Cousin joined the four riders lined up at the tree. With Cousin on the outside as the last rider, they stopped next to Laurent Callahoo.

Laurent rode his beloved Chickadee looking fine as the night I stole him. Laurent rested his repeating rifle across his lap.

Hélène Ducharme rode beside Laurent. A smoky pipe hung from her mouth. Papa Brisson's repeating rifle flickered morning firelight in her hands.

Mathilde Little Bull rode next to Hélène. She held Constable Vale's stole rifle.

Nimama rode beside Mathilde nearest the spruce tree. She rested Winnie on her thigh, barrel skyward.

Roped to the trunk of the spruce sat Wagner. Wagner's trousers was tugged to his boots. His revolver was stole from his holster too. The loop of the lariat on Nimama's saddle horn was laced around Wagner's private parts. Pinger and such included.

"Sara, sweetheart," cooed Odin. "You look well. If a tad slender."

"Odin! Stop!" Wagner's body was roped tight to the trunk of spruce. His boots scuttled the dirt, whipping dust. "This has to end!"

Nimama kicked Pony forward. She ambled a few steps. The coil in the lariat between Nimama and Wagner stretched. His pinger turned ghost white. The lariat was damn near taut.

Hooves clambered the path behind us. I turned to see Auntie lope into the burn scar with her revolver. Behind Auntie rode Bella Gervais with Étienne sitting in the front of her saddle; Madame Morin rode in with Jean-Baptiste gripping her waist from behind. Narcisse Little Bull arrived last riding the boys' runaway pinto with Odin's sash tied around his waist. A polished Enfield revolver shined in his grip. Bella, Madame Morin, and Narcisse sealed the entry to the burn scar.

"Guille!" screamed Auntie when she seen Cousin. She

kicked her heels into Viking. His hooves flung ash. He raced to take Auntie to her boy. Auntie yanked Viking's reins and glided next to Cousin. Viking smushed his barrel tight against Cousin's pinto. Auntie leaned far over Viking to pour herself over her son. "Mon fils! My sweet, sweet boy."

"Maman!" Cousin cried into Auntie's shoulder. She pecked her lips all over his scalp. She was alive again. "Tu m'as manqué!"

Odin squeezed my arm and scoffed at Auntie and Cousin. His eyes inspected everyone like he kept tally of visitors at his own wake.

"Everything's going to be okay, Niko." Nimama smothered her cigarette against her saddle horn. She dropped the butt in her jacket pocket and grabbed Winnie with both hands. "We got you."

"You know, Sara, *I* bought that rifle for dear kohkôm." Odin tugged Apocalypse's reins. He squeezed me. "I'm entitled to what's mine. Aren't I?"

Click-click!

Nimama cocked the repeater. A cold bullet popped out the ejector.

Odin outhaled heavy against my neck.

"Ponygirl." Nimama nudged Pony forward.

"No! No!" The rope between Nimama and Wagner tightened. Wagner's bits tore slow off his crotch. Blood spilled between his thighs like he miscarried. *"Mama!"*

Odin waited.

"You'll never take my dear boys from me, nitânisak! *Heeyah!*"

Odin spurred Apocalypse. We galloped to cross the burn

scar. There was no way out. I squeezed the saddle horn. My body flopped like a fish.

"Go!" Nimama shouted. She pointed the rifle skyward.

CRACK!

Wagner screamed his lungs dry. Smoke oozed into the meadow from all sides.

Odin hammered Apocalypse. The Pussy Posse rushed behind us. Horse hooves pounded Maman Earth louder and louder, closer and closer.

Parrup! parrup! parrup! parrup!

"Come on, sweetheart!" Odin lashed Apocalypse's reins. Spurred her belly. My way-too-long hairs flapped against Odin's chin.

"Yup!" Nimama galloped beside us. She cocked the gun lever.

Click-click!

A smoking shell leaped out the ejector. It landed on my lap.

Nimama mounted Winnie against her shoulder. She barrelled down at Odin like she was the buffalo hunter and Odin her prey.

"Niko! Duck!"

I grabbed the saddle horn and pulled myself forward. I squished my face against Apocalypse's neck. Even scrunched my pinger into the horn. Apocalypse raced for hellfire ahead. Her pale mane tickled my nose.

CRACK!

APPENDIX

CHRONOLOGY OF MAJOR EVENTS

Fall 1869 to December 8, 1869	Louis Riel forms provisional government to establish Métis land rights in Red River, initiating uprising
Late August 1870	Canadian forces arrive in Red River, ending uprising
1870s and early 1880s	Métis communities grow throughout Northern Plains following exodus of some Métis from Red River
1884 to mid-March 1885	Riel forms provisional government in Batoche to establish Indigenous land and food rights in North-West
March 26, 1885	Métis victory at Battle of Duck Lake, initiating war
March 30, 1885	nehiyaw siege of Fort Battleford
April 2, 1885	Mass murder at Frog Lake by hungry nehiyaw dissidents
April 17, 1885	nehiyaw seizure of Fort Pitt
April 24, 1885	Métis victory at Battle of Tourond's Coulee/ Fish Creek
May 2, 1885	nehiyaw victory at Battle of Cut Knife Hill
May 9–12, 1885	Métis loss at Battle of Batoche
May 15, 1885	Louis Riel surrenders to NWMP
May 26, 1885	Poundmaker surrenders to NWMP

May 28, 1885	nehiyaw victory at Battle of Frenchman Butte
June 3, 1885	nehiyaw loss at Battle of Loon Lake
July 2, 1885	Big Bear surrenders to NWMP, ending war
November 16, 1885	Crown hangs Louis Riel in Regina
November 27, 1885	Crown mass hangs eight First Nations men at Fort Battleford

SELECT CREE TRANSLATIONS

RELATIONS

nikosis. My son.

nitânis. My daughter.

nikâwiy. My mother.

nikâwis. My aunt.

nisîmis. My younger sibling.

nimis. My older sibling.

nohkôm. My grandmother.

nicâpân. My great-grandparent.

nîwa. My wife.

ninâpem. My husband.

nitôtem. My friend.

kokum. [diminutive] Grandma.

chapan. [diminutive] Great-grandma.

PEOPLES

nehiyaw. Cree.

PERSONS

okimâw. Leader.

iskwew. Woman.

nâpew. Man.

PREFIXES

ni- my

ki- your

SUFFIXES

-ak plural

-is [diminutive] little

NOTES ON LANGUAGE

Treat Them as Buffalo uses *half-breed* and *Métis* to refer to contemporary citizens of the Métis Nation. The Métis are a unique

Indigenous people (such as Native Hawaiians or Inuit) who trace their Indigeneity to mixed-race communities in the historical Red River Colony during the North American fur trade, and whose distinct culture persists thereafter across the Northern Plains to the present day. In this sense, the terms *half-breed* and *Métis* do not accurately describe a Métis person's individual parentage. Rather, *half-breed* and *Métis* describe ancestors who belonged to these mixed-race communities of the Red River Colony. In *Treat Them as Buffalo, half-breed* and *Métis* are ethnic identifiers. They are not racial descriptors.

Although *half-breed* was an acceptable English translation for Métis in 1885 when *Treat Them as Buffalo* takes place, *half-breed* is now considered derogatory outside most contexts. Its presence and the presence of other terms in *Treat Them as Buffalo* are not necessarily endorsements by the author.

All French, Cree, Michif, and other translations and spellings are the author's own.

TREAT THEM AS BUFFALO ON SPOTIFY AND REDDIT

Playlists on Spotify: Treat Them as Buffalo

Connect on Reddit: r/TreatThemAsBuffalo

Playlists and subreddit created but not moderated by the author.

ACKNOWLEDGEMENTS

Sara Desjarlais and John Palmer. *Treat Them as Buffalo* is for you.

My mom, Wendy, who trusted me, took good care of me, believed in me when I needed believing. Thanks for everything. Love you, nikâwiy.

My dad, Terry, who was the father all kids deserve. Miss you, Rocket Man. I'll make you proud.

My MA supervisors, Keavy Martin and Marilyn Dumont, who trusted me to break ground. Thanks for believing in me.

My agent, Samantha Haywood, and her associates at Transatlantic, who supported this story to its bones. Shoutouts to Eva Oakes, as well as Cody Caetano, for their early and earnest support for *Treat Them as Buffalo*.

My editorial team, Jenn Lambert and Jovanna Brinck, as well as Evan Hansen-Bundy and Nadxieli Nieto, whose support built *Treat Them as Buffalo* into the home it is today.

My MA committee, Thomas Wharton and Paul Gareau, who gave that early tome of shit direction, legitimization, and encouragement.

My beta readers, Ashley, CJ, Drew, Kaitlyn, and most especially Lauren, who believed in the story hidden in the shit. I kept my promise and donated charitably anonymously on your behalf. I will continue when I'm able. The kids who use these resources thank you.

My artistic elders, especially racialized Indigenous writers, who made the literary landscape safer and hungrier for stories like mine. Maarsii. This book could never pay my debt.

My cousin, Rhonda, who gave my family home when there was no home. I owe you, kid.

My aunties, Sandy and Carol, who supported Mom and me when times were what they were. Love you, hooligans.

My uncles, Albert and Ben, who keep home in the family. Thanks for hosting us on our pilgrimages. Your mom and grandparents would be proud.

My kitty girl, who supported me through it all and more. You're real people, sweetie.

My writing friends from Lethbridge and Edmonton and Calgary, who support me from a good place. The community rides together.

My childhood friends and fishing buddies in Calgary, the ones who love me for me. Thanks for being real people. Special shoutout to Geoff for stepping up in Summer 2023. If you read this, know all Métis and Cree people agree—you look like Justin Timberlake.

My bud Janie, who motivated and inspired me every step of this ride.

The University of Alberta, Métis Nation of Alberta, and Government of Alberta, who supported this project in its infancy as my Master of Arts thesis at the University of Alberta.

Special thank you to the Edmonton Arts Council, who generously supported this project when bad things happened in 2020 through the Creators' Reserve Grant. Maarsii à vous. Your trust in me is worth it all these years later.

Special thank you as well to the Writers' Trust of Canada, who kindly supported this project through the Woodcock

Fund when more bad things happened in 2024. Maarsii à vous aussi. You've made a world of difference.

To other artists and Indigenous people living real lives: we got this.

To all people globally facing and fighting organized oppression: we got you.

To everyone who exploited me, deceived me, doubted me, disrespected me: fuck you.

To everyone who hosted me, fed me, fuelled me, taught me, trusted me, assisted me, loved me, believed in me: thank you.

We raised *Treat Them as Buffalo* together.

Thank you for reading this book and for being a reader of books in general. We are so grateful to share being part of a community of readers with you, and we hope you will join us in passing our love of books on to the next generation of readers.

Did you know that reading for enjoyment is the single biggest predictor of a child's future happiness and success?

More than family circumstances, parents' educational background, or income, reading impacts a child's future academic performance, emotional well-being, communication skills, economic security, ambition, and happiness.

Studies show that kids reading for enjoyment in the US is in rapid decline:

- In 2012, 53% of 9-year-olds read almost every day. Just 10 years later, in 2022, the number had fallen to 39%.
- In 2012, 27% of 13-year-olds read for fun daily. By 2023, that number was just 14%.

Together, we can commit to **Raising Readers** and change this trend. How?

- Read to children in your life daily.
- Model reading as a fun activity.
- Reduce screen time.
- Start a family, school, or community book club.
- Visit bookstores and libraries regularly.
- Listen to audiobooks.
- Read the book before you see the movie.
- Encourage your child to read aloud to a pet or stuffed animal.
- Give books as gifts.
- Donate books to families and communities in need.

BOB1217

Books build bright futures, and **Raising Readers** is our shared responsibility.

For more information, visit **JoinRaisingReaders.com**

Sources: National Endowment for the Arts, National Assessment of Educational Progress, WorldBookDay.com, Nielsen BookData's 2023 "Understanding the Children's Book Consumer"